FOR
A
FEW
SOULS
MORE

First published 2015 by Solaris
an imprint of Rebellion Publishing Ltd,
Riverside House, Osney Mead,
Oxford, OX2 0ES, UK

www.solarisbooks.com

ISBN: 978 1 78108 288 1

10 9 8 7 6 5 4 3 2 1

A CIP catalogue record for this book is available
from the British Library.

Designed & typeset by Rebellion Publishing

REBELLION

Printed in the US

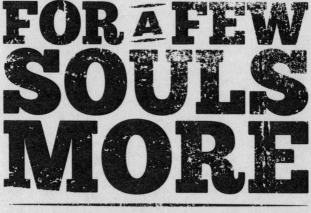

FOR A FEW SOULS MORE

BOOK THREE OF THE HEAVEN'S GATE TRILOGY

GUY ADAMS

WITHDRAWN

SOLARIS

Dedication:
The reviewers and readers that
have travelled this three-book road.
The kind words from you is what kept
this stupid outlaw in the saddle. I hope you're
happy with where the wagon train has settled.

CHAPTER ONE
MAN WHO CAME TO KILL

1.

TWO BULLETS CHANGED the world. The first had already been fired, the second was still to come, resting in its box in the left hand pocket of Atherton's coat as he rode towards the town of Wormwood.

It was the end of a rushed and uncomfortable journey and Atherton was in no mood for the atrocities that surrounded him. He'd heard the stories and read the report but words on a page don't prepare you for the sight of a demon.

"Spare a few cents?" one asked him, brushing a plume of gelatinous, weeping fronds away from its mouth.

Atherton had once watched a table of Chinamen eat noodles with chopsticks. The passage of edible string from bowl to lip had seemed endless, as if they had been trying to consume an infinite clutch of twine. He had thought it like an ancient illustration of hellish torment and was reminded of it now. The demon coughed and the fronds whipped forward, some of them sticking to the creature's forehead, hanging and quivering in front of its small, blue eyes like a mucus-splattered cobweb.

"Damned sickness," the demon said, brushing the fronds free with its scaly hand. "The things you humans spread around."

"If I give you money will you buy medicine?" Atherton asked. He had no intention of doing so but the question intrigued him.

"Heavens, no," it replied, "waste of dollar. I'll spend it on whisky. It won't make me better but it'll make me not care."

"I'll save my money then," Atherton replied, moving on.

"Fuck you very much," the demon said, falling into a coughing fit.

Atherton continued on towards Wormwood.

According to the reports, it had appeared out of nowhere. Atherton's natural inclination would have been to dismiss such talk. He had once watched the illusionist, John Nevil Maskelyne seem to conjure a woman out of thin air but he doubted even that august performer could achieve the same with an entire town. Yet Atherton accepted his concept of reality was now in need of refreshment. While his superiors talked politics, terrified of the global ramifications of this new land in their midst, it seemed to Atherton that the real victim was science. He glanced up at a shape in the sky, it had the wings of a vulture but a human body. It swooped and curled in the air, either for the joy of it or on the hunt for a meal, Atherton couldn't tell. Science, he thought, science may never recover from the presence of Wormwood.

The flying creature issued a cry that brought a hungry seagull to mind. Atherton kept one eye on it, wary in case it should swoop down onto him.

He couldn't resist guiding his horse in a circuit of the town. He had been told that, while it might appear to be nothing more than a small collection of buildings and streets, once entered it was a gateway to almost infinite space. Impossibility after impossibility.

From a distance the place looked empty. That too was a lie, he was assured. His employers had sent a team of local men to investigate—Atherton had been on the other side of the country and a train could only run so fast—and they had all commented on the difference between the town's external appearance and the sights that unfolded once you crossed its threshold. The real town lay hidden, only visible once you were inside it.

As he watched, this was proven as a small group emerged from one of the side streets and out onto the open plain. They appeared like the resolution of a mirage, a shimmering of silver light, indistinct and liquid, that solidified as they left the influence of the town. There were two men, between them a young girl riding on a horse. They appeared perfectly human but Atherton knew better than to jump to conclusions.

"Good day," said one of the men, nodding at him and smiling so widely that his thick beard rippled, like a dog shuffling into a comfy position to sleep on his face.

Atherton nodded and smiled back. "Been exploring?" he asked.

"More than that," the other man said, "setting up house."

This fellow was clean-shaven and less friendly. When he looked at Atherton it was with analytical eyes. Sensible man, Atherton thought. It was the English accent, that always brought people up short.

"Really?" Atherton asked, looking at the kid. "Seems a funny place to call home to me."

"You new here?" asked the man with the beard. Atherton nodded. "Then maybe you need to get a feel for the place before passing judgment."

Atherton shrugged. "You hear stories."

"Yeah," the man continued, "that's as maybe but Wormwood's something you've got to experience for yourself."

The girl smiled at Atherton and he noticed her teeth were moving, rolling up and down like the keys on a clockwork piano.

"Kid needs a dentist," he said, encouraging his horse past them, continuing towards the town.

He entered Wormwood, passing through the invisible barrier that stood between it and the rest of the world.

The town was bloated with people. Great crowds, both human and demon, making their way along the wide, dirt streets. Everywhere he looked, Atherton saw the species intermingling. America, he thought, the melting pot of the world. He had been stationed over here only two months but he had grown to hate the country. Its chaos. Its contradiction. Its sickening enthusiasm.

A pair of children scuffled together in the dust. One looked perfectly human whereas the other had all the right body parts, just in the wrong places. The human kid laughed and threw a small ball, the demon child leapt to give chase, the legs that sprouted from his rosy cheeks paddling in the dirt as they dragged the rest of his torso behind him, arms clenching and clapping at the rear like a dual tail.

It made Atherton sick.

He tied up his horse outside a tavern, the riotous sound of cheering and laughter washing over him as he pushed open its doors and stepped inside.

It smelled like a place whisky went to die.

An obese creature navigated her way towards him on three legs. Her blouse was torn open to reveal multiple teats, all damp and pink from suckling. "Want milk?" she asked, the nipples turning towards him like the heads of flowers searching for sunlight. Atherton shoved her aside, repelled by the sensation of her bloated torso rippling against his arm.

He made his way towards the bar, teeth gritted. His skin crawled. He fantasised about drawing his gun and shooting indiscriminately into the crowd. Did demons bleed? What colour would the blood be as it splashed its wet heat onto the dirty floorboards?

A man with a separate chunk of flesh for each of his features turned away from the bar, clearing a space. His head reminded Atherton of a book, opened to reveal a handful of thick, fleshy pages. On either side, the 'covers' held an ear, then a wedge each for the eyes, the nose and a perpendicular mouth that waved back and forth in the centre with the shifting of the creature's neck. Atherton didn't manage to conceal his disgust and the creature's lopsided mouth sneered to see the man's revulsion.

"Problem?" the creature asked. It reached up towards its mouth with a three-fingered hand and parted the lips. They creaked like rubber and Atherton turned away from the sight of the distended, pink innards revealing themselves like a bloodless wound. The demon threw the contents of his whisky glass into the aperture and then let it slap shut.

"No problem," said Atherton, though he would love to see if the creature's mouth could accommodate something larger than a shot of bourbon, a fist perhaps, or a broken bottle.

"What can I get you?" asked the barman, who at least appeared human.

Atherton had given up finding anything that suited his palate in this godforsaken land. "Whisky," he said, because it couldn't make his stomach more uncomfortable than the sights that surrounded him.

He gazed into the warped mirror behind the bar as his drink was poured, watching what appeared to be a chimp in a suit as it clambered up the stairs in pursuit of a young woman. She giggled, an enticement, though her suitor needed none; he screeched and raised his hairy fists in the air, a daunting bulge in his trousers proving his appetite was already perfectly sharpened.

"Join me?" asked a woman sat at a table to his right. How her voice had carried over the raucous cheering and cackling was beyond him but, as trickery went, it was small beer considering what else he had experienced.

She was dressed in a frock of satin and lace, the garment blooming in all the places that a proper lady's would not. A whore, he decided. He had no interest in paying for what fought to expose itself from beneath her skirts but she might be useful in providing information. He sat down.

"New in town?" she asked and he noticed her mouth wasn't moving.

"Yes," he replied. "How do you do that?"

"What?" she asked and then touched her lips with her fingers. "Oh, the voice," she continued and this time her lips moved and her tone was different, as if another person was speaking entirely. "I'm a woman of multitudes. Pay me and you can count them."

"Maybe," he said, not wanting to put her off, "but first, tell me a bit about the town, would you?"

"What do you want to know?"

"Well, you hear stories on the trail, I guess I just want to know how true they are."

"It's hard to exaggerate about this place, honey, take a look around you. I imagine that, whatever you've heard, the truth is richer and harder to believe." She leaned forward and the next time she spoke it was the other voice, the first voice he had first heard. "Why don't you explore?"

"The town or you?" he asked.

She shifted her chair and hoisted her skirts to reveal the source of her second voice. "There's nothing out there to compare with what you can find in here," her sex said, its lips parting slightly as it spoke.

The look of disgust on his face didn't anger her as it had the man at the bar, instead she laughed. "Oh, you *are* new around here aren't you? Or are you one of those boys from the mountains? Here to fire up your righteous anger?"

"He just doesn't know what he's missing," whispered the voice between her thighs, "one kiss from me and he'll be smiling again."

Atherton drew his gun beneath the table, leaned forward and stoppered her secondary voice with its barrel.

"I think I'd rather only hear from one of you," he said, looking into the woman's eyes. "Now tell me about the people in the mountains."

"They're like you," she sneered, "typical men, cold and afraid of what they don't understand. They look down on us and pray for deliverance, sweet little words to a God who would have ignored them anyway, even if He weren't dead."

"You can't kill God," Atherton replied. Her sex mumbled its disagreement around an inch of metal but he cocked the trigger and it ceased its complaints. "Can you say the same about yourself?"

"Oh, it would take more than you've got to ruin me," she said, her words heavy with double meaning, "and the minute you pull that trigger you'll have half of this bar wanting to make games of your offal. So, by all means, shoot your load, boy, I'll make children of your bullets and invite them to dance on your grave."

He met her gaze for a few moments more then withdrew his pistol, stood up and marched out of the bar, ignoring the dual peals of laughter that followed him.

2.

ATHERTON WAS ANGRY to be leaving the town so shortly after he'd entered it. He had let his anger get in the way of his common sense and could only hope he'd find something of worth in the whore's words.

He urged his horse towards the mountains that surrounded the town, scanning the horizon for signs of life.

After half an hour's ride he was forced to accept that he would have to continue on foot. The landscape was too steep for his horse, the route through the rocks too narrow.

Angry and aware that he might never see the animal again, he did his best to find it some shade and cinched the reins between a pair of rocks.

He had been climbing for twenty minutes or so, the sun beating down on him, when he realised he was no longer alone.

He turned to look down at Wormwood, feigning casual interest, a man out for a hike, all the while keeping his hand close to his holster. As he turned he glimpsed a pair of shadows dart out of sight and he tracked their owners to an outcrop just above him and to the left.

"Why don't you come out?" he asked, keeping his hand close to his gun and looking around for the best natural cover should they decided to reply with gunfire. "I'm no enemy of yours. Quite the opposite."

"You came from Wormwood?" the voice asked. Atherton was surprised to note the speaker's accent, it was as British as his own.

"I've just been there," he admitted. "I was sent to investigate it."

"Sent by whom?"

"Come out and I'll tell you."

"Tell me one other thing first: what's the purpose of your investigation? What do your superiors want to do with the town?"

Atherton smiled. "They have yet to make their intentions wholly clear but I imagine they'll want me to destroy it. As both a political and spiritual abomination."

There was a scuffle from behind the rocks and a man stood up. He was wearing a monk's habit. "Then I can see we are, indeed, allies. I'm Father Martin and I welcome you to our little commune."

3.

ATHERTON FOLLOWED THE monk and his companion, a frail-looking man who remained silent, throwing the occasional concerned look in Atherton's direction.

"You're from England?" Father Martin asked as they climbed up through the rocks.

"Yes, though I've been here a few months."

"A spy?"

"An observer."

"Semantics, something I am well versed in as a religious man."

"What brought you here?" Atherton asked.

"The town. I travelled over with a larger party. We had all heard the myths about Wormwood and wanted to be here for when it appeared." Father Martin glanced over his shoulder where the town was still visible. "At the time I had thought I was on a holy mission. Perhaps I was, though it's hard to cling to that."

"And the rest of your party?"

Father Martin sighed. "Some are still with me, the majority of my brothers. The rest are lost to me. I'm afraid we suffered from a divergence in philosophy."

"Not unusual for someone in your line of work I'd have thought."

"My 'line of work' has irrevocably changed. We've moved from the dust of the library to the open plain. No more discussion of beliefs and theoretical ethics, now the work of Hell is as physical as these rocks, an inarguable thing for all to gaze on."

"Perhaps that's a good thing for faith?"

"The very point of faith is that it's a matter of belief. Fighting against that," Father Martin gestured towards the town, "is not about faith, it's about fear."

"Did you see it appear?"

Father Martin nodded. "And I saw it collide."

"Collide?"

The monk nodded. "That's our word for it. The moment when it became a fixed part of our world. We can discuss that later. We're here."

The track through the mountain dropped down, leading into a hollow space where Father Martin's people had made their camp. Being a man of practical considerations, the first thing Atherton analysed was the camp's security. It was well hidden, surrounded on all sides by rocks, and would remain unseen until you were right upon it. That said, once discovered, the advantage would rest with the attacker, able to maintain the high ground and shoot into the crater. The camp's residents would be captive targets. Fish in a barrel. All of this rushed through Atherton's head before he took in the human details.

It reminded him, unsurprisingly, of a travelling church congregation. The kind of evangelical folk who toured the country en masse, pitching their tent and preaching to the locals before folding the words of Jesus away into their packs and trunks and carting them off to the next town. The people looked drawn and severe, a flock of hungry birds wrapped up in plain feathers. Here and there, fires burned, heating thin stews and watery soups. It was a place of abstinence. A camp of grey people. A place of puritanism and disapproval. Atherton liked it.

"Are you hungry?" Father Martin asked.

Atherton had travelled too far and too hard to refuse a meal when it was offered so Father

Martin led him through the camp to a small tent on the far side.

Their companion, sparing just enough time to offer Atherton one last cautious glance, peeled away to rejoin his family.

The monk's tent was just large enough for two, and they sat in its mouth and ate a meagre portion of bread and cured meat.

Once done, Atherton filled his small pipe and listened to the monk's tale.

4.

FATHER MARTIN TOLD Atherton of his trip from England. He detailed the rest of his party: his fellow members in the Order of Ruth; Lord Forset and his daughter Elisabeth; the engineer Billy Herbert and, finally, Roderick Quartershaft, the man of fiction who, as well as Wormwood, found his real self, Patrick Irish, at the end of his journey.

He told him of the things they had seen on the road to find their impossible town. Of swarms of bats and tribesmen of iron and coke.

He told him how Wormwood had finally appeared before them, the solidifying of a mirage, a dream writ large in timber and slate.

He told him about Alonzo, the self-appointed voice of God who had pronounced to those gathered on the plain.

He detailed the long hours of waiting, of the near tragedy as Lord Forset's Land Carriage was stolen and aimed at Wormwood like a steam-powered bullet.

Finally, and by now the sun was beginning to set behind the mountains that surrounded them, he told him of the collision.

"Light flooded the entire valley. There was the sound of a gunshot, such a simple, earthly noise, and then the air itself felt as if it was being sucked out of the world. A wind roared and we stumbled, blind and deaf as the reality we had always known shifted around us."

This was not news to Atherton. It had been felt the world over. A blank moment of thunder and awe, experienced by all.

At the time, Atherton had been in New York, regretting his transfer from Africa, assisting with the Empire's expansion. Africa had been a land of monsters too, Atherton felt. Heat and rebellion. Bullets and blood. He had done good work there. When the light had come, washing over him, he had half hoped it was the hand of God, coming to claim him from his new station, a city of boredom, and relocate him to somewhere worthwhile. Perhaps, in a way, that was exactly what it had been.

"Then, all was normal again," the monk continued. "The light vanished, the wind faded and the town lay before us. Only now its streets were open, the way no longer obstructed by the unseen barrier."

"What caused it?"

"They say..." and here Father Martin's nerves truly began to show. "It was the death of God. Felled by a bullet."

"You can't kill God," Atherton said for the second time that day. This time he found some agreement.

"I would hope not. Though they say He wanted to die. They say He was wearing the body of a mortal. A child. They say He wanted to know what it felt like to be human. To be finite."

"Who are 'they' that do all this talking?"

Father Martin shrugged. "Stories pass around here as freely as the air. I don't know how much credence I can give any of them. All I can say is that this has become the accepted version of the events that took place on the other side of Wormwood."

"In Heaven?" Atherton didn't bother to keep the cynicism from his voice.

"I know, it's a hard concept to grasp, isn't it? Again the ethereal, the spiritual, given flesh. Heaven is not a place we would ever have granted geography. Even those of us who believed unequivocally in its presence would think of it as abstract, a place of the mind, not somewhere solid. Hell too. These were domains of the soul, that insubstantial, intangible essence. What use did the soul have of walkways? Bricks and mortar?"

He was looking towards Wormwood, Atherton knew, even though it was not visible here in the crater.

"I would always have suspected," the monk continued, "that, however we visualised the afterlife, God or the Devil, we would be doing so in a reductive fashion. The reality would be even more abstract than our human minds could picture. Actually, the opposite is the case. It's as solid as we are. Perhaps, given that, it's not so absurd to believe God may be dead after all. Maybe he was as ruined, as tethered by the flesh as we all are."

"I remain to be convinced."

Father Martin smiled. "And to think, earlier I complained that the intangibility of theology was lost to us. Perhaps we have just as many mysteries as we always did. Except now the answers may be found by explorers not philosophers, archeologists not clerics."

"If our government has its way, that soil will never be dug. They will want the doorway closed. Heaven and Hell, if they exist as physical continents, must be vaster than any other on the map. That they should exist, here... That cannot be allowed."

"I wonder if that would have been the case had Wormwood appeared in England?" Father Martin asked.

Atherton was not going to be drawn into a political argument, however much he knew that the monk had put his finger on the truth. "You said yourself, that place should not exist."

"Indeed not. Whatever my beliefs I am no idiot. To have Heaven and Hell on our doorsteps, to be able to walk directly into either..."

"Or to have whatever inhabits them walk into our world."

"Exactly. It would have been better were that not to have happened. I cannot believe it is what God wants, or, perhaps *wanted*. What chance does any human soul have if it can simply stroll into paradise? The chaos you saw down there, the monstrosities and the aberrations, they will only be the beginning, of that I'm quite sure. Soon, mankind will match it for its excesses. Can you imagine what our world will be like once people realise there are no limitations? That there is no need to await heavenly reward? That Hell can simply be walked away from? Do you think the human race is strong enough to retain its morality, its sense of propriety, in the face of that?"

Atherton held the morality of the world in low esteem and always had. "No."

"And so, if the doorway can be closed it must, for all our sakes."

"God's work?" Atherton smiled.

Father Martin, for all he knew he was being mocked, nodded. "I believe so. And even if that is the only belief I am left with, I will hold onto it."

5.

AFTER ATHERTON ANNOUNCED his intention to remain in the camp, at least for now, Father Martin instructed a couple of men to gather the man some supplies. A bed roll, a canopy, a little food and water. These people didn't have much but they did their best to share.

That night, as the camp slept under the stars, the air filled with the faint sound of smouldering fires and snoring, Atherton lay awake and imagined what might lie ahead.

Father Martin had been right, of course, his government's concern was not a spiritual one. The idea that America now possessed both Heaven and Hell on its soil, vast, powerful landscapes with undreamed of populations; such a thing was terrifying to every other country in the world. Certainly he would not be the only agent of a foreign power currently charged to investigate. He imagined swarms of them were descending from all over the globe. Would those who called the afterlife home ally themselves with the country they were tethered to? Would they attack it? Would they occupy it?

What of the dead? Did they still walk on the other side of Wormwood? How many English citizens were now transported to American soil? How many French? Spanish?

It was an impossible situation and one that his mechanical, rational mind couldn't readily process. He was not a politician, he was a weapon, a scalpel whose blade was turned onto the body politic so that it could have its diseased flesh removed.

After an hour or so, he thought of his horse and, as he was still unable to sleep, decided he would make the short walk down the mountainside to attend to the animal. He had no feelings for it but it was his transport and a man like Atherton always kept an escape route easily to hand.

He walked quietly between the sleeping people. He was used to moving stealthily at night. The moon was the assassin's ally and he had worked beneath its light many times over the years.

He scaled the outcrop that hid the camp from view and began to descend, moving carefully over the uneven terrain. As he got lower, Wormwood was revealed. It burned at night. He had proven earlier that the real town could not be seen from outside so the lights that flickered in its windows, the fires that burned in its grates, must be illusory. Real or not, they cast an orange glow on the plain around it that brought infernal imagery to Atherton's mind. Perhaps Heaven was, indeed, on the other side of that gateway but so far all he had seen was Hell.

His mood was not improved when he discovered the remains of his horse. It was half-eaten, its belly open to the stars, their lights reflected in the black pool that seeped from it.

"There are wild animals in the mountains," said a voice behind him and his gun was in his hand before he had even turned around to face the speaker.

Atherton's first assumption was that one of the residents of Wormwood had climbed up here to take a look at the opposition. Even by moonlight he could tell that the man's skin was raw, a mess of shining flesh and scabs.

"I mean no harm," the man said, raising his hands, "and I'm as human as you, whatever my face may make you think." He smiled and his teeth glinted unnaturally.

"You look like a demon to me," said Atherton. "You do this to my horse?"

The man shrugged. "What sort of man would eat a living animal?" He smiled again and Atherton thought the man's teeth might be false, metal embedded in the gums. "Like I say, there are dangerous creatures out here."

"Clever ones too. The beast's mouth is strapped shut with a belt, to stop it from screaming as it was attacked I assume?"

"They call me the Geek," the man said, ignoring the question.

"What sort of name is that?"

"The only one God left me with. Just ask Father Martin, he used to dream of me. Maybe he still does when the moon's full."

The Geek sat down on a rock, refusing to show concern towards the gun Atherton pointed at him.

"I was listening to you earlier," he continued, "when you were talking to the Father."

"I didn't see you."

"Not many do. I'm not so pretty as I used to be and I prefer to keep to the shadows. But I keep my ears open. I like to know what's going on. You're here to kill the devils."

"I'm here to try."

"I imagine they take some killing. I ain't tried myself, as tempting as it is." The Geek looked towards Wormwood. "I'm always interested in unusual creatures, things I ain't got my hands on before."

To Atherton this sounded dangerously close to perversion and he was quick to move the subject along.

"How long have you been here?" he asked.

"Since the beginning. I saw it born. Maybe I'll see it die too. You ain't alone in wanting that. Can't imagine you'll struggle to find an army." He laughed. "I don't mean the little mice up there, neither," he said. "They mean well I guess but they ain't got a strong arm between them. It'll take more'n prayers to kill Hell."

"You're right," Atherton admitted. He holstered his gun. It wasn't as if it scared the man anyway. "But I imagine Hell has an army too."

"For sure," the Geek agreed. He smiled and, again, those metallic teeth glinted by the light of the moon. "I wonder if any of us will be alive by the end of it? Not that it matters."

"Why?"

"If we die, it ain't like we have so far to go these days is it? It ain't nothing but a short walk."

So saying, the Geek stood up, turned around and vanished into the night.

Atherton, his audience over, took one last look at his gutted horse and returned to the camp and to his plans.

Once he was gone, the Geek re-emerged from the shadows to retrieve his belt from the dead horse's mouth.

"He seems a mite intense," he said, aware that he once more had company.

"Doesn't he?" the man replied. The Geek looked up and smiled to see the look on the man's face as he gazed down on the dead horse.

"Sight of blood troubles you?" The Geek asked. "I'm surprised, with what you're planning I reckon you'll be ankle deep in it before long."

"Maybe," the man agreed. "I hope not. So," he paused for a moment, "you'll do as I ask?"

The Geek shrugged. "I can't exactly refuse God, now can I?"

WHAT AM I DOING IN THE MIDDLE OF THE REVOLUTION?

(An excerpt from the book
by Patrick Irish)

HISTORY IS BUILT on uncertainty. Nothing grows in barren soil, it needs rain storms, it needs the food brought by rot, it needs heat. The status quo can be a pleasant place to live, but nothing great will ever flourish from it.

When Wormwood appeared it changed the world. At the time of writing, I cannot accurately predict what will come from it. I am still too close; it will be for historians to judge, looking back from the vantage point of years gone by, as to what those changes were and what damage they caused. Still, I am a writer, it is the one and only worthwhile skill I possess, and it would be impossible for me not to put pen to paper and attempt to document my place within it all. Perhaps it will be of use to those future historians as they sift through the reports and the articles and draw their conclusions.

I have no doubt that many books will be written about our current times. Though it may seem arrogant, I chance to suggest that mine will be the most valuable. After all, I do not write simply as a spectator. I write as a man who played a part in these proceedings. When the bullet was fired that changed everything, it rang out across the world. That was something we all experienced, every single person on the planet.

But I saw it land. I watched it open a hole in the forehead of its victim. I watched God die.

I was there.

I later discovered how that moment impacted elsewhere, the light, the sound, the shared knowledge that something of universal importance had just happened. From my front row seat, there at the storm's heart, I fear my experience may seem anticlimactical. It appeared to us, those few in the room, as nothing more or less important as the death of a child. We knew our eyes deceived us; Henry Jones, the blind gunslinger, was a man capable of great horrors but I dare to suggest that even he would think twice before emptying his gun into the head of an innocent infant. The child, the young girl, her toy train pulled along behind her by a length of string, was not all she appeared. She was a skin worn by a greater other, the Greatest in fact. Hankering after a mortal existence, God had poured itself into the flesh and bone of a human child. Jones, having a knife to grind with the Almighty, saw a chance and took it. God had wanted to experience mortality. God did so. At least, that is what we have to assume. Certainly the aftershocks lend credence to the act. As tragic and horrendous as the death of a child might be it doesn't alter reality. Our history, built on the countless corpses of children, has proven as much.

Many have argued since that God cannot die, whatever complex game He might wish to play. I don't know. I suspect that is the (understandable) response of a devout mind in fear of losing its anchor in the world. All I can say is: if God is all powerful, God can do anything. That includes putting Himself in a position where his own extinction was not only possible but somehow desired.

Jones certainly considered his work successful, holstering his gun and walking out of that immaculate room with a renewed sense of purpose. I suppose you think one of us should have stopped him? The execution of God is certainly a crime that most would consider worthy of punishment. I can only admit that I—and I presume my companions also—were so shocked at his sudden slaughter that we hadn't the power to move. I know we were still stood there for long moments after he left, staring at the body of the dead girl—and however much we knew she had been more than that, it was the image we were faced with, a child shot in the head.

It was Soldier Joe that made the first move. He removed his jacket and laid it over her. It wasn't long enough for the task, her feet poking out from beneath the hem, and the slowly expanding pool of her blood would not be concealed by it for long. It was better though, not to have to look at that face fallen slack, the small, red hole just above her left eye.

"I don't know what else to do," he admitted, running his hands through his own hair, touching, or so I imagined, the old scar of his own bullet-wound. He had survived his, after a fashion.

I know his history now, of course. All of those years as the brain-damaged messiah for the unscrupulous preacher Obeisance Hicks. Here, in the Dominion of Clouds, he had his faculties, could think and speak and express himself. In the world of the mortals all of these things had been beyond him. He had been at the mercy of his owner, his only friend the woman who stood with him now, his nurse Hope Lane. She doted on him, her feelings for him clearly more than those of nurse and patient. I wonder whether that was another blessing that might only be fully enjoyed now that they had been removed from the narrow-minded beliefs of the mortal world. I am sure the colour of her skin would have been a source of victimisation and disapproval were they to have tried to become a couple. We are not a species known for our acceptance of those we view as different to ourselves, though, of course, the median by which we judged such things was soon to change.

Soldier Joe. I wish I knew his real name, it seems foolish referring to him by such a childlike nickname. On reflection though, perhaps not. Whoever he had been before his accident, it had been a rebirthing. A long and painful one that had only just concluded. Perhaps it is only right in such circumstances that a man be allowed to shed his old name along with his old life.

"What will it mean?" Hope Lane asked, the first of us, I think, to really grasp that the murder we had just witnessed was a beginning, not an end. "Will all of this," she gestured around us, "just crumble? How can the world go on without its God?"

The peculiar, bright white world we had been brought to showed no sign of failing. There was no tremor beneath our feet or distant sound of devastation. While it would be understandable for one brought up on the notion of God as the Almighty glue that both birthed the world and, indeed, controlled it, to expect the Apocalypse in his absence, there was no sign of the End of Days just yet. I am now speaking with the advantage of hindsight of course, I know that life continued, much as a son or daughter might outlive their mother or father. Even then, with Hope's question fresh from her lips I don't think I truly feared Armageddon. I think it was partly the fact that we had already been led to believe that God was an absent ruler. We had been brought to the Dominion of Clouds by Alonzo with a view to us helping him fill the vacuum he already claimed to be there. Wormwood, the very myth of it, was purely a method of securing the living souls he had set his sights on. I was to be the author of his new bible, Soldier Joe was the noble martyr, Jones the Devil. In that role, he had certainly made a most promising start.

"We need to speak to Alonzo," said Joe. "He's the only one who can explain any of this."

He moved to the window as if expecting to be able to see the man—if that word fits, and it doesn't, but forgive me, our lexicon was not built for the stories I must tell.

"He meant this to happen," said Hope. "You heard what Mr Jones said. They'd talked about him killing God. Alonzo planned it."

I found myself staring at the remains of our food, splattered against one of the white walls by a sweep of Alonzo's arm. "He planned a lot of things. What was he saying before he left? A sacrifice?"

"He certainly got one of those," said Joe, looking at the body beneath his jacket.

Again, my hindsight comes into play. The sacrifice Alonzo intended was not the death of God—or, not *just* that—it was the planned collision of the vehicle on which I had so recently travelled, the Forset Land Carriage, with the impenetrable barrier that surrounded Wormwood. A rather dull sacrifice you might think, but the Land Carriage contained a number of highly-delicate and dangerous pieces of equipment, some of which, if ignited, would have reduced the entire plain, and the many that camped on it, to ash. It would have been a disaster of suitably Biblical proportions. It is thanks to the sterling work of my old colleagues, most particularly Forset's daughter, Elisabeth, that the accident was averted. At the time, however, none of us could have known that.

"The room," said Hope. "His..." she struggled to remember the name Alonzo had given it, "Observation Lounge."

The name was unfamiliar to me, but they soon explained it was a room in which Alonzo had maintained a watch on all of creation.

"If he's not there, we'll certainly be able to find him," Joe said.

We filed out of the dining room, making our way along one of the many featureless corridors. I remember thinking, as I had several times, how it could be that Heaven was so empty. Surely, even in a place so vast one would expect to occasionally chance upon another holy soul. Could Heaven really be as vacant as it seemed?

CHAPTER TWO
DEATH KNOWS NO TIME

1.

ARNO JAMES HAD always been told that his charity would be the death of him.

"One day," his long-suffering wife had insisted, "someone's going to take advantage of that big, soft head of yours and put a bullet in it."

It was some small consolation to him as he lay bleeding, his final thoughts fixated on the weathered state of the barn roof struts above him, that she had been wrong. It hadn't been his charity work, it had been her lover, deciding that, after a couple of months of sneaking behind his back, it would be altogether easier to just brain him with a spade.

"We thought it was one of the Klinton Gang," his wife sobbed in a performance of considerable weight as the sheriff looked down at his cold body. "Who knows what he was doing sneaking around in the barn like an intruder? Thank the Lord that Zeke had dropped by, otherwise I would have been defenceless."

The sheriff, a wily old bastard that had no doubt as to the real story, pointed out that maybe it hadn't been such a blessing after all. If Zeke had been at home in his own bed, Arno James would still be working the fields rather than growing as stiff as wood.

However much he may have known in his gut that poor old Arno had been removed as an unwanted complication, he couldn't offer proof. Within a week, the man's widow and her new beau had been on the trail to Denver with their combined savings.

Arno, meanwhile, had woken in a garden. Albeit not the sort of garden he could ever have imagined tending himself. This wasn't a place of dry lawn and patchy daisies, it was a bright, dreamy landscape of the mind. The trees above his head glistened, their branches creaking and waving despite the lack of wind. The grass beneath his fingers felt as crisp as sugar and, sitting up, he was forced to squint as the reflections from a nearby stream flickered in front of his eyes. He touched his face, wanting to feel something he could believe in. He covered his eyes for a moment, pushing the vision of the garden away so that he could think. His ears still rang with the resounding clatter of the spade connecting against his skull. There was no pain, just a sense of dislocation, an awareness, right down in his very soul, that he had stepped out of one existence and into another.

The religious implications of this took a moment to kick in. Arno, despite having regularly bent his knee within the narrow confines of the ramshackle pews of the St. Bartholomew tabernacle, did not automatically assume himself to be in Heaven. His religious devotions, while deeply felt, were singularly elsewhere as his logical mind looked around and tried to put two and two together. Dying is something you never develop any experience in and, consequently, most folks hesitate to assume it's just happened to them.

Uncovering his eyes, Arno got to his feet and began to explore the world he'd been re-born into. The ground gave slightly beneath his feet, soft and pliant as only earth can be.

He looked down at his clothes. They were dreams of garments that had hung in his own closet. He ran his thumb along the hem of the jacket, finding none of the loose threads or repairs that were as much a part of the original as the scar on his temple. Reminded of it, he reached to touch that little nub of white skin, an imperfection he'd carried for years ever since catching it on the underside of a shelf in the barn. It was there. It was a comfort.

He made his way towards the stream, his eyes slowly adapting to the sparkling light.

Squatting down on the bank, he extended his hand into the water. There was no chill and he could barely feel it, rushing over his hand like thick air.

"Paradise?" he wondered. And again, that thought of where he might be crossed his mind only for him to dismiss it again.

What was needed, he decided, was to find someone else.

He followed the bank of the stream, the grass crunching beneath his feet like winter frost.

The trees around him were like those drawn by a lazy artist; they were trees of the imagination, not any species he recognised. Pulling down a branch he looked closer at the cluster of fruit growing on one of them. It appeared to be a bunch of precious stones, cut as if for royalty to hang on their puffy, white necks. As he squeezed them between thumb and forefinger they crumbled, wet and sticky. He raised his fingers to his lips and then decided against it, who knew if it was safe? He wiped the glistening dirt on his trousers instead, happy to make the cloth a little less perfect.

After a short while he came to a bridge that crossed the stream. He crossed it, figuring a bridge had to lead to somewhere.

On the other side, a narrow path made its way through a forest of the unknown trees, the fruit different from branch to branch.

As the trees began to thin out he found himself facing a large building, built from white stone that seemed to glow with an inner light all of its own. The building rose up further than he could see, a stretch of white bricks and windows that grew more indistinct as it soared upwards into the clear sky. To his right there was a wall vanishing back into the forest through which he had just walked. To his left, in the far distance, he thought he could just about make out another. It would seem he had been in a courtyard all this time, one big enough to hold Wyoming.

Cloisters lined the walls. At the junction to his right, a stairway led upwards.

It was as good a direction as any and Arno climbed the stairs to the next floor.

He found himself in a corridor lined with doors on one side and windows on the other.

"Hello?" he called. "Anyone here?"

His voice echoed along the corridor but there was no reply.

He walked to the first door and opened it. Inside was a completely empty room. A large white box, no furniture, no decoration.

Arno stepped back out and moved along the corridor to the next. It was the same. As was the next.

Sharp enough to sense a theme when presented with it, he returned to the stairs and decided to climb higher. If nothing else he would be able to get a good view of the courtyard from a few more floors up.

As he walked up the stairs the only sound was his own footsteps. As they echoed around the white walls his thoughts turned back to philosophical matters. Was it possible that this was Hell rather than Heaven? For all its sterile beauty he couldn't imagine passing a pleasant eternity in it.

After he'd ascended a few more floors, he stepped out into an identical corridor to the one below. He walked to the first room and put his hand on the door handle. It buzzed beneath his skin with a prickling sensation that he would have immediately thought of as a faint electrical charge had he been born a few decades later. For all such a sensation might have seemed an omen of revelations, the door opened once more onto a blank room. He tried one more, with the same result, before moving to look out over the expansive courtyard, a genuine sense of panic building inside him.

Surely this excessive place, a building that bordered on the infinite, couldn't be empty? If so then he must be in Hell, destined to endure the passing decades opening door after door onto nothing.

He looked down on the trees and the garden, tracing the path of the stream. Even this felt like a pretence of perfection, a fragile, child's idea of paradise that glittered only on the surface.

Arno James began to consider what he'd done wrong in life to end up in this candy-coated shell of a world. Had he not tried to be a good man? Had he not dedicated much of his life to helping others? Indeed, that had been his wife's persistent complaint, that he lavished more time on strangers than he did on her. Maybe that had been his mistake. Was this fabricated Heaven the Hell where all bad husbands found themselves? Was it a kind of mockery? A joke? The bitter punchline at the end of a life lived with an eye on sanctity?

His mood was sinking lower and lower, when a sudden glimpse of movement in the trees below tugged him out of self-pity. It was a woman, dressed in light, summer clothes. Her head was down, watching where she placed her feet.

"Hey!" he called, as the figure vanished beneath the cover of the trees. "Hey, wait!"

He ran for the stairs, trying not to calculate how long it would take him to reach the ground level and move back into the garden. Surely, if she hadn't heard him—and she had made no sign of having done so—she would be long gone before he was even back in the open air.

In his panic, he lost his footing on the stairs and the world around him spun in confusion as he tumbled, a brief, disorientating moment of up becoming down and left becoming right. There was just time for a spark of fear, anticipating the damage he might be about to do to himself, his body colliding with the hard steps, before he suddenly came to rest, flat on his back. He was unhurt—how can you hurt something that's already dead? he wondered—and, against all reason, back in the courtyard, having somehow bypassed the several floors he'd climbed.

His sense of urgency returned. He could wonder about the geographic rules of this place later, the most important thing was to catch up with the woman.

"Hello!" he called, running towards the bridge and the spot in the trees where he estimated he had last seen her. "Please, wait."

He crossed the stream and crashed clumsily through the thin lower branches of the trees, their wood and fruit spraying around him like wedding rice.

She was gone, he was sure of it. Despite the time he had gained by somehow skipping the several floors of stairs, he had been too slow and the key to understanding his new world had slipped through his fingers. He hadn't imagined her, there was that at least; he refused to doubt what he had seen and something seen once could be seen again, even in this massive place.

"Hello," said a voice from above. "Are you the one who's been shouting?"

He looked up to see the woman sat on a branch, her feet a few inches from the top of his head.

"Yes," he admitted, "sorry, but I wanted to talk to you."

"So talk," she smiled, swinging her legs like a child on a swing, a woman utterly at peace with her day.

"Well, I woke up here," he explained, "a short while ago and I don't know where I am and what to do and..."

"You don't know much, do you?" she laughed.

"I don't know anything," he admitted.

"Except for one little thing, I imagine?" she asked.

"I'm dead?"

She nodded. "And what a relief that is, isn't it? If I'd known that I could find such peace as this I would have tied a noose around my neck long ago."

"Suicide's a sin."

"Sins are what we make them."

She swung her leg over the branch and slowly lowered herself to the ground.

She was, Arno realised, much older than her behaviour suggested. She was a woman in her late forties, perhaps early fifties, once more returned to a state of carefree childhood. Her face bore only happy lines, creases caused by cheerfulness, the after-effects of countless smiles. Her hair was greying here and there but she wore it long and it trailed down her back like a light coloured shawl over her bright, white cotton dress.

"Veronica," she said, holding out her hand for him to take.

He shook it gently. "Arno. Arno James."

"So you're confused by the afterlife, Arno James?" she asked. "And so you should be. It's a confusing, if miraculous, place."

"It seems so empty."

"That's part of its charm, isn't it? Who wants to spend eternity in a crowd?"

"Well, maybe," Arno considered himself a fairly social person, and while it would depend on the crowd he had no problem with the idea of a little company in Heaven.

"Am I the first person you've met?" she asked. Arno nodded. "Oh dear, how disorganised of them. I'm sure Alonzo should have greeted you. Shown you the ropes, as I believe they say in naval circles."

"Alonzo?"

"He's in charge," she explained, "well, no, I suppose He's in charge." She gestured upwards and then laughed. "How silly, I'm pointing towards the heavens even though I'm stood in them. Still, we never see Him, or hear Him for that matter. Alonzo is the manager I suppose, the human face that makes us feel at home. He really should have found you, you know."

"Oh." Arno tried to shake the feeling that she somehow considered this to be his fault. "Well I have been walking around a lot."

"And shouting."

"I thought there was nobody else here, I was..." Arno decided there was no point in being less than honest, "scared."

"Silly boy," she said, taking his arm and leading him back towards the stream. "There's nothing to be scared of here. All that's behind us now."

"I was exploring the building over there."

"The Junction. The place of travelling."

"Just a lot of empty rooms from what I could tell."

"Then you were looking at them wrong. Come on, I'll show you."

She led him back towards the cloisters at the edge of the courtyard.

"Where were you from?" he asked as the building grew large before them.

"Oh, nowhere important," she said, "a boring little town filled with boring little people. I lived through a succession of droning conversations, a grey old life where I didn't fit in. Here's much nicer. Which, of course, is exactly as it should be."

"I came from Walsenburg, Colorado," he told her, though she hadn't asked. "I had my skull beaten in by a spade."

"It sounds perfectly dreary."

He tapped at his scalp with his fingers. "Maybe I'm just dreaming all this."

"Don't start doubting," she told him, "it's tiresome. You're dead and that's that."

"Yes," he admitted, because he knew the truth of it, despite his momentary thought otherwise, had done so from the very moment he'd woken up.

They had reached the cloisters now and Veronica led him to the door of the first room he'd tried earlier.

"I've already looked in there," he said. "It was nothing but an empty, white chamber."

"Shush now, let me show you the secret of it. The Junction is where we come to travel. To experience whatever our minds can imagine."

She opened the door and Arno found himself looking in on a pebbled beach. The sea crashed against the stones, retreating with the soft crackle of water sucked out from between the pebbles.

"After you," said Veronica, gesturing for him to step inside.

Arno did as he was told, walking cautiously on the stones and gazing out on a wide horizon as pale as milk, the sea and sky blurring where they touched.

"It was empty before," he said, "I assure you."

"It's as empty as you allow it to be," she said, and tapped at her temple. "These doors lead to wherever we dream of but the suggestion has to come from us. These are our rooms, built to our design. You'll get the hang of it."

Arno looked up the shore. The cliffs that marked the edge of the beach rose up to plain grass. Against the sun he saw a group of children playing. The sound of singing filtered down, just audible over the waves.

"That's me up there," said Veronica. "One of them at least. So many years ago."

As he turned to look at her, he was struck by the absurd image of her leaning in the doorway, the cloisters visible over her shoulder.

He turned back to look at the beach again. "How far does it go?" he asked. "If I just kept walking would I eventually reach the wall?"

"You're thinking the old-fashioned way. This is Heaven, it's not bound by the old rules. This is a place of miracles, not brick walls. Come out and I'll show you something else."

Arno hesitated for a moment, wanting to take in the beach a little longer. He could feel the damp of the sea spray as he breathed in. Feel the slight chill of the breeze. It was a miracle indeed.

He stepped back through the doorway into the cloister and Veronica closed the door.

"What's in the next room then?" he asked, moving along the corridor. "A meadow? A town square?"

"You don't have to go to the next room," she said, reaching for the door she had just closed, "this one will do."

She opened the door again and the silence of the cloister was broken by the sound of a crackling fire. Arno imagined a cosy hearth, or perhaps a garden bonfire filling the air with the rich, wholesome smoke of burned leaves.

Stepping through into the dark of night, the smell of burning was, indeed, pronounced but it possessed a meaty odour. A hog roast, he decided, noting the large crowd of people, all in good cheer.

He said as much to Veronica, who smiled. "It's a celebration, certainly," she admitted.

He pushed his way through the crowd, marvelling at their physical presence. He could feel their bodies against him, and they in turn were clearly aware of him, turning to smile in his direction as he passed, encouraging him to be part of their goodwill.

Two young boys chased one another through the crowd, momentarily using him as a barrier in their game, tugging at his jacket and darting around him before running off towards the door that still stood open a short way behind him.

"Can they get out?" he asked Veronica.

"Of course not," she told him. "They're not real, however much they may seem it. They're just memories given weight."

"So what's the celebration?" he asked as she came alongside him, leading him towards the fire. Its flames cracked and flexed, soaring upwards, tapering like the tip of a painter's brush. He could see the silhouettes of the bonfire's structure, the black skeleton of timber that sat at the heart of the flames. Looking upwards he saw another silhouette, one it took him a moment to recognise as a human figure, head bowed, limbs constricted as the heat drew the body inward, shrinking muscle and tendon.

"It's the day I died," Veronica told him, "burned as a witch in front of the town. A source of celebration, relief and, most importantly on a cold night in October, heat."

Arno stared at the bonfire, unable to understand how Veronica could be so easygoing about it.

"That's awful!"

"That's superstition. But it's also the end of a life of being an outsider and the start of something much nicer so I consider it a good day. Don't misunderstand me, it hurt at the time, the human body is not quick to burn. For all our fat and hair we're just big sacks of water. It took a while for the flames to burn enough that I didn't feel them anymore. Those long minutes were full of agony and the choking smoke of my own ruination, weighed down with the certainty that help was never going to come.

"In some way, that last was almost a relief. The long hours waiting in the town gaol while the fire was built, being marched out here and tied in place as the crowds began to gather, singing their happy hymns and calling out their jolly prayers. That was hard, because waiting always is.

"Most suspected witches were hanged. I envied them that when I heard the kindling begin to smoulder. Hanging is at least relatively quick, though perhaps it's no better really. I've seen people dance on the end of a rope, faces popping like overripe fruit, eyes slowly emerging onto their cheeks, tongues fattening. Perhaps death is always long and ignoble. Paradise has to be paid for."

"I was barely aware of mine," Arno admitted. "Just a clanging noise, a momentary sense of heat and wet, a blinding pain and then a gradual slip into darkness."

"Good for you," said Veronica, "I'm glad."

Arno felt absurdly guilty, as if he had let the side down by expiring swiftly.

"I'm still not sure I'd want to revisit it though," he said. "Why would I want to witness my own death?"

"It's liberating. It can't hurt you anymore, it's just an event, the beginning of something new. Why not take the time to stand back, get a little perspective on it? I come here all the time and watch the woman who used to be me as she withers and blackens."

"Were you a witch?"

"Oh yes," she smiled, "at least, in any meaningful sense. I practiced medicine using old recipes my mother had taught me, I sold folk cures, I buried things beneath the moon, I uttered old prayers. I did not, however, raise the dead or worship the devil."

"I suppose you would hardly have ended up here if you had."

"I don't know, I get the impression that the decision as to where a soul washes up is almost entirely down to the owner of the soul in question."

Arno found that an uncomfortable idea to accept.

"But surely, God..."

"God minds his own business, Arno, much as we do ours."

This was a theological point too far for Arno, clashing as it did with many years of religious conviction that dictated otherwise.

The heat of the fire seemed stifling, the smell of Veronica's cooking flesh, the press of the crowd. And now he was being asked to accept that his God, the God to whom he had prayed throughout his life, was a disinterested deity who had no strong feelings as to the life his creations led.

It occurred to him then that maybe this was not Heaven at all, but rather the domain more readily brought to mind when one thought of flames and the burning of human meat.

"How do I know any of this is true?" he asked Veronica. "How do I know you're even who you say you are?"

"How do we know anything?" She shrugged. "I'm not the one to convince you. I'm not your nursemaid. I'm just trying to help. You were the one who came chasing after me, remember?

Arno nodded but his mind was a mess of conflicting thoughts, a building nest of panic. "I know, I know..." he looked around, "I just... I think I need to..."

He ran towards the door, pushing his way through the people, ignoring their shouts of surprise or recrimination. He needed to breathe cold, clean air. He needed to think for a minute, he needed silence.

Back in the cloisters he sat down looking out over the garden and took several deep breaths.

After a moment Veronica joined him. "I don't mean to be insensitive," she said, "but I really don't need someone to worry over. Or to doubt my word. I don't mind showing you around but I'm not going to hold your hand forever." She looked around. "This is why it's better if Alonzo does it. He's better at the calm, patient business. I just want to go walking in the trees again."

"I'm sorry," Arno replied, unable to keep the irritation from his voice, "but this is a great deal to take in."

"Yes. Well, when you've managed to do that come and find me in the garden, it's far too nice a day for an argument."

Could he afford to lose her? In a place as large as this he might never find her again. Did he really want to go back to wandering up and down the corridors in confused silence?

"Wait," he said, "I'm sorry. Please don't go. Not just yet. I'm not sure I can take being on my own again. Not yet."

She sighed and he heard her mutter to herself. He didn't hear most of it but caught the word 'nanny' and felt an unpleasant blend of irritation and shame.

"Just a short while," he said, "just until I get the hang of it."

She nodded. "Alright, but only as long as you promise not to start hurling accusations around. If there's one thing I was glad to consign to the flames it was that."

"Agreed."

2.

FOR A WHILE, Veronica continued to show him the secret of the dreaming rooms. After an hour so she even seemed to relish it, the earlier threats fading away as she began to enjoy the fun of making the rooms do as she wished, seeing the magic through new eyes.

Soon, Arno was able to work a little of their magic himself, though to begin with they were rough, fragile illusions.

"This is where I grew up," he explained to Veronica as he led her through a small field of corn. In the distance there was a cabin; a man, Arno's father, sweated his way through a pile of firewood.

Every few seconds, the air was filled with a grunt and the heavy slap of axe on timber.

"Charming," she said, plucking at an ear of corn. It crumbled in her hand. "Though you need to think in more detail, I can see through your dreaming."

Arno nodded, looking towards his father whose face was a blur of pink skin. "He died when I was quite young," he told her. "I can't quite recall his face."

"Then give him one you can remember," she suggested. "This is your world, you can do what you like with it."

Arno closed his eyes and tried to pull features together.

Once, a few years ago, and much to his wife's exasperation, he had taken to sketching. He was never very good at it, always struggling to get the perspective of the world to sit right on the flat dimension of the paper, but he had enjoyed the process of hashing out the lines. There was something magical about filling a blank area with the black of charcoal, pulling shapes out of nowhere and pinning them down on the page. This was no different, except this time the muscles he needed to train were not in his hands; it was no longer about translating what he saw through the tip of a pencil, rather it was about recalling with clarity. He imagined a moustache, and focused on each hair, imagined it dark at the root and fading to light grey at the tip. He looked through that imaginary bush to the skin beneath, pricked with follicles like holes for thread. He thought of the skin of the lips, shiny and creased. He imagined the eyes, light grey, filled with filaments and swirls.

"Much better," said Veronica, looking at the man who was his newly-imagined father. "You'll be a master at this in no time."

At her prompting, he even showed her the moment of his death, or at least how he imagined it. It was difficult to be precise under the circumstances. They sat on a sack of corn, hiding in the shadows and watching the memory of Arno as he finished unloading his cart of supplies, wiping the sweat of heavy lifting from his brow with the handkerchief his wife had embroidered in happier times. The cloth was scarlet, his initials stitched in white. The treacherous Zeke loomed behind him, spade in hand as his wife looked on from behind the crack of the half-open door.

Arno wondered if Zeke was still hot from his exertions in the marriage bed, corrupting its sheets with an intruder's sweat and seed. He supposed it likely. Perhaps it was the intensity of the lovemaking that had brought the strength of conviction to his shoulders and biceps as he hefted the spade and swung it. There was a faint whisper of displaced air, and then a musical clang, the ringing of a dinner gong or a cheap church bell.

Arno flinched at the sight of it. The face of his imagined shadow contorted in an ugly, unflattering collection of features, puffy and folded. He looked, Arno decided, like a man in the grip of a sneeze so violent it had blown off the back of his head.

"What a way to go," said Veronica. "Quick and percussive. There's a lot to be said for a surprise killing."

"I would have rather avoided it," Arno admitted.

Zeke the Murderer, spade still in hand, looked around. "Who's there?" he called, his voice thick with panic.

"Oh," said Arno, "he heard us."

"Doesn't matter," said Veronica, stepping out into the light. "What's he going to do? Even if he were more than a memory, you can only kill a person once."

She gave a scream and jumped on Zeke, tugging at his thinning hair. He dropped the bloodied spade, raising his hands to defend himself. They spun around, Zeke's boots connecting with the still-twitching body of the man he had just brained, sending them tumbling into the dirt and straw that lined the floor.

From the doorway, Arno's wife entered, coming to the aid of her lover.

Arno, knowing an act of catharsis when presented with one, picked up the discarded spade and brought out its music by swinging it straight at her face. It's good for the soul, this slapstick of memory, he thought as the clang of metal against teeth rang loud and clear.

"Better?" Veronica asked, bouncing up and down on the now wailing Zeke, a whirl of arms and legs, pummelling at a man who had never quite regained the sense to defend himself after the initial attack.

Arno looked down at his wife, her face now a comical grotesque of flattened nose and bloodied lips. "I'm not sure," he said, "can it ever be right to take pleasure in hurting someone else?"

"Ah..." Veronica sighed, taking a rest from beating Zeke's head against the ground, "I can see how you ended up here. What a pure soul you are."

"I loved her after all," Arno admitted, "even if that love wasn't always returned."

"She encouraged her lover to empty your skull of its contents, Arno, she wasn't worthy of love."

"We're all worthy of love, some of us just aren't terribly good at receiving it."

"What a sweet little man you are." She stood up, wiped her bloodied hands on her dress and took him by the arm. "And an utter wet blanket."

He sighed. "She certainly thought so," he admitted. "Say what you like about Zeke, he was never boring."

"He is now," she laughed, "though I'll admit he entertained for a while. Come on, let's go out and find some sun to push away all this gloom."

They returned to the garden, having had their fill of dreaming for a while.

For some time, they just sat in silence, Arno pleased that Veronica now appeared happy to be in his company. He didn't know how many hours they had been in The Junction, the passage of time was slippery here in the afterlife, but the reticence she had shown earlier had completely evaporated.

He looked at his watch. It claimed to be twenty past eight but the second hand was frozen and he knew that it showed the time of his death, that final second when time still mattered. What business did hours and minutes have here in Heaven? You couldn't break an eternity down on a clock. Or could you? The horizon showed signs of darkening, so even the everafter knew the passage of day and night.

"It does get dark here then?" he asked.

"Oh yes," she said. "What would paradise be without a cool evening or a midnight full of stars? God knows the beauty of a sunset or a dawn and is happy to share them."

One thought led to another as the sky continued to darken.

"Where do we sleep?" he asked.

"Wherever we like," she said. "You can imagine whatever you like in The Junction, dream up a bed or a warm hearth."

"Is that what you do?"

"No," she admitted, taking hold of his hand. "I like to sleep beneath the stars."

They appeared above them, as if summoned, and perhaps they were; after all, if Arno had learned anything about Heaven he had learned it was a place that shifted with the desires of its inhabitants.

She pulled him down next to her and guided his awkward fingers as to the way of her dress. As he stripped her of it, he was pleased to note it no longer bore her bloodied handprints from earlier. If their crimes were so transient that their evidence vanished so quickly, they couldn't be mortal sins. The thought led him to consider other acts that might once have shamed him and he busied himself with them as the forest glowed around them, the trees filled with starlight.

Two lovers in a garden in Paradise. Naked. Unburdened.

To Hell with serpents.

3.

FOR THE FIRST few days, Arno managed to mark the passage of time but eventually he stopped bothering. It hardly mattered.

He and Veronica split their time between the garden and The Junction, sleeping together under the open sky.

For the first couple of nights, Arno found sleep hard. He didn't feel tiredness so profoundly now, he supposed you had to be alive to really grow tired. But, as Veronica explained, sleep was a pleasure in and of itself. How blissful was it to open one's eyes as the warmth of the sun heated your cheeks, gazing out onto a fresh day? Why give up on any pleasures now they were your life? Soon, he caught the trick of it, the earth a better mattress than any other his back had known.

It didn't take him long to realise that Veronica had been as happy to meet him as he her. For all her bravado and insistence that she had been happy on her own, she never left his side now and he recognised a soul retrieved from loneliness.

It was a strange Heaven, he decided, that contained so few of the blessed. Of all the questions that had been on his mind during that first day in the afterlife, that was the only one that clung. Where was everyone?

"It's a big place," Veronica said, "bigger than we could ever really conceive of. Is it so strange that we don't bump into others?"

And perhaps that was the truth of it. If the acreage of Heaven was as vast as God could imagine, a place unbound from the geography of rock and ocean, then how could it ever be filled? Still, in the quiet moments, when he and Veronica weren't exploring landscapes in The Junction, or exploring each other in the garden, the question rolled around in Arno's head. It was the one thing that didn't let him rest.

Then finally, that one question robbing him of his peace, he found a serpent he could ask for an answer. He found Alonzo.

"Good afternoon!" the man called, walking through the trees towards them. "A lovely day as always?"

He was dressed well, his fine blond hair capturing the sunlight and glistening almost as much as the grass or the water of the stream.

"This," said Veronica to Arno, "is Alonzo."

"Pleased to meet you," Arno said, wondering on the etiquette with angels, did you shake one's hand? Bow?

Alonzo gave him a hug, solving the problem with admirable enthusiasm.

"My dear Arno," he said, "how lovely to finally meet you. I can't apologise enough for ignoring you on your arrival. I've been hatefully slack on my duties of late. I find myself unreasonably consumed with other projects and allowed the business of meeting and greeting to pass me by."

"That's alright," said Arno. "Veronica has been taking good care of me."

"Wonderful! That's what I like to hear. So good when souls meet, a paradise shared is a paradise doubled."

"I'm surprised we haven't come across anyone else," said Arno, circling around the question that plagued him.

"Not that we need anyone else," added Veronica, perhaps knowing, on some deep level, that the answer to Arno's question would break the pleasure they had found.

"Not that surprising, sadly," said Arno. "You find Heaven in hard times, my friend. So few come here. It's a sad reflection on the state of the human heart that most consider themselves worthy only of Hell. All would be welcome here if only they had the convictions to make the journey as you two did. That's the ultimate truth, my dear Arno, we get the eternity we wish, and so few wish for—or feel deserving of—this..." He opened his arms crucifixion wide, gesturing around them.

Arno tried to get his head around this. "You're saying that everyone's in Hell?"

"Well," Arno replied, pointing at the two of them, "not everyone, obviously. There are other souls here like you. But it's a majority, yes."

"But they would be welcome here?"

"Indeed. Our Father has always believed in second chances, though it's a concept that has fallen out of favour in the mortal coil."

"Then why don't you tell them?"

"It's not my place," Alonzo admitted. "I could make the journey to the Dominion of Circles, certainly. It's simple enough. But there are laws, even here. I can't simply walk into Hell and hand out tickets. I'm afraid that would be a breach of protocol too far." He took Arno's arm. "I'm pleased to see the situation chimes with you though, my friend. It is a sorry state of affairs is it not? You can rest assured that I am, in my own way, attempting to turn the tide."

"Oh?"

"Indeed. I won't bore you with the details but I am hard at work on a solution." He stepped back and, clapping his hands with enthusiasm, opened his arms as if to embrace them. "On the subject of which, you're clearly in no need of my intrusion. I shall return to my endeavours and leave you to yours."

He turned and walked back into the trees, leaving Arno to think about what he had said.

4.

"YOU'RE STILL DWELLING on it aren't you?" Veronica asked him that night.

There were dancing lights like mobile candle flames, flittering about them. Earlier, Veronica had caught one between cupped palms, letting its glow light up her smiling face.

"Thinking about what?" he replied.

"What Alonzo said, about all the people trapped in Hell."

"Yes," he admitted. "It just doesn't seem right."

"Who are we to question?"

Arno shrugged, but it didn't feel like an excuse he could live with.

He tried to push the thoughts away, to focus on Veronica and their life together in Paradise. Some days he managed, some days he realised he was playing at the role, fixing a smile in place when really, deep down, his mood boiled. How could he enjoy what they had when he knew that others were suffering needlessly? Alonzo had said a paradise shared was a paradise doubled, how great an ecstasy would it be if he could bring those lost souls to the afterlife they deserved?

One night, as they lay on the bank of the stream, their naked bodies crackling pleasantly against the grass, Veronica turned to him and he saw she had tears in her eyes.

"I've lost you, haven't I?" she asked. "The spark's gone, you're only half here."

"I'm sorry," he said. "I've tried to leave the thoughts alone. I just..." He felt a surge of anger, having to express himself, to justify these worries when surely she should share them. "You see it's wrong, don't you?"

"I owe them nothing. Perhaps it's right they're trapped where they are. Who am I to say what their souls deserve? The people who watched me burn, who laughed as the flames turned my skin to crackling, should I want them here with me?"

"You could forgive them."

"Why should I?"

He sat up, frustrated and confused, miserable that he had lost his grip on contentment. "I don't know, perhaps you shouldn't, I just can't enjoy all this anymore."

"Not even me?"

"It's not about you. I don't want to lose you but I can't stay here either. I have to try and do something. I have to make the effort."

"Even if you have to make it on your own?" No 'we' anymore, he noticed.

"Yes," he admitted, "if that's the way it has to be."

"I don't need you," she said, "I was perfectly happy here on my own. I can always dream new lovers. Maybe that's best, that way they cease to trouble you once you close the door on them."

"I'm sorry. But if we have all eternity here what does it matter if I go? One day we'll be back on this grass, looking up at that sky."

"Such confidence."

"You know what I mean. It's not like any of this is going anywhere, is it? Heaven's not going to fall. The Junction will always be there to do our dreaming in, the stream will be there to cool our feet. The grass will be here as our bed. Why not make the journey? Why not try? You said yourself, you can only kill a person once. What do we have to lose?"

She thought about that for awhile. Gazing up at the stars.

"To Hell," she said after a few minutes, "back to the flames." She looked at him and smiled; it wasn't a good smile, hesitant and uncertain, but it would do for now. "I survived it once, I suppose I'll survive it again."

"Do you know the way?" he asked.

She shook her head. "But I know how to find out."

She closed her eyes and between them a point of light appeared, slowly expanding until it hung between them, a small glowing orb.

"Take me to Arno James," Veronica said.

The orb bobbed the couple of feet between them and hovered over Arno's head. He looked up at it and it slowly dissipated and vanished.

"That's a trick you didn't teach me," he said.

She shrugged. "Alonzo showed me when I first got here. But what did you need to find? I was here all along."

He smiled at her and they lay down to sleep, his mind the clearest it had been for some time.

5.

IN THE MORNING, Arno was relieved to see that Veronica hadn't changed her mind. Part of him had expected to wake alone, abandoned to his folly. If anything, she was more cheerful than ever.

"You seem happy," he said, partly worried that drawing attention to it might break the magic.

"I was thinking about it before I fell asleep," she said, "and I decided you were right. What's the point of living forever if you can't occasionally change your horizon? Wherever we go we can always come back, so let's see some fresh sights."

He kissed her. "Thank you," he said.

He looked towards The Junction and realised part of him was tempted to abandon the journey before they had even begun. Did he really want to leave all this behind? To seek out its very opposite? Why not just return to their dreaming and their life of pleasure?

Because, he thought, pleasure, like anything, palls if you have nothing to compare it to. And guilt will always be the vinegar that sours any meal.

They would come back here soon enough. When they did it would be in the company of other lost souls. A paradise shared.

He looked to Veronica who had conjured an orb out of the air. "All you have to do is imagine it," she explained, "just like the rooms in The Junction. You dream it and it's here."

The orb hovered in front of them and he took her hand. He looked at her and she nodded, giving him her permission to change their lives.

"Take us to Hell," he said.

6.

ARNO AND VERONICA followed the glowing orb until it led them into land that seemed as indistinct as a dream. If much of the Dominion of Clouds was a place that built itself on the human imagination, this was the hinterland, a place where thoughts became vague and details blurred.

There was a thin, white fog that curled around them as they walked, the sand beneath their feet just as nondescript.

"I don't like it here," Veronica announced, hugging herself though it wasn't cold, the air around them as ambivalent as everything else. "It feels like everything's fading. A few more steps and there'll be nothing around us at all."

"It seems to know the way," said Arno, pointing at the orb as it slowly hovered a few feet ahead of them.

"Well, I wish it would take us somewhere worthwhile. Hell can't be worse than this."

The orb drew to a halt, dropped to a foot or so above the ground and began moving back and forth.

"It's gone mad with the boredom of the place," said Veronica. "We should tell it to take us back while it still has some semblance of life."

"It's not that," said Arno, squatting down and looking ahead. "The ground stops here."

Ahead of them was a chasm vanishing down into the white fog.

"How deep is it?" Veronica asked.

"No idea," Arno replied. "Can't tell how wide it is either, not with all this fog."

"How are we supposed to get across then?"

The orb continued to move backwards and forwards and then shot directly at Veronica. On instinct, she caught it in her hands as it pressed against her belly, pushing her back several feet.

"I told you!" she said, "it's gone mad!"

"No," said Arno, "I think it's trying to help."

"Help? It's going to help wind me that's all."

"Hold onto it, grip it hard."

She did so and then gave a shocked cry as it lifted her from the ground.

"That's how we get across!" he said. "It carries us."

Veronica let go, dropping a foot or so before the chasm. "You're joking," she said. "Who knows how far it is? What if we can't hold on that long?"

Arno thought about this for a moment and then nodded. "I'll go first. Just in case. You can follow when we know it's safe." He waved at the orb. "Come here."

It floated over to him and he walked around it, trying to think of the best way to ride on it. Eventually he pressed it to his lower belly, grabbing it with both hands and trying to find his point of balance.

"I don't like this," said Veronica.

"I'm not that enthusiastic myself," admitted Arno, "but what's the worst thing that can happen? You can only die once."

The orb lifted slowly and he fought to shift his balance, trying to find the most secure grip as it floated out over the chasm. The skin of it felt soft under his fingers, like a well-stuffed leather cushion.

"I'm fine!" he shouted, thinking he should reassure Veronica as he went. His voice echoed back up at him from below, and he had to shake the impression that the chasm was mocking him with his own words. There were other sounds, some like voices, some musical, always at the very edge of his hearing, unable to be pinned down, ghost noises. He tried to see what might be making them but the fog continued to obscure his view and he didn't want to move around too much in case it robbed him of his precarious hold.

The orb moved slowly, maintaining a straight line, clearly trying to make it as safe for him as possible. A soft wind blew up from below and, for a moment, the fog swirled around him, the orb bobbing slightly in the current. It wasn't much, but it was enough to make him unsteady, rocking to and fro, his balance lost for the moment. He gave a shout as he toppled backwards, his hands digging into the surface of the orb, trying to find some form of purchase.

He heard Veronica calling to him but he didn't respond, concentrating on trying to maintain his grip. The orb suddenly dropped and for a brief moment he thought it was abandoning him to his fate. Then it pushed up against him once more, letting him get a stronger hold. It had consciously acted to help him. This thought reassured him as he shouted back to Veronica.

"I'm fine! My hand slipped but the orb kept me safe." He hoped that would give her a little more confidence when it was her turn to make the journey.

The orb began to descend, and the fog cleared ahead of him to reveal a set of jagged mountains, their stone black and volcanic. They looked sharp enough to cut you just by walking on them.

He was lowered gently to the ground, which crunched beneath his feet.

"I'm over!" he shouted, as the orb retreated back over the chasm. "You'll be fine!"

There was no response, maybe she hadn't heard him.

He wondered if she would make the journey. He knew she had been reluctant to leave the Dominion of Clouds and this was the first moment their journey had represented genuine danger. This was the lost point at which it would be easy to simply turn around and return. If she was willing to do this, he knew, she would stay with him whatever the future held.

He paced up and down at the edge of the chasm, staring towards the fog and waiting.

After a few minutes he began calling her name, convinced that she had decided against making the crossing.

Another couple of minutes and he had decided that she *had* tried to make the journey but had fallen. If that was the case, his common sense argued, surely he would have heard her fall? Wouldn't the orb have continued its journey and reappeared by now?

Just as he was convinced he would never see Veronica again, the orb appeared through the mist. She was clutching it to her so tightly he could see the cords rising up in her neck, her teeth clenched.

"I was worried," he said as she came to rest on solid ground.

"I wasn't exactly relaxed," she replied, her legs shaking as the tension finally left her body. "Oh boy." She sat down. "So stupid. I've never been so scared in all my life. And I'm not even alive. Oh Lord..." She put her hands over her face. "I hate heights so much."

"I'm sorry," he said, trying to console her. "I didn't realise."

"Just don't ask me to do it again." Then a thought occurred to her. "We'll have to go back the same way!" She gave a moan and shook her head. "Should have stayed in the garden."

He didn't know what to say to that so he just sat next to her and held her.

After a few minutes she got her breathing back under control and got to her feet. "I nearly left you," she said, "you know that? I stood on the edge of that thing and tried to think of all the sensible reasons why I should turn around and walk back the way we had come."

"Why didn't you?"

"I don't know," she said. "Because I'm as stupid as you are."

He smiled and kissed her on the head. "I'm glad."

She looked around at the volcanic landscape. "I'm not. This place is grim."

Arno was about to say something reassuring, to tell her it could have been worse (though maybe it soon would be) when there was a blinding flash of light and the sound of a gunshot.

They both turned back towards the chasm they had just crossed, sure, despite the fact that the light and sound had seemed to wash over everywhere, that it had come from the Dominion of Clouds.

"What just happened?" Arno wondered. His face was wet and he wiped at it with his dusty hands. He was crying and he had no idea why.

"Something awful," said Veronica. "Something really, really awful."

They stared out into the mist for a few minutes, neither of them saying another word.

Then they turned their back on paradise and began their walk into Hell.

WHAT AM I DOING IN THE MIDDLE OF THE REVOLUTION?

(An excerpt from the book
by Patrick Irish)

I MIGHT HAVE expected that the finding of Alonzo's Observation Lounge would be an act beyond us. To explain why I must clarify a number of natural assumptions you must have with regards to the geography of the Dominion of Clouds. Put simply, it was a preternaturally large building that housed a massive courtyard garden. Yet that is, in itself, a reductive description. By physicalising it, rendering it as a place of bricks and mortar, I steal away some of its scope. This is, again, where our language, designed to pin things down, simplify them into descriptions and natures we can understand, is a hindrance rather than a help. The geography of the place was not a simple matter of feet and inches. The place shifted, altered, adapting itself around you as you walked. I have mentioned already the seeming absence of population but there can be no doubt the Dominion of Clouds had been designed for inhabitation. It was a place designed to hold every soul there ever had been or ever would be. The idea that a place on that scale can be summed up as a 'large building that housed a massive courtyard garden' is patently absurd. It must have had the capacity for our entire globe multiple times over. It was a place beyond description. That is why I think it presented itself as something far simpler.

Yet the briefest of investigations broke down the lie. Corridors appeared where they hadn't been before, sometimes running at an angle that contradicted the sense of location you had already developed. An example: we had walked through a set of cloisters, the beginnings of the garden to our right. After ascending a set of steps we found ourselves faced with a large hallway that was extending out to where we knew there should be nothing but fresh air. There had been no sign of such a construction from the floor below, the perfect line of the cloister unbroken, but there the hallway was. I believe the entire building was far more a place of the mind than it was an actual, physical object. I suggested as much to my companions, moreover, I wondered whether the best way of finding the Observation Lounge was simply to expect it—to wish it, if you like—and let the building respond accordingly.

"If we ask it to be in there," said Joe, gesturing to a doorway, "it will be?"

"It's a theory," I replied, "and there really is only one way to prove it."

Filling myself with as much conviction as I could muster, an utter, unshakeable belief that I would open that door and find what we needed, I marched up to it, turned the handle and found myself face to face with a saloon bar. I closed the door immediately, accepting that this building might know me better than I had given it credit for.

"Well?" asked Hope.

I decided to experiment.

"Looks about right to me," I said, "though I've not seen it before, take a look for yourselves."

They opened the door and stepped inside.

"You were right," said Hope, "it is the Observation Lounge."

Which proved that my theory was right in principle but would take some getting used to in practice. What was needed in this place was a clarity of thought and intent that I had spent the vast majority of my life striving to avoid. I could only hope I'd develop the skill of it; if I planned on staying in the Dominion any longer it was something I needed to learn.

Simply stepping into the Observation Lounge was an act of bravery. It seemed to be entirely made of glass, hovering over the world, its walls and ceiling filled with sky, its floor looking down on the earth beneath. Currently, that view was of the plain outside Wormwood, the large camp that we had all so recently been a part of until Alonzo had brought us in here, ignorant cogs in the lunatic machine of his plan.

"The view changes," Hope was explaining, walking across the invisible floor in utter fearlessness, "depending on what you ask to see." She closed her eyes, focusing on Alonzo's face. "Find him," she commanded and the plain blurred and sped away, making me fall to my knees in disorientation. I could only imagine the effect the room would have on a drunken man, or one let loose from his senses by opium. It would be more than either could bear.

The view was now closer to home, the white walls of this very building visible to one side. We were looking on the outside of the Dominion, though, not the garden at its centre but a desert of off-white sand. Lying in this sand was Alonzo, his face vacant, a pair of ragged holes in the front of his shirt, blood seeping into the cotton. The first thought that entered my head was surprise that he could even bleed; surely, I thought, that was the province of mortals. Then, the absurdity of that came second, he clearly was mortal: he was dead.

"The celestial are not quite as invulnerable as I always assumed," I said, leaning back against the far wall so as to remind myself that the room was solid and that I wasn't about to fall anywhere.

"How can he be dead?" Hope wondered.

"If God can take a bullet that doesn't offer much hope for anyone else, does it?" suggested Joe.

The view was changing once more.

"What did you do?" I asked, slapping my hands against the wall to steady myself.

"Nothing," insisted Hope, Joe shaking his head.

"It has something else to show us," I said.

The view now was of a white circle, pulsing with a liquid light. It was like molten rock, rippling and glowing with a brightness that suggested unimaginable heat. Around this circle, the ground was also on the move, rocks swaying, sand undulating, as if the entire area was living, unable to be still.

"What is it?" Joe wondered.

"Who can tell?" I said.

"It's the Fundament," came a voice from the air above us and we looked to see an ethereal form moving around the uppermost corners of the room. The shape descended and, briefly, it took on a face we all recognised: Alonzo.

"You're not dead then," said Joe.

"Death is just a change of state," the voice said. "When mortals experience it they pass from their world to one of the Dominions. When one of the inhabitants of the Dominions experiences it they pass into the Fundament. It's where our essence, our souls if you like, go. It's the core of all life, in a few moments, my essence will merge with it and, one day, I will have flesh again. It will be different flesh and I won't remember the actions of the old but that's probably for the best." The form soared towards the ceiling once more, hitting it and dissipating in all directions, like smoke blown against a wall. After a moment it coalesced again. "I did my best," it said, "but I'm not sure I will be fondly remembered so ignorance will be a blessing."

"On the subject of ignorance," I said, "what exactly are we supposed to do now?"

"Whatever you like," it replied. "It's no longer any of my concern."

And with that, it vanished.

"Well," said Hope, "that was helpful."

We sat there for a few moments, continuing to stare at the Fundament. Then Joe got to his feet. "I'm not going to hang around here," he said, "not if there's Paradise to explore." He looked towards Hope.

"I'm coming," she said.

"I'd like to stay a little longer," I said. "Maybe see what's happening to my friends."

"There's nobody left behind I care for," said Joe, "the future's here." He extended his hand towards Hope who took it with a happy smile.

"I'll find you later," I told them.

They left and I settled down to get to grips with the workings of the Observation Lounge.

CHAPTER THREE
PRICE OF POWER

1.

ON THE PLAINS of Balthazar, just north of that viscous and unpleasant place known locally as the Bristle, a lone rider made his way towards the city of Golgotha.

The Choir of the Heat watched him as he passed, their cracked and dusty eyes grinding in their sockets as he crossed the horizon, trailing a dissipating tail of red earth behind him. As always, they sang their opinion on the matter, the birds in the sky above them circling away from the advances of those sharp and lethal notes. The rider, pre-warned, had taken his own precautions, his ears clogged shut with mud from the banks of the Bristle. It fizzed and popped, filling his head with a sound like cradles burning.

He skirted around the Forest of Truth, having no wish to hear its leaves pronounce on his future.

Whether their name was accurate or not, he wasn't a man who believed in destiny. You made your own way in this world or any world, you carved it out with bullet, knife or tooth.

As Golgotha rose in the distance, the road widened and began to fill with other travellers. Carriages of people, carts of produce, the occasional car, foul, black smoke pouring forth from their exhaust pipes. The rider stayed to one side, not comfortable negotiating so much traffic.

At the edge of the city, a lone beggar baked in the dirt by the road. Desperate for cool air, he had pulled the flesh of his head away to hang around his neck like a glistening scarf. The low sun glistened off his wet skull as he brushed the flies away from their egg-laying in his shed cheeks. As the rider drew close, the beggar stared at him, eyeballs dry from a lack of blinking. If he had lips he'd not have looked so happy.

"Spare a memory?" the beggar asked.

"None I'd be willing to share," the rider replied.

He continued along the road as it began to curl between the buildings.

He had once spent a little time in New York. The city had felt suffocating to a man like him, used to the feeling of space and distance. Of course, later had come prison and then he had known real suffocation.

Golgotha was not unlike New York. As in so many parts of the Dominion of Circles the landscape was influenced by the mortal world, some would say infected by it.

He was surrounded by demands on his attention. Signs begged him to buy their wares, everything from a hot meal to a hearty fuck presented to him at bargain rates. Their pleas went unnoticed. So much smoke and steam billowed from the sidewalk gratings and the open windows that the whole city looked to have been built on a fire, every building on every street ready to become kindling. To him it was just chaos, a crowding in on his senses that made him desperate for the simple, easily negotiated world of the plains.

"Long time on the road?" a man shouted from the sidewalk, scratching at a face of shedding skin. "Got what you need to relax and unwind."

"Doubt that," the rider told him, continuing past him.

"Don't know what you're missing!" the man shouted after him.

"I know exactly," the rider replied, more to himself than the seller. "Wouldn't be here otherwise."

After a few more minutes, he had to stop. The constant barrage of people and buildings felt as if they were choking him. He had sunk low in his saddle, flinching from things that weren't there, sick to his stomach by the smells of cooking, sweat and death.

"You look just about done in," said a voice to his left. "Not used to the city life?"

It was a young girl, though he knew better than to take such things on face value. He was about to tell her to begone when common sense kicked in.

"I'm heading for The Exchange," he said. "Lead me there and I'll see you well paid."

"How about I see some proof of your worth first?" she said. "I'm not stupid."

He took off his hat and scarf, the latter stiff with dust and spittle. He turned his face towards her. "You can take me at my word or not at all."

She gave a small laugh. "Maybe I can at that. You the man they're all talking about? You don't smell familiar."

"Maybe. What are they saying?"

"That they want you dead, for the most part. Reckon I could be set up just fine if I took you there. Bet there's a reward."

"Then it's your considerable good fortune that I want to go. Hop on and lead me there."

"And I can get whatever they're paying for you?"

"As long as they pay upfront, and don't make no stipulations about my being dead first. I don't think you want to take on a deal that risky."

"I don't want to kill you, what would be the point these days?" She climbed up onto the rakh. "Now cover your face back up. I don't want someone else trying to take you off me."

"I'm all yours."

As they moved through the streets he tried to blank out the ceaseless assault on his senses. The crowds moved like a storm raging around the buildings, flowing in and out of every available space. While some appeared human, other species loomed on either side of them that could not be so easily placed, absurd, grotesque shapes that he didn't even try to process. Monstrousness was not something you judged from the outside, it lay at the heart of you. How could he not know that with a heart as black as his?

Shadows passed over them, cast by unseen behemoths in the sky. If the beasts wished to hunt they'd need to do so on open ground, there was no way that creatures of such size could pass between these buildings.

"We're here," said the kid, halting the rakh opposite a tower of grey brick that reared up in front of them. It stood at the heart of a paved, circular space, the stones winding in a screw towards the building, making it look like it was a long, brick shaft that had been forced into the earth, perhaps to stab the world in its corrupted heart.

"You need to announce yourself before they let you in," the kid said. "They like their privacy, turn up unwanted and you'll be a stain on the sidewalk begging for a bucket to pour yourself into."

"You do it," he said, "it's your bounty."

Her confidence wavered slightly as she made her way towards the entrance to the building, a large revolving door of stained glass. "I've found him for you!" she shouted. "And wish to claim my reward."

For a moment there was silence then the revolving doors began to spin, a low whisper of cushioned metal sliding through its groove.

"You've found who?" asked a voice so barely audible it sounded like its speaker was some distance away, possibly underground.

The creature that spoke was a corpulent thing, dressed immaculately in a concierge's uniform complete with gold braid and the woven hair of innocents.

The rider stepped off his rakh and walked forward, unwrapping the scarf from his face as he did so.

"You want to keep back, boy?" said the concierge. "You don't want to get me on the defensive, I can be unsettling when riled."

"I'm no boy," the rider replied, tucking the scarf in his pocket and lifting his face up to be seen. "I'm Henry Jones, and I'm the man who shot God in the head, so forgive me if I'm slow to unsettle."

The concierge inclined his head in acquiescence. "I can see that might be the case." It inclined its head towards the girl. "You claim this man as yours?"

"I do if there's a bounty."

"There is. A generous one. There is also a penalty for anyone found harbouring him. Surely both are your due. Which do you wish to claim first?"

The kid thought for a moment and then sighed. She knew when she'd been outmanoeuvred. "Fucking cheat," she cursed, turning on her heels. She spared a final look to Jones, though she knew his sightless eyes wouldn't appreciate the fact. "Watch out for them, my little outlaw," she said, "they're tricksters all."

"I know it," he replied.

"Can the man that killed God be tricked?" asked the concierge, amusement in his voice.

"Of course," Jones replied, "but he can bite back pretty fucking hard when it happens."

"I just bet he probably doesn't need my arm to guide him either?"

"He does not."

"Walk this way then, God Killer, the council have been looking forward to meeting you."

As Henry Jones entered the building, the cool air that washed over him was most welcome. His boot heels echoed around him, bouncing between marble floor and a vaulted ceiling.

Out of the chaos of Golgotha's streets, his 'sight' began to return to him, that heightened sense of his place in a room. He could map out the size of the foyer, could sense the spiralling stairwell that ran from its end, descending down into the earth for an immeasurable distance. He could also sense the solitary elevator, its doors open, that lay next to the stairwell. Had there been anyone else in the foyer but himself and the concierge, he would have sensed them too, rocks around which the air of the room flowed.

None of which allowed him to fully appreciate the tone of the place. He could sense a sculpted structure at the centre of the room, could even discern its shape. He couldn't, however, take in its subject. He didn't recognise the various human forms that went into its construction. Perhaps, had they been more isolated by the sculptor, he would have recognised them for what they were. That had not been the artist's vision. The bodies curled and flowed into one another, as if the subjects were terrified at the thought of being unique. It was a grotesque sight as they fought to enter and be entered, not a sexual image, not given the look of terror on their faces, rather a curse that forced them to try and bond, fist into gullet, foot into anus, until there would be only one, amorphous mass left at the centre.

He could tell that they were surrounded by paintings, their heavy gilt frames standing proud from the walls. But he couldn't see their subjects.

In one, a procession of schoolchildren formed a happy queue at the open door of their headmaster. They laughed and jostled one another, peering inside to watch him as he slit and carved, a master butcher at work, breaking them down into their respective cuts on the tiled floor. At the head of the queue, a child, eager to help, was sketching out dotted lines across his skin, helpful directions for the knife to follow. The headmaster appeared quite content in his work, though the artist had worked to bring a sense of exhaustion to the man's face—when would this work be done?

In another, while the brushwork was different, a theme was shared: the human animal. Man, woman and child frolicked in the pig pen, naked and jubilant. They ran, copulated, defecated and fought, wild and happy in the straw and shit.

Yet another, this the product of a very angry painter if the brushwork was anything to go by. In places the canvas looked at the very threshold of having torn, distended and uneven, held together by the paint. The subject was presumably the infernal equivalent of Bosch or Blake, wishing to purge the horrific into art. Not for this artist the landscapes of Hell or depictions of a medieval devil. Instead they had presented a lamb, its fleece aglow with sickly light.

The concierge stood back to allow Jones into the elevator. For a moment, the outlaw wondered if this small steel box was a trap, but he entered it anyway. If the residents of The Exchange wanted him captured they would have plenty of opportunities to do so. In truth, he had been theirs from the moment he had crossed the threshold.

"Someone will escort you once you arrive," the concierge said. "I never leave the foyer."

"Who wants to get in here anyway?" Jones asked.

"Oh, nobody," the concierge said. "My job is to keep people in, not out."

It reached inside the elevator and pressed the final button on the panel, the lowest floor. The Exchange was nothing if not traditional. In the world of mortals, the most important residents occupied the penthouse, reaching up towards the heavens. In the Dominion of Circles honour went in the opposite direction.

As the elevator descended, Jones' sensitive ears began to pick up other sounds over the creak of winch and cable. As he passed each floor, sounds faded in and out: laughing; screaming; a rattling of sewing machines; the chinking of metal; the lowing of animals in captivity, abattoir music; a sound like, but not quite, the chopping of firewood; the plucking of tuneless harp strings; the stretching of rubber; the whisper of the confessional... The work of the Exchange was busy and varied.

Finally, the elevator reached the bottom and, after a pause that felt like a breath, the doors opened and the cool of the foyer had been replaced with an icy cold that brought clouds of condensation from his lips.

"Welcome, Mr Jones," came a woman's voice. It was as sharp and precise as a newly minted coin, a voice of business and professionalism. "May I welcome you to the corporate floor? It's an honour to meet you, I'm a great fan of your work."

"Nice to know." Jones stepped out of the elevator, taking a 'read' on his new companion. She was small, wrapped in what he assumed from the smell was a fur coat. "What is that?" he asked, leaning in and taking a sniff. "Rabbit?"

"The coat?" She laughed. "Not quite. It gets quite cold down here, one has to take measures."

She reached behind her to where a short rack of coats were hung, selecting one from its hanger and opening it up for him. "Please, I'm not sure how long you could stand the temperature in the boardroom without it."

He let her help him as he pulled on the coat. It clung to him with warmth and the musk of the dead.

"Do follow me," she said, leading him along a narrow corridor that opened out into a large cavern after a few steps.

He couldn't get an accurate sense of how big the place was. Their feet rattled on a metal gantry as they crossed the space but it was so large the echo was all but nonexistent. The cold that surrounded them made him glad of the coat. He had recently survived a bout of exposure, his skin frostbitten, his fingers turned ragged until the attentions of a deluded angel had healed them. This was far colder. This was ice colder than the mortal world could ever create. He leaned over the gantry. As far as his senses could tell there was nothing beneath them.

"If you had eyes," the woman said, "that would have been more than your mortal soul could bear."

"My mortal soul can bear more than you might think."

"You've proven as much, true. But even a dangerous animal like you has its limits."

Jones was aware that she was intending compliment rather than insult.

"The abyss," she continued, "is not something that should ever be stared into."

"What's down there?"

"Nothing. At all. Which is why it's more than most can stomach."

To Jones, not a man with a mind that leaned towards the philosophical, this sounded like a nonsense. He had no interest in pursuing the matter and they continued on their way.

At the end of the gantry, his escort pushed open a pair of large doors and Jones once again found himself in an environment he could partially understand.

It was a large room, dominated by a central desk. The light in the boardroom was dim, offered by three flickering lamps spaced across the arced wall. Twelve figures surrounded the desk and from a distance, or to a blind man, they might appear perfectly normal. But look beyond their silhouettes and their true nature was revealed. Six male, six female, dressed in formal suits, the magic of them began at cuff, collar and hem. Wherever skin would be exposed there was nothing but dark shadow. Look closer, if you could bear it, and perhaps you might get the impression that the blackness had depth; it wasn't simply an absence of the person in the clothes, cut from reality as if with a pair of sharp scissors, it was an opening to the abyss. These people had given themselves to that absence and it had sucked them from the world.

"Mr Jones," said the woman at their centre. She lifted her hole of a head as if to look at Jones and her auburn hair twitched, revealing itself to be a wig. If Jones could see the true nature of these figures he might wonder what was keeping that wig in place, and indeed, what was filling out the shirts, blouses and jackets they wore. Or perhaps he would simply accept it as another dark miracle of the Dominion of Circles. It takes a lightness of heart to be impressed by the otherworldly, an inclination towards wonder and fear. Jones was too grim to acknowledge either.

"It's excellent to have found you," the woman continued, her voice carrying a slight echo as it travelled up through the emptiness at her heart.

"You didn't find me," said Jones. "I came of my own free will."

"Which is interesting," said one of the male figures, a solitary monocle hovering where his left eye should be. "And leads us to conclude we have something you want."

"Is that true?" Auburn Wig asked. "Have you come to make bargains?"

"We do respect a good bargain," added another woman, her absent head capped off with a smart bonnet, its ribbon tightly knotted around nothing at all. "They're the oil that greases our engine."

"The salt that flavours our meat," said another

man, polishing the lens of his wire-framed spectacles with a silk handkerchief. He placed them back on the memory of his face and the lenses magnified the emptiness beyond.

"I think you wouldn't have let me be here if it wasn't you who was after the bargain," Jones replied.

"Ah," sighed Auburn Wig, "even if that were true then you couldn't have known as much when you entered the city. You bluff well but you came with an offer in mind, I think."

"An enticing offer," said Monocle. "A tasty offer. Perhaps we let you get this far purely because we were curious to hear it?"

Jones couldn't argue the logic of this.

"The Dominion no longer has a ruler," he said, "that's what people tell me. Once it was a kingdom, now it's nothing but a collection of sovereign states."

"This is true," agreed Spectacles, "though we like to think we have a certain influence over those states."

"But do you have all the influence you want?" Jones asked.

"We are the Exchange," said Auburn Wig. "We are the heart through which all the blood of the Dominion must be pumped. We control the worth of power, we are the measuring stick by which power is measured."

"You're bankers," said Jones.

"By mortal standards," Auburn Wig replied, "that is accurate. Power is worth nothing unless it has comparative value. How much is a memory worth? What is the going price for a fix of Buzz? How much the price for another's head? We are the balance, the scales that measure each state against another. In return they all pay a percentage of their earnings to us."

"Which makes you the wealthiest of all?"

"Naturally," Bonnet agreed, with a trill of amusement. "How better to place a value on power than being the most powerful of all? We are what they aspire to."

"For how long?"

"We do not understand," said Spectacles.

"How many times do the states pay you what they owe? How often do they hold back a little? How often do they screw the figures? I hear one of them, a guy by the name of Greaser, even worked in partnership with the opposition, not paying you a cut at all."

"We don't really see the Dominion of Clouds as opposition," said Auburn Wig.

"That's not the point and you know it. Your power's been slipping. People are deciding they'd rather keep what's theirs and cut you out of it. And that's only going to get worse."

"Explain," said Spectacles.

"You have a whole new Dominion to take into consideration, the mortal world."

"That is not a Dominion," Bonnet insisted, "it is simply a place of transience."

"Don't kid yourselves," Jones replied, "it's a whole world of new business opportunities. Dollars and dimes. You're going to be weaker than ever if you don't take advantage of it. You need to go back to the old system. One ruler, one power."

"The Exchange is not interested in war," said Monocle, "at least, not as a participant. There is no profit in it when you're the one fighting."

"There's no need for war," said Jones, "power is won by fear. I'm offering you something the rest of the Dominion will fear, something they will bow to and call their one true king."

Bonnet laughed. "You?"

"Yes," said Jones, "me. I killed God. That's why you wanted me, isn't it? You knew that if one of the other states got hold of me they would use me as a figurehead. I'm the one who walked into the Dominion of Clouds and blew the Almighty away. I achieved the impossible."

"You could not have killed Him had He not wished it."

"That's neither here nor there. Nobody knows that for sure, one more show of power and nobody in the Dominion of Circles would dare stand up to me."

"Show of power?" said Bonnet. "What power? You're just a mortal, a damaged one at that."

"You said yourselves, power is about comparisons. It's about perception. It doesn't matter how powerful I am, what matters is how powerful I *appear* to be. And with you on my side I could appear to be pretty fucking powerful indeed."

The Exchange were silent for a moment, deliberation curling around in their hollow heads.

"There is merit to your plan," announced Auburn

Wig, finally. "But we would have to be clear as to our agreement. You may be the figurehead but we would be the authority. We will not simply be a tool for you to use as and when you wish."

"I'm a man of simple needs," said Jones, "and there's really only one thing I want."

"Your eyes?" suggested Bonnet. "That would be easily done."

"No," said Jones. He had thought about it but what use did he have for that which he'd never known? He had never seen the world as others did and was by no means sure that changing that now would be a benefit. "I want my wife. She's somewhere here in the Dominion of Circles. The way things are, with no central control, it could take me lifetimes to find her. But if the whole Dominion was mine to govern..."

"Then she would be brought to you," said Monocle. "How sweet. He wishes to rule Hell out of love."

"Does the reason matter?"

"No," Monocle admitted, "in fact it's entirely acceptable. Your wife is our penalty. If you attempt to trick us, if you betray us in any way, it won't be you who feels the pain and suffering. It will be her."

"We will lay eggs of agony in her heart," said Bonnet.

"We will make legends of her misery," agreed Spectacles.

Jones had expected such threats. They were just words. He wasn't lying when he said he had no real interest in the power. He would let The Exchange use him as they saw fit. There was no shame in it. "Agreed," he said.

"Which leaves us with only one question," said Auburn Wig. "What show of power did you have in mind?"

For the first time, Jones experienced genuine discomfort. "You're not going to like it..."

2.

THERE ARE THOSE who have described cities as living things, likening the streets to veins (or perhaps, in less attractive districts, lengths of bowel). They name its thriving centre as the heart, the food quarter as its stomach, the financial district as its brain. In this somewhat contorted analogy, the city's population are often likened to ants, or fleas, scurrying across the body of the great beast, feeding and destroying with equal measure. Of course, in truth, not even the most enlightened metropolises have quite attained such autonomy, not even in the loose domain of metaphor. Golgotha, for all it may have appeared miraculous to the mortal eye, was no different. Its streets had been paved not grown, its buildings the slow accumulation of hard work, bricks and mortar laid by hand layer by aching layer. It would have been nothing were it not for the hard work, patience and investment of each and every one of its founding citizens.

Still, much of that work, certainly much of the investment, had been provided by the Exchange.

It was there, at that awesome tower, that the poets would have claimed Golgotha's heart.

For Golgotha's residents, the Exchange was the shadow that fell over them. It was the raised hand, ready to strike. That it should fall was something not one of them would ever have dreamed or hoped.

Yet fall it did.

Beetle Elmutt was tired from a day of manning his food stand, face sweating from the glow of its flames, hair slick from the oil vapour that surrounded him. He was turning off the gas, mentally accumulating his take. You didn't get rich filling the bellies of passersby. He had only the briefest of memories in his purse: the smiles of loved ones; the feeling of cool water on the skin after hours in the sun; the odd laugh at a joke or rise of excitement from a story well told; an orgasm or two. You had to have one of the classy places on fifty-ninth if you wanted to get rich from food, the sort of joints where you waited aeons for a table and offered up years of your life for a solitary plate. That was OK though, he didn't have the skill to run a kitchen like that. He was just a man who knew how to heat meat and pour sauce.

Looking around to make sure none of the guards were watching, he poured the dirty oil from his pans into the gutter where it slowly crept down the street gathering dirt.

Putting the empty pans on the lower shelf of his cart along with his uncooked food, he prepared to wheel his way home.

He passed by Riligius, one of the lower demonic caste. Riligius used to joke with the few in Golgotha that put memories in his begging bowl, that he had fallen even further than Lucifer. The last time he had consumed his day with actual work was in the middle ages, plaguing a neurotic baker from Ghent who eventually expired in one of his own ovens rather that than put up with Riligius's ham-fisted attempts at possession any longer. He had been found by his overworked apprentice, a blackened loaf of meat. The apprentice hadn't shed a tear, at least not in mourning, he had kept the bakery going throughout his master's 'lunatic spell' and considered this the final act of irritation from a supremely annoying employer.

Riligius had returned to the Dominion, out of work, out of pocket and down at heel. He had been begging ever since.

"Not much for you," said Beetle, tossing the demon the memory of a particularly fine Chinese meal, "but at least it'll make you think your belly's full for awhile."

"They never last," said Riligius, "you're hungry again an hour after experiencing them. Thanks anyway."

Across the road, Sylvestre de Vroot was winding down the shutter on his store. He knew the metal wouldn't keep the determined burglar out; if they wanted his charms and poisons enough, they'd soon break through. Of course, everyone in the area knew that de Vroot had extra protection, a curse across the threshold that threatened to desiccate anyone fool enough to enter without muttering the right safe code.

"Good day?" he asked Beetle.

"Shit and corruption," Beetle replied. "If I wasn't eating my own wares I'd starve to death."

De Vroot had strong opinions on Beetle's wares and thought he'd rather die than subsist on them. He wasn't callous enough to mention as much though, just shrugged as if to say 'what can you do?'

"I used to think life would get better," said Riligius, "now I just hope it doesn't get worse."

"Not sure it could," said Beetle.

It was the sort of dramatic irony that would have pleased the poets, still fresh from describing Golgotha as a living, breathing beast.

The hot air was filled with the sound of tearing foundations, stone, concrete and earth torn apart as the Exchange tower suddenly thrust upwards, as if in a last fighting attempt to stab that boiling sky to its core.

Thousands of heads turned, including those of Beetle, Riligius and de Vroot.

"What in all the fucks was that?" wondered Riligius as the tower hung for a moment, as if trying to find its balance.

Then it toppled, the long finger slowly sinking towards the earth. There was a rush of displaced air that sent Beetle's cart toppling. Riligius, damned if he was going to be pulverised on an empty belly, savoured his donated memory of a meal, distracting himself from the impending pain. De Vroot looked to his steel shutters and sighed, throwing the keys to the floor.

The tower hit, crumbling buildings and residents with equal ease, reducing Beetle, Riligius, de Vroot and several hundred others like them to paste of meat and powdered stone.

Death in the Dominion was never a permanent affair, flesh corrupted but souls lingered. Golgotha would be a haunted city for years to come as those souls drifted, awaiting the call of the Fundament and a chance to inhabit new bodies and new lives.

In the aftermath, a voice was heard. It carried it with more strength than a human throat could give it, greater even than the sound of the tower hitting the ground.

"Now hear me," said Henry Jones. "I am the God Killer, I am the wasting, I am the bullet in a thousand backs. I have taken the Exchange and toppled it. It didn't please me. Will you risk the same? There's a new power in the Dominion, and it is the ultimate power, the only power. It is me. And you would do well to remember before I come looking for you too."

In the rubble, the sound of his words still echoing through what was left of the streets, Henry Jones turned to his rakh, left standing by magic or luck he neither knew nor cared. He climbed on its back, a young girl's voice calling up to him before he could ride away.

"I got my reward," she said. He recognised the voice, the kid that had led him here in the first place. "And my punishment."

He couldn't see her eyes of course, now absent, windows to the abyss at the heart of The Exchange; but he knew she was now nothing more than a vessel for the powers that controlled him.

"We thought it best to borrow this body," she said, and Jones wondered which of the Exchange was speaking, if indeed they truly existed as individuals rather than several facets of one entity. "That way we can keep an eye on you."

He nodded, and held out his hand to pull the girl onto his rakh. "Fine," he said, "then you can start as you mean to go on and steer me out of this place."

WHAT AM I DOING IN THE MIDDLE OF THE REVOLUTION?

(An excerpt from the book
by Patrick Irish)

I WAS NOT alone.

"I knew this place would capture you," said Alonzo's voice, proving his spirit had not dissipated as quickly as he had led us to believe. "As a storyteller, how could it not?"

I looked around for him, eventually spotting the faintest of glimpses in the far corner. He was little more than a breath on a cold day, a wisp of white in which I could just about discern a single eye, perhaps a nose.

"I can't say I've quite got the method of it yet," I admitted, pacing across the floor which still showed the glowing heart of the Fundament.

"That's why I stayed," he admitted. "One last bit of assistance. Or interference perhaps, I'm no longer sure I can differentiate between the two."

"I'll take either," I told him. "Better that than to be in a room filled with possibilities and never master them."

"It's all about thought," he said, "like everything here. You need to be clear in your thinking. Visualise what you want it to do and it will do it."

"I always did struggle with clarity," I admitted.

"Drinkers do."

"I don't drink anymore," I told him, wondering if he knew that the first thing this room had offered me was a chance to break that pledge. I realise my coyness may seem absurd as clearly I'm happy enough to admit what happened in print, where anyone can read of my weakness. I suppose, however much as his actions may have proven to the contrary, I still looked upon him as something heavenly, something I should aspire to. He certainly seemed to have similar thoughts as he began to tutor me in the ways of the Observation Lounge.

"This place," he explained, "it's a great gift I'm offering."

I didn't know what he expected me to say to that. Was he after my thanks? If so he had it, profusely expressed.

"You must understand though," he explained, "it is not just about witnessing. There is that, of course; from here you can see everything, anywhere, at any time. But by witnessing these things you will become involved."

"How?" If this place was a book, with all of the history of the worlds written on it, then that I could understand. It was amazing but I could understand it. But how could I affect them? A reader doesn't alter the flow of words simply by reading them.

"How can you not? That was my problem. I was incapable of knowing so much, seeing so much, without wishing to involve myself. And, as I told you, this place responds to thoughts and desires. It helped me."

I didn't understand and it seemed he was reluctant—or perhaps unable to—be clear. "You are in a place of power. This room gives you a kind of omniscience. It changes your perspective. You are used to a life lived from a single perspective, experienced in a chronological line. That is not how this room works. Here you will move forward and back in time, following threads of the world's story as you switch between perspectives. You wish to see your friends?"

"Of course."

"But when? Do you want to see how they die? Do you want the end of their story? Or do you want find out what they were before you crossed their paths?"

"I just want to know how they're doing now."

"What is 'now'? I've already told you time is inconsistent outside the mortal world. There is no 'now'. It is simply lives lived, only a straight line when viewed by the person living it. To us, here, now, that line is complete, it can all be viewed. So what is the point of 'now'?'"

"That's terribly confusing."

"It's omniscience. Or close to it. You cannot hear their thoughts, know their inner selves, but you can know everything else. Let me show you."

And he did so. I found myself watching a man I didn't know as he visited Wormwood, then travelled up into the mountains to find Father Martin, a man broken, I fear, by so many of his recent experiences. Then he showed me two people in the Dominion of Clouds. I watched as they made their decision to travel to the Dominion of Circles to rescue lost human souls. Finally, I saw Henry Jones, countless miles away, hatching plans in the city of Golgotha.

"How did he get there so fast?" I asked.

"You still don't understand. There is no now, it doesn't matter whether what you have just seen happened, will happen or is happening in this moment. You need to stop thinking in linear terms. Time moves differently in the Dominions anyway, it has less meaning than you're used to. You have to start thinking bigger. Henry Jones rode from here to Golgotha, no doubt he talked to several people on his way, gathering information, making plans."

"Which must have taken him time."

"For him, not for you. His time is not yours, you're not riding with him, you don't share his line. When it intersects with yours you synchronise, your time runs in parallel, then, when you part, you go your own way."

"That's ridiculous."

"It is the way of the Dominion of Clouds. You'll get used to it."

I wasn't sure that was true. So I changed the subject. "Why have you been showing me these things? That man outside Wormwood, the couple in the garden. I don't even know them."

"All of these stories intersect, they are all part of the greater story. The story of what we have done here."

"We?" I wasn't being humble, I was far from willing to take my portion of blame in these matters. It was responsibility I was avoiding, not credit. "I think this was all your doing."

"That's what you think at the moment, but this is only because you have yet to see what lies ahead on your own personal line."

"And can I do that here?" It was an obvious question, though I was by no means sure I wanted to do so.

"No, only He could ever do that. This room gives us powers close to His but we're not God."

I was relieved, the decision removed from me. His answer exposed another question.

"You think He knew Jones was going to kill Him?"

Alonzo didn't answer. The smoke shifted slightly, perhaps the ethereal equivalent of a shrug.

"I can't stay much longer," he said. "You must carry on on your own."

"But I don't know what I'm doing!"

"Do any of us? For all our power? Just do what feels right. That's all you can ever do."

I looked to the floor which still showed the ruins of Golgotha.

"My friends," I said, "the Forsets, Billy... I want to know what happened to them." I corrected myself. "Is happening."

"Will happen?" came Alonzo's voice, weak and fading as the smoke disappeared.

I stared at the floor and, slowly, it began to show me the plain outside Wormwood.

CHAPTER FOUR
A TOWN CALLED HELL

1.

As THE SKY filled with light and the sound of a gunshot echoed across the plain, Lord Jeremy Forset had an epiphany.

It would seem to him later, after the chaos had died down to be replaced with conviction and decision, that a great weight had been lifted. Something obvious was now understood, the idiocy that had cluttered his life was finally washed away.

There was a time when he hadn't been obsessed with Wormwood of course, he hadn't been born with the curiosity that had dogged him for so many years. Try as he might, however, it was almost impossible to remember those days, the young man unburdened. He must have existed, growing into manhood with hopes and dreams. He must have had his fill of things to stuff his head, to occupy and thrill him. Forset wondered what they had been.

There had always been the inventing of course but that was a subconscious act, the solving of puzzles that had never concerned others. The physicalisation of the abstract. The wonder of flight turned into metal, cogs, gears, chemical reactions. It was, in its own way, an extension of his obsession with Wormwood. It was the rationalisation that stopped him from losing his marbles when the real secret, the real mystery, refused to be solved.

And still he had littered his life with the shadows of that mystery—notes, sketches, the miraculous pinned down and robbed of its magic. His entire library of research was like a cabinet of mounted butterflies, their colour dimmed behind glass, their real miracle, that of flight, stripped away by the killing jar and a pin. Magic was not to be found on paper. You couldn't paint a sunset, you could create a painting that had a sunset in it, and maybe it was beautiful in its own right, but the actual sunset, the explosion on the horizon, needed to be experienced in the flesh.

So it was with Wormwood. He had waited outside the town with notebooks and pens, a camera and the urge to document. No, he decided, as the light began to fade, the world taking shape around him again, faint lines at first then the solid shapes of the mountains, the dirt, the town that had ruled his life. *No pens, no sketches. Just sight, that's all I need. Just to experience it.*

His wife had known this truth all along of course, she had despaired of his obsession for precisely that reason. "You're lost in books and the real world passes you by," she had said. "Look up once in a while and see the things that are really important. Such a shame that she had never lived to see that penny finally drop.

"It only took a lifetime, my love," he said, speaking aloud, though everyone around him was far too disorientated to notice, "but I finally understand."

2.

THE AFTERMATH OF that moment, when God ceased to be and his worlds became ours, affected those gathered on the plain in two distinct ways.

It wasn't long before it was discovered that the barrier that had kept them away from the afterlife was gone. The sign of its vanishing came from within Wormwood itself, as a creature with the hide of an elephant but the wings of a fly came bursting from what appeared an empty street and took flight over the plain. It filled the air with a low, vibrating hum, its wings beating so fast they were nothing but a blur bookmarking the sagging, rough body. Its mouth was in its belly, a thing of multiple lips that peeled back to expose the hungry space beneath, howling to be filled.

The people ran for cover, hiding beneath their canopies or carts, sure that it could only be a matter of time before this thing descended and began plucking them from the ground to satiate its hunger.

Some reached for their guns and began shooting into the air but it would take more force than was possessed by their bullets to pierce that tough skin. Perhaps they still irritated it, however, as the creature circled a couple of times before returning the way it had come and vanishing.

The nerves of the crowd had already been at breaking point. The sense that the gunshot they had heard, and the blinding light that had followed it, had caused some essential change in the fabric of the world was something they all felt. They couldn't begin to guess at the details but they knew their reality had changed and likely not for the better. For many, the sight of such a creature let loose in their skies finally eroded the bravery that had seen them this far. Many had seen worse during their travels but a journey of horrors is tolerable when paradise lies at the end of it. Once you begin to suspect your destination is as terrible as everything else it's hard not to turn around and abandon the enterprise altogether. Heaven had turned out to be Hell, that was the pervasive belief, and they had been duped into offering themselves to it.

The evacuation spread contagiously, first a couple of wagons hit the trail and then the exodus thickened. Within a few hours, the camp that had become a town itself was reduced once more to a scattering of nomads. The plain was littered with junk, abandoned to the dust and the shadows of Wormwood.

There were those who stayed of course, those with strong enough reasons to still want what

Wormwood contained—absent loved ones for the most part—and those who weighed the business up and felt they had so little to return to that there was little point in the journey. Bridges had been burned, lives committed, for better or worse.

It was no surprise that Forset was amongst those that stayed, his recent epiphany having, if anything, sharpened his compulsion to cross the town line. Elisabeth remained with him; she hadn't abandoned her father yet through a lifetime of obsessions and wouldn't do so now. Billy Herbert stayed too, under a pretence of 'seeing through what they'd started' but really because it would have taken more than the threat of monsters to pull him away from Elisabeth.

The Order of Ruth were not quite so devoted. They had lost some of their number to the cause. The results of Brother Clement's conviction in the righteousness of their goals still lingered, both in their minds and spattered across the windows and carpets of the sleeping carriage. It's hard to remain philosophical about death when you're forced to clean up the results of it with a mop. Their leader was absent, last seen wandering in the mountains. After a brief conversation, all but one of his order decided to follow his example. They were sure that once they found Father Martin, conviction would be restored and the way forward would be clear.

It was Brother William who stayed. The young novice had slowly begun to feel more at home with the rest of the party than his ecclesiastical brothers and now, when the choice had to be made between them, he knew which way his future lay. He had changed his clothes and shed the name that went with them. William had made his choice.

No more than an hour after the death of God and the exodus it inspired had started, the crew of the Forset Land Carriage was reduced to four.

3.

"I WANT TO go in," Forset announced. "No more waiting. Alonzo isn't coming for us, and neither," he added after a moment's consideration, "is anyone else."

"I'm in," said Billy.

"Me too," agreed William, "I didn't come all this way just to stare at it."

Elisabeth looked at her father and smiled. "No pleas for me to stay here?"

"Would there be any point?" he replied.

"None whatsoever."

"Then no, we all go." He patted one of the wheels of the Land Carriage. "And we take this."

"It's hardly worth it, surely," said Billy. "It's only a short walk."

"If there's one thing we do know," Forset replied, "it's that the town is only a door. A gateway that leads to the worlds beyond."

"It'll have to be a big gateway," said Billy, looking at the town. "I reckon it'll fit between the buildings but we'll struggle to turn her."

"We'll ditch one of the carriages," said Forset. "There's only four of us now, I'm sure we can manage with just one plus the engine."

"True," Billy agreed. "Even then..."

"We'll manage," Forset insisted. "It will let us through, I'm sure of it."

"You speak like the town's a living thing," said Elisabeth.

"Yes," Forset admitted. "I do rather. I somehow feel like it is."

4.

IT TOOK THEM some time to effect repairs. The Land Carriage had been through a fair ordeal over the last few hours, driven to breaking point, shot at and attacked by an angry mob.

The work was rough, they had little choice about that. This was not an engine yard and materials were limited to what they had onboard, or could salvage from the carriage they intended to abandon or pick up from the detritus left behind by the parties who had given up the plain. Windows that couldn't be replaced were boarded up, holes patched, rough edges cut loose and made safe. The vehicle that took form over those hours, with the four of them working until the sun set and the moon rose over the plain, was an ugly thing. But the following morning, having forced himself to take a few hours' sleep, Forset watched the dawn light pour itself over every harsh line and tatty edge and fell in love with it all over again. It seemed to him to be the perfect example of practicality over draftsmanship. His initial designs were just lines on paper, the beginnings of beauty; here was the real thing, hard, powerful and awe-inspiring.

"You'll do," he told it. "You'll have to."

Throughout the night, there had been further signs of life from Wormwood. Flashes of light as a slow traffic began to build in both directions, some of those on the plain gathering up a few belongings and setting out to explore its streets just as a few of those from the dominions beyond decided to step out and take a taste of mortal air.

After a hasty breakfast, they made the few final checks before setting off.

"Fuel is going to be our first problem," said Billy. "She can burn pretty much anything and I've topped us up with whatever I can find that's combustible. She's designed to run more efficiently than a lot of commercial steam engines but we've still used two-thirds of our coke reserve and we really don't want to grind to a halt in the middle of nowhere. If we see anything we can use we should get it onboard, I don't want to be on the run and losing power."

"Noted," said Forset. "We'll top up when we have the chance."

"Food's fine," said William, who had checked the stores. "Now there's just the four of us, our supplies will stretch a lot further."

"We're short on munitions," said Elisabeth. "I'd like to think we wouldn't need them but given where we're going that's probably naive."

"Not that bullets were much use against that creature yesterday," said Billy.

"No," she admitted, "but knowing we have something with which to defend ourselves will make me feel safer."

"Agreed," said her father. "Perhaps Wormwood will be more than just the facade of a town? Maybe some of its stores will contain supplies we can use?"

"No harm in looking," said William.

"I wonder if we'll find Patrick?" said Elisabeth.

"I imagine the odds of us stumbling upon him are slim," said her father, "though we owe it to him to try. If we can find someone in authority we can ask where the chosen were taken."

"What an English answer," joked his daughter.

"Yes, 'if all else fails ask a policeman'. Still, it's all we can do."

Billy had lit the firebox, building up the pressure in the boiler. Once the gauge began to rise he called the others onboard and they moved out.

5.

BILLY COULDN'T HELP but grind his teeth as they drew close to the edge of town. Judging the width of the street ahead, they had several feet of clearance on either side and there were no obstructions. The last time he had been this close, however, they had been rattling at an almost uncontrollable speed staring death in the face.

Forset was in the cabin with him and he patted the engineer on the shoulder. "Just take her in as slow as we can," he said, "to be on the safe side."

"Damn right," Billy replied, taking her forward at a crawl.

The nose of the engine pierced the skin of Wormwood, what had once been an impenetrable barrier now a slick bubble that stretched and parted as they forced their way through.

On the other side of the barrier, the nose of the engine appeared as if out of nowhere, sending the gathered residents into a panic as they jumped clear, running onto the boardwalk or into the stores.

"What machines these mortals make," announced one, an ancient demon which prided itself on the fact that it had sharpened its claws during the halcyon days of Torquemada's Spanish Inquisition. It could barely flex those bamboo-like fingers these days, but sometimes it would tap a long, yellow nail against its sole remaining tooth and dream.

"It's as loud as it is ugly," announced another, flipping up its feet so the mouths on the souls of its feet could spit out their dust and join in the conversation.

"Horrid," said Left.

"Abominable," concurred Right.

In the Land Carriage, Billy and Forset were still unaware of the effect they were causing, inching themselves through the barrier. It was only as its surface passed over their heads, stretching momentarily at their faces with a tickle of static electricity, that they saw the street ahead as it actually was.

The Dominion of Circles had already expanded into Wormwood, mingling with the mortals from the outside, both groups eyeing each other warily.

The stores were opening for business, the saloons were pouring liquor and one enterprising young Incubus had already laid claim to the hotel that lay at the centre of main street.

"If there's one thing people will always need," it said, scratching at its permanently erect groin, "it's beds."

A family from Canada who had made the journey south to brush close to the celestial were sat on the boardwalk and watching the infernal parade.

"I like it here," said the son, working his way through a bag of nuts so spicy they made him fear for his tongue, "the people are funny."

"That they are," his mother agreed, casting a surreptitious, admiring glance towards the Incubus.

"Well," said the father, "I can't say it's what I had in mind but they don't seem interested in doing harm."

And this was the truth. Despite the caution evident on both sides, nobody raised a hand towards one another, curiosity won out over aggression. In Wormwood at least, it seemed the mortal and the mythical could co-exist just fine.

"What a place," said Forset, his eyes wide and his mouth agape.

Billy could only nod as he pulled the engine all the way through, casting a glance behind to see how much further they had to go.

A group of children—at least Forset assumed they were children, given their size and exuberance—came running up to the engine and began climbing up it. They were spindly looking, their arms and legs flesh but jointed like those of an insect. Their bodies were smooth and as purple as a bruise, segmented and plump. Their faces were round and fat, cherubic if not for the cat-like whiskers that sprouted from beneath their stubby noses.

"Careful!" he shouted as one leaped onto the smoke box. "That's hot!"

The creature stuck its face into the plumes of smoke and then turned to the others to show off its sooty grin. They all laughed, taking it in turns to repeat the trick. Soon the front of the engine was covered with soot-covered creatures laughing and choking in equal measure.

"They like your machine." Forset followed the woman's voice to find the children's mother. She had the same basic physique but leaner, the fat spread out over an adult body, her face thinner and more refined. She walked along next to the Land Carriage, stopping as Billy applied the brakes, the rear carriage having finally cleared the barrier.

"It's impressive," he replied, feeling foolish saying such a thing when surrounded by such sights.

"It's loud and smelly," she said, "that sort of thing appeals to the young."

"Right, yes." He realised she was not being as complimentary as he assumed.

"We had no idea the town was so populated," said Forset, fairly spinning around, trying to take in as much as he could.

"Well," the woman said, "it would have been a waste to leave it empty after the barrier fell, wouldn't it?"

"But that was less than a day ago."

"Time moves differently between here and your mortal world," she explained. "That's half the reason I haven't visited it as yet. I could come back to find my babies all grown."

"So," said Billy, "even though we've only been here a few minutes, hours could have passed back there?" He gestured back towards the barrier.

"Or days," she shrugged. "I imagine as time goes on they will synchronise. As the Dominions merge fully with the mortal world. I'm no expert mind you, what do I know?"

She clapped her hands, calling for her children's attention.

"Come come!" she called and they all jumped from the Land Carriage and followed their mother away into the crowds.

"It's unbelievable," said Elisabeth, she and William walking up to the engine to join Billy and her father. "Such creatures."

"I think," said a gruff voice behind them, "the term you're looking for is 'people'."

She turned around to find herself face to face with a man who appeared to have a good deal of the canine in him. He stood upright but was covered in long, greying hair. Great tufts of it were escaping from the sleeves and collar of his jacket and the cuffs of his trousers. His mouth, though not quite a snout, certainly protruded further than would be normal and she could see he had fangs rather than teeth.

"Sorry," she said, "I didn't mean any disrespect."

"Sweet cheeks," he replied, "I'd listen to any old shit if it was coming out of a mouth as pretty as yours. For the sake of the peace though, I'll have to ask you to mind your tongue." He pointed to the large sheriff's badge on the lapel of his jacket. "The name's Biter and I'm the law around here."

6.

FORSET WAS BY no means sure how he felt about a dog in a suit flirting with his daughter. He came to the conclusion that he needed to let go of his old morals and sense of propriety. After all, such things were a product of one's social rules and social rules fluctuated from one country to another. If there was one thing he could say with some certainty, breaching the barrier into Wormwood they had travelled much further in real terms than the scant few feet they had actually crossed. They were now in Shakespeare's 'undiscovered country' and it was only logical that they would do things differently here.

Besides, if he argued, there was no guarantee the creature wouldn't just bite his head off.

"I'm making it my business," said Biter, "to welcome as many of the newcomers here as I can. This is a new world we're stood on." Forset couldn't help but note the creature was mirroring his own thoughts. "And it's my job to make sure people know the rules we all need to follow to make sure it ain't drowning in blood and guts before it's got through its first week."

"Sounds fair enough," said Billy, hopping down from the engine and moving to stand next to Elisabeth.

Biter noticed the man's defensiveness. "Oh," he said, with a grin, "the lady's already got herself a man. Fair enough." He gave her a wink. "Can't blame an old dog for taking a sniff."

"Sniff away," she replied with a smile. Billy smiled too, because she hadn't contradicted Biter's assumption that they were a couple.

Biter chuckled with a sound like a cat trying to shift a hairball.

"Leave your machine there," he said, "nobody's going to steal it."

"Are you sure?" Forset asked, looking around.

"Sure I'm sure. That's the second of our rules. No stealing other people's stuff."

"What's the first?"

"No killing," Biter replied, before raising his voice and pointing to a creature leaning back against the wall of one of the stores, its body a mass of reptilian skin, several tentacles bursting from its voluminous gut and tapping on the ground in what appeared to be impatience. "However frigging hungry you are!"

He turned back to Forset's party and rolled his eyes as if they would understand the ludicrousness of his predicament. "Walk this way, folks," he said, "we'll soon see you settled."

"Well," said Forset, "to be perfectly honest, we weren't planning on staying. We didn't think there was really anything here."

"Nothing here? We've got ourselves a thriving little town!" Biter reached out and grabbed someone who had been running past. It was a boy of about fifteen, and Biter lifted him off the ground with no apparent effort. "Problem, kid?"

"There's a thing in the general store," the kid said breathlessly, "its stomach burst open and all these worms... purple and gold..."

"Oh," said Biter, setting him back down, "sounds like one of the Annelides giving birth. No big deal. I mean, Abernathy will be mopping up after that son of a bitch for a week but they ain't going to do no harm. Get a thicker skin, kid! You can't have a hissy fit every time you see something new!"

The boy nodded but his face was still terrified as he turned and ran away.

"You mortals freak easily," said Biter with a laugh. "You'd think you came from a world where there was only one species."

"In all fairness," said Forset, "and correct me if I'm wrong, but you do all come from Hell?"

"The Dominion of Circles," Biter agreed, "yeah. So what?"

"Well, traditionally your role has been to torture human souls, has it not?"

"You've got a lot to learn, boy," Biter replied. "I ain't saying everything from the Dominion is sweet as sugar but it's never been our 'role' to do anything. We ain't your slaves your know."

"That wasn't quite what I meant."

"Oh, I know what you meant but we've got more important things to do than poke your sorry asses with toasting forks and shit. What you kinky sons of bitches like is your own business, we're not judging you, but we're not being blamed for it either."

"So mortal souls aren't sent to Hell," Elisabeth corrected herself, "the Dominion of Circles, for punishment?"

"Nah... nobody's soul is sent anywhere, you can go where you like. The fact most of you chose the Dominion of Circles says a lot about you as a species. Why you can't just live a simple life I don't know. Do what you do and accept responsibility, it ain't difficult, it's how most of us get by after all. But no, you have to look to a higher power to judge everything from your poetry to your bowel movements. If nothing else, all of this is going to change that." He waved around his head. "Now we're all on a level playing field, you'll just have to accept your own natures, won't you?"

"I'm not sure it's *our* natures that will be the problem," said Elisabeth, watching as an obese, feathered woman vomited into the upturned mouths of her squawking young.

"Sure," said Biter, "feel superior, then go and squirt milk at them from your titties."

Forset grimaced at his crude tone but had to concede his point. "You are right that we shouldn't judge. It is a failing of man."

"We believe ourselves refined," said William, "but we just keep our horrors on the inside."

"That's the last place you should put something unpleasant," said Biter. "Bury something rancid and it'll only slowly start to smell worse."

They looked either side of them at the stores and

the people. The people, in return, stared right back. Everyone is strange to somebody.

The stores seemed designed to appeal to a market none of the party could ever imagine having existed. Windows filled with everything from string puppets to dried flowers, doll's house furniture to leather goods that didn't look designed to fit a horse.

William looked through the open doorway of the barber's shop, watching for a moment as the bony creature inside dragged its razor-blade fingers over its customer's cheek. In a sudden chatter of movement, its off-white teeth chewed at the man's hair, sending great flurries of it into a cloud around their heads. As it settled, William was forced to admit the creature had left its client with a perfectly respectable short back and sides.

The client wasn't happy though, dabbing at his ear. "You fucking bit me!"

"Never did," the skeletal barber insisted. "I am the definition of professional. Show me blood or pay in full."

William chose not to linger to see the result of the argument.

"Herbs for life?" an elderly woman asked Elisabeth, proffering a bunch of dried leaves. "Herbs for death? Herbs for sin? I sell all the herbs."

"No thank you," Elisabeth replied, "though I'm sure they're lovely."

"Everything from the bedroom to the mortuary my dear, you just stop by when you know what you want."

"We should call in at the general store," said Biter, waving the old woman aside. "Just to make sure the Annelide isn't causing problems."

He crossed the road and Forset looked to their left, where the street opened out into a small square dominated by a large house. It was an intimidating construction in the mid-Atlantic colonial style. It loomed over the square which was empty but for a carved wooden statue of a Native American that stood in its centre.

"That's charming," Forset said, walking towards it.

"Charming?" Biter changed direction and led Forset over to the statue. "That's my damned deputy. Say hello, Branches."

The statue remained silent, for all the world a solid piece of wood. It possessed a deputy's badge, hammered into its chest like a piece of absurd decoration. Forset looked to his daughter who had joined them.

"Damn it, Branches," shouted Biter, "stop making me look like an idiot. Say hello to the folks."

Still, it refused to move.

"Screw you then, you stiff," Biter said, smacking it on its chest.

He turned around and marched back in the direction they'd been walking in in the first place. "He's kind of quiet," he said, "doesn't really move unless we have some kind of emergency."

Billy raised an eyebrow as the Forsets passed but they kept quiet, not wishing to offend their guide. William was staring towards the general store which had begun to gather quite a crowd.

"You just can't beat fresh Annelides young," said one of the bystanders. At least William assumed he was a single individual, it was difficult to tell as he seemed to be built from several inert human bodies, a profusion of spare limbs and dull, inanimate heads sprouting from all over his body. "Come on!" the creature shouted towards the store, "some of us have got a lot of mouths to feed." He looked back at William and chuckled at his own joke. "It's not true," he said, as if William had asked. "I shove food in one of these puppies and there's no saying where it'll turn up. Trust me, you haven't experienced discomfort until you've forced your appendix to try and digest steak."

William couldn't think of a single thing to say, so he just smiled and hoped he appeared sufficiently in agreement not to risk being eaten.

"Come on folks," said Biter, "there's nothing to see here, get about your business damn it or I'll be forced to start roughing some of you up."

"You think you can take all us of on, you mutt?" came a shout from the crowd.

Biter snarled. "Sure I do. Then I'll have a nice chat with the governor about how deep to bury your sorry asses."

"The governor?" Forset asked, not wanting to distract Biter from the crowd but too intrigued to keep silent.

"Sure," said Biter, "he's the one who lives in the big house you were just looking at." He raised his voice so others could hear clearly. "He's the one who gave me my damned badge too, which some of you would do well to remember, sorry sons of bitches."

He stepped inside the general store, followed by Forset's party.

"Mind your feet," Biter warned.

"Mind their feet?" came an aged voice, "who gives a cup of warm milk and rat turd about their feet? It's my stock I'm worried about." A tiny man appeared from behind one of the shelves, three foot tall and looking as old as a twenty-years-in-the-earth corpse. He was holding a mop that was longer than him.

"Ben Abernathy," said Biter, "store owner and misery."

"Misery? I'm as merry as Christmas when my shop ain't drowning in worm guts."

"Oh Lord." Elisabeth had cleared the edge of a row of shelves and now found herself face to face with the Annelide. It was a fat worm, coiled into a pyramid about four feet high, its skin ridged and glistening with mucus. Its tail, poking out at the top of the pyramid, had parted like a flower revealing a slick orifice that was in the process of pumping out miniature, coiled versions of itself. The offspring came in sacs filled with gobbets of purple and gold goo. As the sacs hit the floor they popped, uncoiling the baby worm and splattering the goo liberally. A good portion of the store was now slick and wriggling.

"If you're going to upchuck," Abernathy told her, "go outside, I've enough problems without you adding to the mess."

"If you mean vomit," she said, "I've a stronger stomach than you give me credit for."

"I'm not sure I have," admitted William, stepping back towards the door. "Maybe I'll just grab a little air."

"Pussy," Abernathy muttered. He poked at the Annelides with the handle of his broom. "You'd better be of a mind to pay for the damages here, damn it, I'd only just got the place stocked before you decided to fill it with your stinking muck." He poked at a pile of the goo. "So disgusting," he moaned. "I'd chew my own fingers off before I got a drop of it on me."

"Annelides mucus fetches high prices," Biter told him. "The higher castes use it as an aphrodisiac."

Abernathy dropped to his hands and knees and began scooping it up in his hands. "Don't just stand there!" he turned to Billy, "fetch me a couple of buckets."

Billy looked around, making sure Abernathy wasn't talking to someone else.

"Would you have an old man do all the work?" Abernathy said. "They're in aisle three, bring the cheap ones not the galvanised."

Billy wandered off in search of them while Abernathy scooped the mucus into a mound. "Fetch a shovel too!" he shouted after him.

"It's amazing," said Forset, "I've never seen a creature the like of it." He squatted down as close as he dared, scrutinising every detail of it. "It's like a worm but clearly not subterranean, the pigmentation's too dark."

"If words cost dollars you'd be one of my favourite customers," said Abernathy. He looked to Elisabeth.

"Don't suppose you've got any dollars have you? I hear they're all the rage with mortals and if I want to do business outside this town I'd better get the hang of 'em."

"I have some back at the Land Carriage," she told him. "Maybe I'll let you keep one or two of them in return for some supplies."

"Explain to me how the damn things work and you've got yourself a deal."

Billy returned with three buckets and a shovel. "Get scraping, boy!" said Abernathy. "Do a decent job and I'll cut you in for a percentage."

The Annelides had finished its birthing as William returned, looking pale. "Folks out there are beginning to clear."

"Good," said Biter, "saves me having to whup 'em till their ears bleed."

"You have a very percussive turn of phrase," said Forset, scowling slightly.

"Why thank you," said Biter with a grin, "good of you to say."

He paced up and down, surveying the brood of young as they began to curl and wriggle. "I guess we should probably gather these up so we don't lose any."

"They're rather sweet," said Elisabeth as one poked at the toe of her boot.

"Damn right," Biter agreed, "like honey dipped in sugar. That's why they were gathering outside. Annelides young are a real delicacy."

"That's awful, how could they eat the poor thing's babies?"

"Well, in my lawless youth, I might have turned a blind eye to one or two," Biter admitted, "but I'm a man of responsibility these days." He grinned, taking pride in the fact. "And I can guarantee you that no son of a bitch is swallowing these puppies 'cept the mother herself."

"I beg your pardon?" Elisabeth backed away slightly as the large Annelides began to uncurl from its pyramid, its blind head probing around for its young.

"That's the life cycle," said Biter. "Annelides can't eat nothing but its own young. If it don't have a big enough litter to satisfy itself it'll start chewing on its own tail and I don't have to tell you what a mess that makes when it meets in the middle."

The Annelides began sucking up its babies, slurping them whole into its distended, toothless maw.

"I'm just going to get a bit more fresh air," said William, dashing towards the door.

"How does it propagate its species?" asked Forset. "Surely if it eats all of the young the line can't continue?"

"It'll spare a couple every few litters," explained Biter, "then, once they're mature, it's off we go again."

"That's horrid," said Elisabeth.

"That, my little bundle of sweetness," explained Biter, "is nature."

7.

WILLIAM SAT ON the boardwalk trying not to listen to the glutinous sounds coming from inside.

He watched the inhabitants of Wormwood going about their business. He wondered what his old brotherhood would have thought of the place. No doubt they would have made the sign of the cross and run off to find a dusty reading room to hide in. He had never really belonged in their order, he decided, he was too active to exist in such a passive regime. He wanted to experience the world, not sit in the dark and imagine it.

What about God? What would He have made of the beings that populated this halfway-house between worlds? If Biter was to be believed, the population of Hell were not the prison wardens traditional Christian study marked them out to be. They were just different. More of His creations living out their lives according to their own beliefs and desires. Perhaps it was his childhood, growing up on streets where even the cruelest, most violent gang member had something to redeem them, be it a sense of fraternal honour or doting love for his mother or dog, but William found he could see the bigger picture when he looked around him. He also knew that most would not. When these beings moved beyond Wormwood, stepping out into the mortal world, they would be greeted with fear. The fear would lead to hate and then the killing would begin. It was miserably predictable. Which side would he be on?

He watched a young couple cutting across the road towards the square. The man was definitely human, lopsided spectacles and unruly hair. The woman was harder to judge, she looked perfectly normal but there was an air to her that somehow set her apart. His instincts told him she was not of the mortal world. Yet here they were, arm in arm, sharing a laugh and, judging from their body language, much else besides. They would be the exception, William decided. A pity.

They walked up to the wooden statue and the man patted it on the shoulder, saying something in its ear. The statue remained immobile and the young couple continued on their way, walking up to the large house. The man opened the door and they stepped inside. After a moment the wooden statue's head inclined slightly, no more than an inch but enough to prove there was life in it.

William smiled, got to his feet and went back inside the store.

8.

DESPITE THEIR INITIAL determination to pass Wormwood by and make their way into the Dominion of Circles, Forset's party agreed to linger.

Forset had been convinced that they'd have more success moving forward with the help of a guide. Securing the services of someone reliable would be time well spent, he decided. Also, the prospect of being able to carry out full repairs on the Land Carriage was attractive to Billy. Why make do with the rough emergency repairs when they had access to materials and tools to do the job properly? They could also get themselves fully stocked for the road, maybe even secure more fuel. After all, Wormwood was a thriving town, becoming more so by the day. Why not take full advantage of the fact?

Of course, as sensible as these excuses might be, they were still excuses. They had been lured by the strangeness of the town, mysteries and monsters on every corner made safe by the attentions of Biter, his immobile deputy and the control of the governor. The latter was, it seemed, a reclusive figure, staying inside his house and only occasionally meeting with his representatives—most notably Biter. Sometimes instructions were given, messages passed. The permission to store the Land Carriage in the square ,for example. It was quite clear it couldn't remain where they had left it, blocking the streets. It could be stationed in the square, the governor instructed, and Billy moved it there, trailing the group of children that had taken such a shine to the vehicle when it first arrived.

The children used the Land Carriage as a climbing frame while Billy worked. Eventually they even began to take an interest in the dull business of repairs, assisting with small jobs, offering up wood to Billy's hammer and nails, balancing glass panes as he replaced the windows.

If this noise disrupted the life of the governor, he gave no mention of it. Which is not to say there wasn't sign of some distress within the walls of his home.

Working late one night, Billy had noticed a small fire burning behind one of the upstairs windows. He had assumed the worst when it began to flit from one window to another, moving around in the darkness like a firework ricocheting off the walls.

He had jumped down from the carriage, meaning to call for help, when the young man that William had seen on their arrival had appeared next to him and reassured him that there was no emergency.

"He gets like this sometimes," the young man said, removing his spectacles and cleaning them on the material of his waistcoat. "He's grieving."

"Who for?" Billy asked.

"His father," the man explained, walking on and entering the house.

To begin with, they slept in the Land Carriage but, after a couple of nights they found themselves convinced to take up rooms in the hotel. Their money was desired in Wormwood, its infernal population intrigued by the concept of currency you could hold in your hand and eager to learn its value.

"This is a far less painful way of working," said Popo, the Incubus manager of the hotel, holding a dollar note up and rubbing it with his fingers. "To think that, if you gather enough of these, you can get whatever your heart desires without having to lose years of your life to pay for it."

He had explained to Elisabeth the system prevalent in the Dominion and she had been grateful they didn't have to subscribe to it. She had so few truly cherished memories that the idea of abandoning them seemed more than she was willing to consider.

"It's not so bad," Popo told her, "at least it stops you living in the past. Mind you, mortals would be very impoverished, so few years to gather the currency of experience."

Both her father and Billy had been extremely wary of Popo talking to her of course but, despite physical evidence that suggested otherwise—something his refusal to wear clothes made brazenly plain—he appeared to have no sexual interest in her. She had mocked them for their clear embarrassment and disgust at the creature's appearance.

"Typical men," she had said, "we're surrounded by physiognomies undreamed of and yet nothing terrifies you more than the sight of someone's sex."

They had not had much to say to that. Though, as the days passed, she noticed they grew used to his appearance and soon seemed to forget the fact. You can get used to anything in time, she thought. Say what you like about mortals but we're adaptable.

If Popo fed on any of his residents none of them were aware of it or suffered ill-effects. He was the most gracious of hosts and they were extremely comfortable beneath his roof.

It was after they'd been in Wormwood a full week that Forset first met the elusive Governor.

9.

"'YOU MORTAL ENGINES, whose rude throats the immortal Jove's dead clamours counterfeit.'"

Forset looked up at the voice. The night was heavy around him as he sat in the Land Carriage, reading his old schematics by candlelight, contemplating improvements on the vehicle.

The man appeared ancient, his skin dry and sunburned. He wore black trousers and a loose shirt which showed the wrinkled flesh at his throat, a dry riverbed flowing down his chest.

"Shakespeare?" Forset asked.

"*Othello*," the old man agreed. "It seemed appropriate."

"You're the governor," said Forset, unsure as to why he was so certain of the fact.

"I am. I thought it would be good to meet you. I haven't been sociable of late," he looked out of the window towards his house, "for decades in fact. I have a feeling you may be of some use."

"Considering your hospitality I'd be only too happy to help if it's in my power to do so."

"You're a man of power in your country?" the governor asked.

"Why would you think that? Oh... my title. I'm a Baron, it's hereditary. I'm afraid it doesn't mean much."

The governor nodded. "Titles of power handed down from father to son, unwanted and unused."

"Pretty much."

"So you don't have the ear of your Queen?"

"Not really."

"A shame. You must be aware that we've got an unpleasant time ahead of us. Consequences. War even."

Forset hadn't really thought that far ahead, too enamoured by the new world around him to think of where the appearance of that world might lead. "I suppose so."

"I would avoid it if at all possible. I have no taste for death." He paused for a moment. "Not any more."

"You're worried that the mortal world will try and stamp you all out?"

The governor looked up at him, a look of confusion on his face. "Quite the opposite. They wouldn't stand a chance. It's them I'm worried for. You can't imagine the sort of power that lies on the other side of this town. I can hold it back, for a while. But sooner or later the mortals are going to make their demands. They're going to threaten. Or just attack. Then I won't be able to stand by and do nothing."

Forset was struck by the man's manner, there was no arrogance in him. He talked of a wave of destructive power that could wipe out the entire mortal world and yet he claimed he could hold it back. What was it about this man that made him such a force to be reckoned with? He decided he could but ask.

"I terrify them all," the governor said. "Every last one of them. But fear is a useless power unless you're willing to feed it. I'd rather think of another way."

"Diplomacy?"

The governor nodded. "So. Will you help?"

How could Forset refuse?

WHAT AM I DOING IN THE MIDDLE OF THE REVOLUTION?

(An excerpt from the book by Patrick Irish)

NATURALLY, IT WAS a relief to see that my friends, indeed, all the inhabitants of the plains outside Wormwood, had survived the fate Alonzo had planned for them. As absurd as it may seem, given my residence within the gleaming corridors of paradise, I found I even envied them. Religious preoccupations aside, the Dominion of Circles will always make for more interesting sights than its heavenly counterpart.

I had made my considerable living writing about the monstrous and the uncanny—a genre I will be so bold as to suggest will offer little interest in the near future as the notion of the bizarre loses all meaning—and yet my imagination had been poor indeed. The barest glimpse of the denizens of that town soon made me look to my oeuvre with nothing less than embarrassment. I had once asked readers to react in awe to the notion of talking apes (*Roderick Quartershaft and the City of Gorillas*), small beer indeed compared to the species that strolled the streets of Wormwood.

But how would the people of the mortal world react? The governor—or, indeed, Lucifer as most knew him—was unquestionably right to assume the worst.

I have no doubt that, in the future, when the world is a different place, made smaller by faster transport and quicker communications (yes, I have seen such things, would you really expect a writer to sit in a room that can show him all of history and not take a peek?) that period between the town's appearance and its global acceptance will seem absurd. A miraculous town—indeed the entire plain and the mountains surrounding it—had forced itself into the grasslands of Nebraska. Surely this would be remarked upon instantly? As a chronicler of these events I am duty bound to point this out to readers who—ah! The hubris!—may come to my words many decades after I have written them. To you, who have forgotten the slow crawl of information and wonder how the afterlife could intrude so forcefully and not immediately be surrounded by forces from countries the globe over, let me remind you of the world in which this happened.

The telephone was in its infancy, both in terms of construction and subscription. While telephony exchanges existed all over the country, they were small, local networks. The telegraph was our only method of long distance communication and, while fast, that relied on traveling to and from a telegraph office. The closest town to Wormwood, now that it had finally settled on a geographical location, was a small town called Alliance, and this was where you had to go if you wanted to send a message or, for that matter, take a train. It was fifty miles away, four hours on horseback, three if your horse was used to keeping up speed over distance.

As much as everyone, worldwide, knew that *something* had happened—that sensation, felt universally, when the Almighty fell to something as ignoble as a bullet—the appreciation of precisely *what* it was took a considerable time.

CHAPTER FIVE
PATHS OF WAR

1.

RAIN FELL OFF the old stone of Victoria Tower, pissing miserably onto the ground at Oscar's feet.

"Is it so unreasonable," he asked, hunkering beneath his umbrella, "that this meeting might have been conducted inside? I have no wish to drown halfway through our conversation."

Oscar was used to suffering the elements. His position in the Foreign Office seemed never to allow him inside, it was one clandestine meeting after another. This, however, seemed a step too far; braving a cold wind in Regent's Park was one thing, this deluge bordered on the apocalyptic. He regretted the thought as soon as it occurred to him, given the events he was hearing about in America. The notion that the apocalypse might indeed be close, chilled him more than the rain.

"I'll be brief," Admiral Frederick Clemence assured him. "It's easy enough, as we still know next to nothing."

"Hurrah." Oscar checked his watch. "I'm meeting the Prime Minister in ten minutes so you have little choice."

"Does he know?"

"Of course he does, as to whether he believes..."

"At this stage, I'm not sure anybody does... a doorway to Hell popping up in the middle of America?"

"Indeed, though if any country were to possess one they are certainly well-suited. What word from your man?"

Clemence retrieved a telegram from his pocket and handed it to his superior. "It's hardly illuminating."

Oscar read it and nodded. "Just so, it simply confirms the newspaper reports. What is the point in having an operative on foreign soil if all he tells you is something you could read in the *Times*?" Not that that was, in itself, unusual, he had to admit. If only he had John Walter's resources he was sure there was little in the world that would escape his attention.

"I have instructed him to continue his observation and report every other day unless something suitably earth-shattering occurs," Clemence continued. "We have a team of people en route, but it will be another three days before they arrive at New York, let alone set their sights on the town itself. At present, Atherton's the only man we have."

"Is he reliable?"

Clemence took a moment to consider the question. After all, Atherton had been perfectly reliable in the work he had undertaken on behalf of Her Majesty, the concern was whether this was really the job for a man of his talents. Given a choice, Clemence would have sent someone with a more gentle temperament. "He's always followed orders," he said in the end, though this wasn't really answering the question.

"Well then," said Oscar, "we shall just have to hope he continues to do so and doesn't cause us any embarrassment in the meantime. He does understand the delicacy of this situation?"

"Of course." Clemence hoped that were true.

"Because this is the unknown staring us in the face," Oscar continued. "I hesitate to even speculate, but can you imagine our response should all of this turn out to be true? What is any world power to do when faced with the possibility that it has become completely, irrevocably, outranked overnight? We own half the damn world, Admiral, we'd own the rest if we had any interest in it, and yet still, compared to this... to possessing the entirety of Heaven and Hell in your back garden, it counts as nothing."

"It can't be true."

"I would agree with you, certainly the alternative is to talk madness. Before the initial reports I considered the living embodiment of Hell to be Brighton on a Bank Holiday, but if it *is* true..."

"If it is then the world as we know it is, if you'll excuse the expression, righteously buggered."

Oscar laughed. "That it is, old chap, that it is. Perhaps it's best we enjoy the last few days we have left, eh? If we're all going to Hell we may as well earn it."

2.

PHINEAS TRUMP ALWAYS got his story. Even if he had to make it up. Still, he had to admit that even on a particularly imaginative day—and he'd been known to invent entire wars—he would never have typed a word of the stories he heard coming out of Nebraska.

"They say it's Heaven itself," his editor had told him, "crash-landed in the dirt like a duck full of buckshot."

"Someone's been drinking," Trump told him. Certainly both of them had.

"There's a mass exodus of folks heading out from there, all telling the same story. Meanwhile, here you are cluttering up the office."

"Working."

"Not on anything like this, get on a train damn you, or I'll stab you to death with your goddamn pen."

When put like that, of course, Trump didn't see he had much room for argument so did as he was told and headed west.

By the time he'd halfway completed his journey, his natural cynicism had taken a pounding. News travelled in a wave and he had met the crest of that news head on. When starting his journey he had been surrounded by nothing but the usual traveller conversation, complaints about service, dents to luggage and the rudeness of porters. By the time he hit Columbus, people were talking about a ridiculous story they had heard from 'this guy in a bar/restroom/ticket line'. Once the train window was looking out at Springfield every passenger was telling the story, a sea of conflicting explanations as to what might have caused the 'hallucinations'. By Des Moines it was a matter of fact and people wanted to know what the President intended to do about it.

Trump had gone from feeling a fool for covering it to an idiot for being so behind the times. Still, he told himself, it was hardly his fault if world-breaking news chose to emerge in Nebraska. I mean, *Nebraska*... Hadn't God heard of the East Coast?

Getting off the train at Alliance, a small town hoping to grow fat on the railroad like a tick latched on to a vein, Trump was relieved to find the *Tribune* had secured him a horse on which to continue his journey. If they hadn't thought to plan ahead Trump would have been walking the rest of the way. Alliance was filled with people who had heard the stories and wanted to see more. Folks were paying a fortune to hire transport and the town was struggling to keep up with demand.

He had imagined riding out there on his own, cursing the heat and the discomfort of a few hours in the saddle for the sake of a drunkard's fable. As it was, the road was filled with travellers. Enterprising locals had set up a business in ferrying the curious, cramming their carts and coaches to intolerable levels as they made the journey to and fro. Copy rushed through his head as he jostled his way amongst the crowds, allusions to the Biblical exodus, evoking the clamour of the faithful and their choruses of hymns as they marched towards enlightenment (this was window-dressing of the highest order, there was no singing as the travellers made their way across the flat grasslands, just the low murmur of conversation and the frequent ejection of gas from the horses).

He ended up in the company of several other reporters, all deciding that the notion of an exclusive was as remote now as their destination so why not just pool resources?

"I heard the place is filled to the brim with monsters," said Jonas Beloved, a writer for the *Boston Daily Advertiser* whose reputation didn't match his name, "things the like of which you never before set your eyes on."

"My eyes have seen a fair amount," Christopher Bridges, of the *Jeffersonian Republican*, replied, "so I'll reserve judgement on that."

Such reserve was in short supply after they had been forced to navigate the body of a creature twice the size of a luxury hotel that had expired blocking the road. To begin with people surrounded it cautiously, waiting for the first soul brave enough to give it a jab with a long stick. After an hour or so, kids were jumping up and down on the tip of its tail and one wily group had begun peeling off its scales with crowbars, mindful of selling them on to the folks back home.

"Still think people are exaggerating?" someone asked Bridges as they continued on their way. He didn't grace the question with a reply.

3.

ATHERTON LAY ON his back beneath the shade of a rock and imagined ways in which he might make his employers suffer. He had only been here two days and he was already suffocated by inaction. For every hour they did nothing, the problem grew bigger and he was at a loss as to why his Whitehall paymasters seemed ignorant of the fact. "Just observe," they ordered. He had seen all he needed to see during the half an hour he had spent on Wormwood's streets. It was a place that simply couldn't be allowed to continue its infestation of the world. The longer it sat there, a wide-open gateway allowing filth to spill out, the more difficult it would ever be to close it. What was needed was action, something major and decisive, and if the people that issued his insipid orders didn't see that then maybe he needed to take matters into his own hands.

But what? And how?

His little private army of monks and worshippers—and he was confident enough in his ability to control people that they *were* his army, not Father Martin's—were hardly worth the box of ammunition he carried in his bag. They were weak, undernourished civilians, not a true fighting man amongst them. If he marched them in to battle then they would die and that would be that.

Atherton had no problem with that, he felt nothing for these people, but he failed to see what advantage their deaths would offer.

Another concern: once the others Admiral Clemence was sending arrived, what would happen then? Politics? Talking? Compromise? He suspected so. He had been present at such deliberations often enough, they began with determined promises and ended with inaction treated as if it were a victory. Besides, once the Americans had become thoroughly entrenched in the business—he had watched what had clearly been an official party enter the town that morning—then the battle would be over. It would no longer be a case of taking on Wormwood, it would be a case of taking on America and he knew for a fact that his government wouldn't give that serious consideration.

So, how to act? What could he do to force the hand of those that would, in his absence, do nothing at all?

He closed his eyes, blanketed out the sound of the camp and began to plan.

4.

FATHER MARTIN TRIED to remember what it had been like not to question every single action. Not so long ago, life had been simple, it had been about books, dust and whatever was eating the leaves of the peach trees in the monastery garden. Now it was one moral confusion after another.

He had no doubt that the existence of Wormwood

was a disaster waiting to happen, but not because of those who lived on the other side of the town but rather the effect they had on the mortals who didn't. He looked at the mood of the camp, the people becoming angrier and more violent day by day, and wondered how bad it would get if things were allowed to continue.

He had tried to preach calmness but that was a hopeless proposition. He no more believed that the problem of Wormwood could be solved by gentle consideration than the rest of the camp. So what did that leave? Violence? And where did that leave him as a man of God? If indeed, there were any God left to be a man of.

He was a man utterly adrift, with no idea of his place in the world.

What he wouldn't give to return to a life of spraying the peach trees.

5.

DUGGAN MCDAID CLUTCHED his satchel of paperwork close to his chest and hoped it might help protect him as his carriage was driven through the barrier into Wormwood. To most people, sheaves of documentation, copies of statutes and legal precedents (for which there were certainly none in this case) would feel like little protection at all but McDaid took great comfort from facts in ink. He preferred the world when it was on paper, inarguable, indelible, black and white.

"Would you just look at this place?" asked one of his companions, "it's..." and there Algernon Sidney Paddock's gift for description failed him. Senator for the state of Nebraska, it had only been a matter of time before he visited Wormwood. His only regret was that he couldn't have put the business off longer than a couple of days. He was by no means sure he was ready for what he was about to meet.

"Sit down, Algernon," said the third passenger, William A. Poynter, Nebraska's Governor. "We're supposed to present the firm and respectable face of America at these people, not gawp like a kiddie in an aquarium."

"Right," Paddock agreed, dropping back into his seat, "yes. Firm and respectable."

Poynter rapped on the roof of the carriage. "Stop here, Jim."

The coach came to a halt and Poynter stared at McDaid. "You ready?"

"I suppose so."

"Dear God, man, I'm not asking you to do much, just get a good look around. I want to know what this place is really like. To do that I need someone who can explore freely, you get me?"

"I get you. Sir. Yes, sir."

"Then get on with it. We'll pick you up later."

McDaid nodded and clambered out of the coach, still holding his satchel in front of him.

Poynter shouted once more at the driver and the coach carried on towards the town square and the governor's house.

McDaid looked around, half tempted just to walk back to the barrier and wait for his employer to finish his business and leave. He could always say they'd thrown him out, he decided, taken him for a spy and threatened him with violence unless he took his leave. He had thought he'd been brought along to take notes, document the talks between his employer and the authorities in Wormwood. That had been terrifying enough but when Poynter had made his real plan clear McDaid had almost been beside himself. A more creative man, he had decided, would have been able to come up with a speedy excuse. He was not a creative man. He had simply nodded and spent the last hour of their journey in a state of miserable terror.

He sat down on the edge of the boardwalk and looked up and down the street. It was busy and his eyes struggled to take in some of the more bizarre sights, creatures that looked like characters from the books his mother had read to him as a child, mythical beasts, all fangs and eyes. He was surprised by quite how many of the folk who went about their business were as human as he—or at least appeared so. He saw a family, mother and father ferrying their children towards the general store; a young couple wandering along eating buttered corn; an elderly lady manhandling a bag of groceries as she made her slow and fragile way home. The old woman finally lost the battle against her unruly shopping as she drew next to him.

"Oh Lord," she sighed, as the boardwalk was suddenly cluttered with vegetables.

"Let me help," he told her, happy to busy himself with something normal, if only to defer acting upon his orders a little longer.

"You're a sweetheart," she told him as he gathered her spilled groceries and placed them back in her bag.

He looked at her. The little hair she possessed was worn long, her body little more than bones wrapped in layers of cotton and wool. She could have been his grandma. Hell, could have been *anybody's* grandma.

"Are you..." he tried to think of the right word, "normal?"

"What's normal, kid?" she asked. "I'd have thought you'd lived enough years to know there ain't no such thing. I'm mortal, if that's what you're asking. Too damned mortal if you ask me, I've been knocking on Heaven's door for years, now I'm so damned weak I have to live next to it in order to reach."

"Sorry," he said, still carrying her bag. "I didn't mean to be rude."

"No matter," she told him, "carry my shopping for me and I'll try and make sure something violent doesn't eat you for being a bigot."

He looked around. "Eat me?"

"Just joshing with you, son, now come on, if I stand still too long I'm liable to take root like Branches over there." She nodded towards the square but he had no idea what she was referring to and decided not to question her.

"How long have you been here?" he asked her.

"Oh, ages," she replied, "had my son move me out here months back. I wasn't going to miss this, not for anyone. Had a little place outside for awhile, watched the others roll up as the months went by. Then watched them all roll out again when they decided they didn't like the look of the place as much as they'd hoped. Course, I'd thought Hodge and I would just come in, take a little look around then go back to Kansas. Didn't expect to set up a home."

"Hodge?"

"My son, pay attention, I'm too old to repeat myself."

"Yes, right, sorry."

They had moved off the main street and into a road beyond where a row of houses were being claimed. Families from the mortal world and the Dominion of Circles alike were moving in, making changes, setting up homes.

"What's you name, son?" she asked him. "If your mother didn't bring you up right enough to offer it, I guess I'll have to do the honours."

"McDaid," he said. "Duggan McDaid. Sorry."

"So you keep saying, maybe we should just take it as read. Mine's Elspeth Gorman."

"Pleased to meet you Mrs Gorman," he smiled, "and my mother brought me up just fine, I'm just a bit in shock is all."

"What you doing here Duggan? Fixing to move or just having a nosey?"

"I'm here with the Governor," he admitted, only thinking afterwards that perhaps he was supposed to keep that secret. "He and Senator Paddock are meeting up with your man here, to discuss what's going to happen now that... well, you know...."

"I suppose you'd think of it as Hell, though, by all accounts, it ain't what most people would imagine. There's two Dominions, the Dominion of Circles and the Dominion of Clouds, though only one of 'em's got much in the way of people in it. From what I understand Heaven's kind of sparse."

"Hi," came a voice from the stairs and McDaid stood up to shake the newcomer's hand.

"Name's Hodge," the man said, "you help Ma with her shopping?"

"That he did," Elspeth said, "he's here with a bunch of politicians but he seems nice enough so don't throw him out just yet."

Hodge smiled and scratched at his unshaven cheeks. "You'll have to forgive her," he said, "she don't like mincing her words."

"Duggan McDaid," McDaid replied, "and I don't mind one bit."

Hodge sat down in another chair, brushing the dust from a pair of tatty looking bib pants. "Been working on the roof," he explained. "God knows why, probably never even rains here. She say you're with politicians?"

"I work for the Governor," he said, "he's here with Senator Paddock."

"Governor of where?"

"Nebraska." McDaid wasn't sure if it was a trick question. "That's where we are after all."

"Not anymore you ain't," said Elspeth, "you left Nebraska behind the minute you crossed the town line."

"Nebraska," said Hodge. "I thought we were in Texas."

"You know how it works, you silly ox," Elspeth told him, "wherever we thought we were, we ain't. Wormwood appeared all over the place. 'Cept when it didn't."

"That's clear then," Hodge laughed. He looked at McDaid. "Lots of people came to find Wormwood, and they went to different places but somehow we all found it. Now that it's actually bolted on to our world I guess it plumped for Nebraska."

Much of this was going over McDaid's head, but he'd decided he couldn't keep asking for explanations. Some if it he'd just have to take on face value.

"So," said Hodge, "you think the Governor's going to try and cause trouble?"

McDaid couldn't find it in himself to give a political answer, these people were being straight with him so he'd be straight right back. "Nobody really believes what's happened," he said, "but when they do they're going to have a hard time accepting it. It's not every day you suddenly have a new world dumped in the middle of your state. Two new worlds, I suppose. I don't know what they're going to do. I guess it won't be down to them anyway. They'll report to the President, then the conversations will really begin."

"The governor... that is *our* governor... worries about war."

"I suppose it could come to that, but it's all so ridiculous. On one hand, these people..." McDaid paused, catching a look on Elspeth's face as she brought him his coffee, "no disrespect intended...

but they've invaded the United States of America. But they've done so in a manner that makes it impossible to withdraw. At least, I assume so? Could this place be lifted up and placed elsewhere?"

"I don't think so," Hodge replied, "nobody's quite sure. It wasn't supposed to have happened at all. Wormwood was a temporary gateway. Something went wrong..."

"God was shot," said Elspeth.

Hodge sighed. "I know that's what they're saying, momma, but I'm trying to keep this purely factual. Let's stick to what we actually know, shall we?"

"Someone shot God?" McDaid asked.

"Ahuh," Elspeth replied, "made Himself mortal and someone took advantage. Bang. That's why we're all in this mess, His good hand is now off the reins and who knows where it'll leave us?"

"The point is," said Hodge, trying to bring things back on track, "Wormwood became fixed. The temporary gateway stays open. It wasn't an invasion, it was an accident."

"Accidental it may have been but the result is the same. In normal circumstances," he shrugged, "and that seems such a pointless thing to say, *nothing* about this is normal, but the invaders would be asked to withdraw. We assume that can't happen. So what's the next step? They're treated as immigrants? How many are there? Would they all be willing to become citizens of America?"

"And if they're not willing," Hodge replied, "you have to realise, there ain't a damn thing anyone could do about it. You're looking at a population that far exceeds that of the rest of the world, many of whom have powers mortal men could only dream of. That's the governor's fear. If the mortal world tries to pick a fight, the Dominion of Circles will just slap it down. Hard. A lot of these folks are nice enough but folks are folks, you know? Some are good, some are bad. And when you're bad with sharp teeth and claws that could open an iron stove like it was made of paper... Well, it don't make for a long fight. He's determined to find a way that we can all co-exist peaceably."

"You think he'll find it?"

Hodge scratched at his face and sipped his coffee. "I don't think he's got a chance. I only wish he had."

6.

BILLY STOOD BACK to let the coach past.

"There they go," he said to Elisabeth, "the powers that be."

"Father barely slept for worrying about it," she said. "He's never liked responsibility. Leave him alone with his books and his inventions and he's happy, force him to discuss things with other adults and all he really wants to do is crawl away and hide."

"Well, I doubt today's talks are going to mean much anyway. They'll posture a little bit, then run back to make their reports and recommendations, all of which will be ignored, then we'll have the President's men down here."

"At which point, the posturing will *really* begin."

She took his arm as they made their way towards the barrier. "Still, it could have been worse, we could be in England, then they'd have Cecil to deal with. He'd have taken one look at the place and resigned."

"Cecil?"

"The Prime Minister."

"Oh. Him."

They'd reached the barrier by now. Billy withdrew his pocket watch. "Let's make sure we're synchronised."

She held her own watch next to his, adjusting it slightly so that it matched. "Thirty-seven minutes past eleven," she said.

"I'll be back in a minute!" he said, and walked through the barrier.

"Probably not," Elisabeth replied, "you never are."

On the other side of the barrier, a few new faces were poking through the ruins left by the abandoned camp. Many of them from the Dominion of Circles.

"What's this for?" one of them asked, recognising Billy as he drew closer. She was one of the Kirby Clutch, an extended family who seemed to share a group mind. Billy had been struck by the way they rarely spoke to one another, their unnaturally small heads twitching as they sat together, pooling their thoughts. It had been Biter that had explained the way of them.

"There's hundreds of them," he'd said, "dotted all over the Dominion. They just gather information. You want to know anything, ask a Kirby, they'll set you straight."

She was holding up a pickled pig's foot, drying out

and covered in dust. "Is it an offering?" she asked, "a prize to the fallen God?"

"If it is," Billy replied, "it ain't much of one." Her head twitched, as if trying to translate his words into a meaningful answer. "It's food," he told her.

The head twitched again and she placed the pig's foot in her mouth.

"No!" Billy laughed, "you don't eat the whole thing, you'll choke. It'll taste disgusting anyway, it's probably rancid from being left in the sun."

She swallowed and smiled. "We like rancid pig's feet. Where can we find more?"

He shook his head. "That you'll have to ask Abernathy."

A mortal had walked up to them, staring at the Kirby. He was middle-aged, his ginger beard twitching as he scrutinised the woman quite openly.

"You new here?" Billy asked him.

The man turned to look at him. "Come from Alliance," he said, "see what's what."

"That's great," said Billy. "What's the time?"

The man seemed confused by the question. "Time?"

"Yes. The time. What is it?"

The man pulled out his pocket watch. "A quarter of four."

"Great. And what day is it?"

"What day?"

"Yes. What day is it? Today."

"Thursday?" The man was utterly bewildered by this line of questioning and was clearly beginning to wonder if Billy were as outlandish as the Kirby.

"The fourteenth?"

The man nodded. As did the Kirby, absorbing all these brilliant facts for the benefit of the Clutch.

"Thanks," said Billy, "you've been very helpful." He walked back towards the barrier.

"Hey!" called the man. "You one of they demons?"

"Nope," Billy replied, "no demons here."

He stepped back through the barrier. Elisabeth had gone, but he wasn't altogether surprised. He walked up the road a little and found her sat on the bench outside the general store talking to Abernathy.

"I need to open up a whole new supply line," the shopkeeper was saying, "find a way of buying this muck you mortals like. You know, cows and peas and stuff."

"I got bored," she told Billy, "so Ben has been entertaining me."

"She's teaching me the point of rhubarb," Abernathy said, "but I'm just not getting it. If you want something sharp that takes the skin off your teeth, drink acid, that's what I say."

"It's the dessert form of acid," she agreed, holding out her watch to Billy. "You've been gone hours." The watch said it was nearly half past two.

"Actually," Billy held up his own watch, "I've been gone five minutes. Guess what day it was."

"Do tell."

"Thursday."

"What day is it over here?" asked Abernathy. "I never really bother with days. When they're all the same who keeps count?"

"I do, darling," said Elisabeth "and it's Sunday."

"Great, that next to a Thursday?"

"No."

"Well it seems to me that I'm better off. If you mortals can't come to an agreement why should I bother?" He went back inside to increase some of his prices. That never failed to make for a cheerful afternoon.

Elisabeth was jotting down the time in her notebook. "The differential is definitely narrowing. I shall tell father when I see him, he'll get all excited and add it to his graph."

"At least, with time moving faster over here, I could hang around for a few months and not lose my job," said Billy. "It certainly stretches your holiday."

"You really think you'll ever go back to it anyway?"

Billy shrugged. "I suppose it seems unlikely. Got to do something for money though, can't survive off fresh air."

"Maybe," she said, pulling him down onto the bench next to her, "you should just marry someone rich."

"I guess that's one solution," he agreed. "Know anyone?"

Elisabeth kissed him on the lips and smiled. "No. You?"

7.

McDAID HAD FINISHED his coffee and chatted awhile,

accepting that his employers were likely to be several hours. After very little prompting he'd even helped Hodge with his repairs. Once he'd decided that loitering any longer was to risk a long walk home, he left Elspeth's house and made his way back towards the main street. Noticing that the carriage was still waiting outside the Governor's house, he decided to take a walk along the main street, if only so that, when the inevitable cross-examination came later, he could say he had.

His time with Elspeth and Hodge had calmed some of his nerves. As grotesque as some of the sights were he tried to approach them with an open mind. He was not always successful—perhaps a braver man than he could come face to teeth with the rotating maw of the voracious Acka and not give out a startled cry, but for him it was involuntary—but he no longer viewed every resident of Wormwood as the enemy.

He even partook in a jug of something that was like, but wasn't quite, iced tea at one of the tables outside Madame Mimi's Refreshatorium. It occurred to him after a couple of glasses that the liquid may have contained something mildly narcotic, as he felt as if he were floating for half an hour or so after drinking it. For a few minutes he panicked slightly, imagining the dressing-down he would likely get from his employer if he appeared insensate when they collected him, but—and no doubt this was also a side-effect of the relaxing brew—he decided it was all in the name of experience and he'd argue as much if pressed. That decided, he found himself enjoying the sensation of weightlessness as he ambled along the street, browsing in the shops and smiling at the folk he passed.

"Well look at you," came a voice from one of the doorways. "Stranger in town?"

He looked up to see what appeared to be a creature entirely composed of hands. Its limbs were extended fingers, its body a cluster of clasped palms, a knuckle raised as if for a head. With mild curiosity—that 'iced tea' really was doing its work, he decided—he looked to see a mouth but the creature seemingly possessed none, the palms that made up its torso merely parting slightly when it spoke, the sound escaping from between them.

"Just visiting," McDaid told it. "I'm here with the Governor."

"Lucifer?"

McDaid was momentarily thrown. "Not really," he said, assuming the creature meant some insult towards his employer, "though certainly Mr Poynter has some enemies. He's here to talk to your people about, well, you know... what's going to happen now you're living in America."

"I'm living in America, am I?" the creature said, its palms clapping together in amused applause, "and here I was thinking you were now living in the Dominion."

"Who you talking to, Fingers?" came a voice from inside. It was so dark inside the building McDaid couldn't discern the speaker, though the shadows appeared to move.

"Some mortal," Fingers replied. It was silent for a moment, then turned back into the doorway. "Come in," it said, one of its digit limbs beckoning him.

McDaid couldn't think of a polite reason why he shouldn't.

As he stepped inside, Fingers extended a limb and pushed the door closed behind him. "Apparently he's here to tell us what we have to do now we're under mortal rule."

"I didn't mean it quite like that," McDaid said, staring into the darkness to find Fingers' friend. The darkness moved once more, shifting across the walls and floor as if a light was being shifted, altering the shadows. McDaid realised that Fingers' friend wasn't in the darkness, they *were* the darkness. "Anyway, it's just talk."

The darkness moved towards him, sliding along the floor like oil.

"There's a lot of talk these days," said Fingers. "Nyck and I don't like it much."

"Nick?" McDaid asked, confused.

"Nyctos," the darkness said, "people just call me Nyck. Are you afraid?"

McDaid wasn't, though, having been asked, he suddenly realised that perhaps he ought to be. "No," he said, "should I be?"

"Mortals always used to be afraid of me," said Nyctos. "I would slide over their heads and they'd lose themselves in my infinity. They'd scream but nobody would hear them except the darkness."

"He's showing off," said Fingers. McDaid, whose nervousness had now returned, was about to insist that he wasn't when he realised Fingers was referring to Nyctos. "He misses the old days when he had power, rather than just moping around in corners with an empty belly."

"I still have power," Nyctos said, "see how it trembles?"

"You're an old ham," Fingers laughed, those palms clapping together again. It prodded at McDaid. "You scared of the dark?"

"Not really," McDaid replied, which wasn't entirely true but it seemed such a childish fear that he was reluctant to admit it here. "I guess I used to be." He made for the door. "I should be going," he said, "my friends will be waiting for me."

"Your mortal friends?" Nyctos asked.

"Yes, they'll probably be finished now and we'll need to be getting back."

Fingers moved so that it was between McDaid and the door.

"What about Biter?" Nyctos asked.

McDaid didn't understand the question, but when Fingers replied he realised it hadn't been addressed to him. "I don't see him around, do you?"

"I guess not. Though if he gets to hear then we'll be on Lucifer's shit list."

"Then I guess," Fingers loomed behind McDaid, pushing him towards Nyctos, "we'd better make sure there's no evidence."

"Evidence of what?" McDaid asked.

Fingers placed two limbs on McDaid's shoulders, forcing him to his knees, staring into the darkness of Nyctos' body.

"I see your fear!" the darkness said. McDaid felt the tips of Fingers' limbs pressing on either side of his head.

"Please don't," he said, "I don't want to..." then Fingers pinched off his head like it was extinguishing a candle. McDaid's body tumbled forward into the darkness of Nyctos' belly, spurting fruitlessly into the black.

8.

INSIDE THE STORE, Abernathy threw William a broom and suggested he got on with the business of using it.

"And stop looking so damned thoughtful all the time," he told him, "it encourages the customers to do the same. A thoughtful man is a man that puts things back on shelves rather than buying them."

William smiled and nodded. He'd taken to helping out in the general store because he needed something to occupy him. Forset had his newfound position in politics and Billy and Elisabeth had become inseparable. He didn't mind, was warmed by it in fact, but it did rather leave him feeling like he was a spare wheel. So he filled shelves, swept floors and enjoyed the sensation of letting go of his old life and taking on something new. Abernathy, for all his harsh words, was a reasonable enough employer and they enjoyed trading information. William told Abernathy about the mortal world, Abernathy sketched him a picture of the Dominions. It was a profitable transaction for them both.

"Hey kid," said a gravelly voice from behind him, "where can I find something to eat that ain't going to fight back?"

He turned to see a dwarf ambling along the aisle, staring at the wares with obvious suspicion.

"You got a problem with my goods, high-pockets?" asked Abernathy, appearing from around the corner and never deaf to any possible complaint.

The dwarf looked down at Abernathy. "What's it to you?"

"My store, my rules," Abernathy replied. "Come in from the mortal world, have you?"

"Yeah, I was travelling here with friends and they all upped and vanished so I thought I'd see what I was missing."

"Left you on your lonesome did they? Don't sound much like friends to me."

The dwarf shrugged. "You may be right. We weren't so much friends as colleagues I guess. We were in a circus together."

"Circus? What, like gladiator sports?" Abernathy was thinking of the Palace of Bones, a popular entertainment spot in the Dominion of Circles.

The dwarf looked confused. "Side show, you know, freaks."

"Freaks? And what were you supposed to be?"

"Take a guess, name's Knee-High."

"What sort of name is that, you lofty son of a bitch? You telling me you was in a freak show because you were shorter than lanky arseholes like him?" He pointed at William.

Knee-High shrugged. "Where I come from it ain't common."

"Freaks my ball sack." Abernathy spat in disgust, stared at the result and then looked at William.

"Fetch a cloth kid, looks like I left half a lung on the canned goods."

William rolled his eyes and went off to find one.

"What's your real name, boy?" he asked Knee-High, "because you're sure as hell taller than my goddamned knees."

"Brian."

"Fine, come with me Brian, we'll get something to eat and drink while the kid minds the store, and you can tell me all about these freaks of yours."

9.

"WE NEED TO act!" Atherton told the gathered crowd, who hung on his every word. "We sit up here, waiting for our leaders to step in on our behalf, but they do nothing. They're in there now, talking, negotiating, making compromises. Is that enough?"

There was a murmur of disagreement.

Atherton's gaze fell on the face of Father Martin who was hanging back, his eyes down.

"Of course it's not. They've had long enough. That's not heaven. That's not God's domain. We've seen nothing holy step out of its influence. That is Hell. That place should be surrounded by the army, guarding us against the monsters that live there. Instead the door lies open and these things are allowed to just wander out, making their way into our world. We've watched them, one after another, strolling off towards our towns and cities. Every minute we stand by and do nothing something else gets free. An invasion force that our leaders chose to ignore. What do they want, these creatures? What does the devil always want?"

There were a few suggestions shouted out from the crowd.

"He wants to corrupt," Atherton said, "he wants to destroy. He wants each and every one of our souls."

He turned towards Wormwood. "And who's going to stop him? Nobody seems to want to try. Nobody seems to care."

The crowd disagreed, they cared, they told him, they cared a great deal.

"So maybe it's down to us to show the way," Atherton said, "maybe it's down to us to act?"

There was a small cheer at that and Atherton knew he had them.

Of course, they didn't stand a chance, as he had accepted earlier. If they attacked Wormwood it would be a massacre. But perhaps that was what was needed. Let his employers preach politics then, when the dirt was stained red. Sometimes, to get something important done, you had to make sacrifices.

10.

"Where in tarnation is he?" asked Governor Poynter, sticking his head out of the carriage window.

It had been a sorely unproductive few hours, the Governor of Wormwood having indulged them with refreshments and courtesy but nothing more.

"I think," the man had said finally, "that I need to talk to someone who can make decisions for the whole country rather than just the state."

Now, with one of their party having wandered off, they weren't even able to make a definitive exit, loitering in the street and looking like idiots.

"He's probably got lost," said Paddock.

"Or run off," said the Senator, falling back into his seat and banging on the carriage roof for their driver to get moving. "We'll probably find him in a dead faint a mile outside the town. We haven't time to waste, he can make his own damned arrangements."

The carriage left Wormwood, one light, and by the time anyone thought to mention the fact that Duggan McDaid still hadn't been found, they all had far more important things to worry about.

WHAT AM I DOING IN THE MIDDLE OF THE REVOLUTION?

(An excerpt from the book
by Patrick Irish)

I DECIDED TO take a break from the Observation Lounge. There was so much to take in, so many threads to think about that I could imagine myself lost in that room forever unless I forced myself to take a step back from it all.

Real stories never begin or end, it's all just different lives crossing over, bouncing off one and another and heading off in new directions. We writers try to hide the fact, we finish our tales with happy resolutions and pretend a line has been drawn under events. But if our fictional characters were real we would only find closure on their death beds. The happy marriages that close our books, the great escapes, the celebratory feasts, the silhouettes growing smaller on the horizon, they're all a nonsense. You never reach the horizon, you just keep riding.

I wanted to find out what the ultimate result of Wormwood's presence would be but, in that, I feared I was asking the impossible. I could spend an eternity watching the ripples as they expanded outward from that defining moment. God, even were he alive, had no interest in typing the words 'The End'. I could—and certainly would—continue to follow the various threads Alonzo had presented but I wanted to stretch my legs and contemplate everything I had seen thus far. Uppermost in my mind was that elusive suggestion of Alonzo's that not only would I find myself increasingly occupied with the things I saw in that room but I would also wish to influence them.

I failed to see how such a thing was possible. I had crawled on my hands and knees above the rain-soaked Thames, eavesdropping on that conversation outside the Houses of Parliament. I had pounded at the floor, absurdly struck by how much I missed the recognisable comforts of my home, however grey and miserable it might appear. Still, I was an observer, held at a distance by the structure of the room that was, however invisible, as impermeable as stone. Watching the trains of people as they flooded towards Wormwood, the reporters and the men of power, I had felt almost close enough to breathe on their hot necks, the angle of vision bringing me down and into their party as if I were riding alongside them. But it was illusion; I could no more reach out and touch them than I could embrace my old friends, intercede on behalf of the unfortunate Duggan McDaid or hurl a stone of dissent at Atherton the rabble rouser. I was a ghost, forever removed.

As I left the room I experienced a momentary fear. I hoped that, having thoroughly interacted with the place, the act of finding it once more would be simple enough, but what if I was wrong? What if I closed the door on it now, never to cross its threshold again?

I decided upon an experiment. I left the door open, crossed, the corridor and focused on a closed door on the opposite side. I visualised that room, showing Atherton in the mountains above Wormwood, filled with a false evangelism. I gripped its handle, my eyes closed, and opened the door. I was, once more in the Observation Lounge. Looking over my shoulder I could see the door I had left open behind me, I could even glimpse the movement of its visions in the wall beyond. It was as I had hoped: the room was not a fixed point, it would be wherever I wished it to be. Reassured, I closed the doors on both and set out to find fresh air and my companions.

When I had first entered the Observation Lounge I had found it disorientating, set adrift above its visions. Now, the reverse was true. Walking on the solid, blank walkways of the Dominion of Clouds, everywhere felt too empty. After the chaos and noise of Wormwood, the silence was unnerving. I felt like a man who had lost one of his senses. All the more reason, I decided, to try and limit my exposure to the Observation Lounge. The very last thing I needed, being in the process of trying to curtail one addiction, was to add another.

I made my way out into the garden, hoping that the feel of real grass beneath my feet might ground me. It worked its magic. I lay there for a short while, running through what I had seen in my head, following each string of events as if they were narrative threads, guessing at their possible conclusions, imagining where they might yet intersect. The situation in Wormwood was clearly coming to a head and I couldn't imagine how it could be successfully resolved. With antagonism on both sides and the political ramifications of Wormwood's location, violence seemed inevitable. World politics is a balance of interest versus power; you use all the power you have to gather as much as you want, imported goods, money and, most importantly, land. The bigger you became, the more power you had. Until the arrival of Wormwood, nobody could rival the British. Now my home country was bordering on obsolescence. While one could understand their wish to see that situation change, I couldn't help but feel a genie cannot be re-bottled. This was Atherton's mistake. However much he hoped to force Britain's hand, there was little they could do. An attack on the Dominions was likely to be met with such an overwhelming force of retaliation that the casualties would outweigh any possible victory. Surely the British government would see that? Indeed, it was to be hoped that every government would, including the Americans, in whose country the forces of the Dominions now resided. The only safe solution was acceptance. Not something politicians are noted for. It was to be hoped that the quality that *did* define them, self-preservation, would outweigh their natural bullishness.

Time would tell. Already I was itching to return to the Observation Lounge and find out but I was determined to limit myself a little, find Soldier Joe and Hope, perhaps eat something (it was hard to judge how long I had been in the Observation Lounge but, unlike a natural resident of the Dominion of Clouds, I was a mortal man with mortal needs and my last meal had been somewhat interrupted by the death of God during the main course).

After a few moments gazing up at the building and wondering quite how I might locate my colleagues I realised I could summon up an orb to lead me; hadn't I seen Veronica explain as much to Arno? Perhaps there was even a quicker method, might I be able to use the same trick that allowed me to find the Observation Lounge? I walked out of the garden and into the cloisters, stepping up to the first door I came to, the faces of Soldier Joe and Hope Lane as fixed as possible in my mind. I opened the door and found myself face to face with a plate of sandwiches on a small table. I was still not thinking clearly enough. I took the sandwiches, reasoning that consuming them would help quiet the inner voice that was diluting my focus, stepped back outside, closed the door and tried again.

The room had transformed itself and I found myself stepping into the garden. It was a small orchard of trees—their fruit would have been unrecognisable had

I not watched Arno and Veronica pluck their like from similar branches. Thoughts of those two lovers made me realise I might be about to intrude on my friends in a similar state; it also, strangely, made me realise quite what an invasion of privacy I had committed earlier. That sense of dislocation I had complained about with the Observation Lounge, of never quite being able to be part of the action, had another effect. I had watched two strangers make love right before me and not for one moment considered the moral implications of doing so. I had simply looked on, like a member of the audience at a theatre. I had seen men die, and others conspire to further slaughter. Acts that, I now realised, had marked me no more than had I viewed them on a stage or read them in a book. These lives I witnessed were not lived for my entertainment, the unfolding saga was history, not fiction. I had known that in my brain but not in my heart. The realisation actually made me fear the room and what further horrors it might show me, though not enough to stop me returning to it. However disturbing, I simply had to see what the future held.

My passing concerns as to whether I might be intruding proved unfounded. Soldier Joe and Hope were paddling in the stream and only too pleased to see me.

"The writer finally steps outside!" Hope laughed. "Have you finished spying on the world?"

"Not quite," I admitted, removing my boots and socks and rolling up the cuffs of my trousers so as to join them. "I can't resist knowing what is to happen to everybody."

"Well," said Soldier Joe, "we've decided what's going to happen to us."

"Not much!" said Hope. "For a long, long time."

"What's the point of being in Paradise if you break a sweat?" Soldier Joe asked. He looked at me. "Do you think that's selfish of me? No doubt, back in the real world it's all panic and fighting but I'd hardly be much use, would I?"

I was by no means sure that his health would return to its previous state simply by his stepping outside the Dominion. I thought it likely that Alonzo had bestowed a permanent cure, much as he had with Henry Jones' useless hands. That said, I appreciated the possibility that it offered him the perfect, guilt-free justification for leaving the fighting behind. Soldier Joe had seen a good deal of misery in his life and I, for one, begrudged him his happiness not one jot. Let him believe he was making a logical decision, a man is entitled to his pride.

"Absolutely," I said. "It would be foolishness for you to leave here, so why not make the most of it?"

He nodded and smiled. "Thank you," he said. "I was beginning to wonder if I was being a coward."

"Hardly, you're making the only sensible decision. Put it from your mind."

"I've been telling him that for hours," said Hope. "I'm glad he'll listen to you at least."

"I listened," he said, "but it's good to hear it from someone else."

"Have you explored far?" I asked.

"Not really," said Hope, "we've just been walking around out here."

I told them what I had learned about the place from watching Arno and Veronica, about the orbs they could summon and the adventures they could experience within the rooms of the Junction. I told them about the couple's mission to retrieve other souls and bring them back here.

"I think there's probably room for a few more," said Soldier Joe, "we don't mind sharing."

"Who knows if we'll even notice?" I said. "There are other souls here for sure, not everyone ended up in the Dominion of Circles, but we've seen no sign of them as yet."

"This place is even bigger than we realise," agreed Hope. "I think it's personal too."

"Personal?" I asked.

"You know, you meet the people you want to meet, see the things you want to see. Maybe we're surrounded by other souls but we don't see them because they're all in their own, private Heaven."

"Maybe. Alonzo talked about the fact that all our lives are personal. He was talking about time but I suppose it extends into everything. We all walk our own path then we interact with others and our paths synchronise with theirs. To be honest he lost me rather..."

"He lost me from the minute I met him," Soldier Joe admitted.

We continued to paddle for a short while but eventually I felt I could delay my return no longer. The compulsion to find out what came next was too strong. Looking around, I realised that the door I had travelled through was now gone so I decided to try Veronica's trick with the orb. I closed my eyes and visualised one hovering in the air before me, hoping that this time I was suitably focused as to not force a bottle of gin to appear in thin air. I opened one eye and was relieved to see that it had worked.

"There you are," I said. "Take me back to the Observation Lounge, please."

I said goodbye to Soldier Joe and Hope, promising to come and find them later, and followed the orb out of the garden.

CHAPTER SIX
ANIMAL CALLED MAN

1.

THE PLAIN OF Salt crowned the peak of Mount Noma, a flat acre that glittered with crystals, allegedly formed by the gallons of tears that had been shed there. While this was doubtless theatrical myth-making, the plain had certainly seen its fair share of activity over the millennia. At its height it had bustled with the presence of penitents, great crowds of human souls desperate to feel the prick of barbed wire or smell the barbecue tang of their own flesh burning. What made the plain so perfect for the task was a little piece of magic that flourished on its surface: whatever atrocities were committed there, however violent, however debilitating, they would vanish at the end of the day leaving the sufferers whole, unblemished and ready to start all over again. This drew people from considerable distances and the locals, disinterested on a moral level but only too wise to the ways of commerce, had been quick to offer their services as torturers.

Then, one wise old demon who had an eye for earning a buck but a lousy right hook had swapped the onerous business of wielding whip or branding iron for a seat in a ticket booth. For a small fee, visitors could take a tour around the site, watch the bloodletting, hear the sordid crimes the penitents had committed during their mortal spans; even take a go on the instruments of instruction, turn a wheel here, yank a chain there. Why tire yourself out when people would pay for the pleasure?

Eventually, like all entertainments, it was superseded by something more innovative, more fashionable. In truth, the customers had always complained about the need to hike up the long mountain trail, more often than not far too tired to do more than take a couple of swings at the guilty. It had been a success while it lasted.

Once the tourists dwindled, it was back to paying for the flagellation. Mortal lives being the butterfly things they are, there were only so many memories to go around and soon, even that revenue stream dried up.

Eventually, bewildered and confused, minds barely strung together after years of spending their contents so freely, even most of the penitents stopped attending the Plain of Salt. Perhaps they simply forgot why they used to attend. There were certainly many mortals, their sense of self so whittled away, wandering the Dominion of Circles with no clear purpose. All that was left were the handful of die-hards, the souls who had made their own way onto the hot coals or broken glass, maintaining just enough of their faculties to keep up the daily grind of self-abjection.

That day there were but three. Their names were lost to them, replaced with more prosaic titles.

Pole, as always, was the last to make it to the top, forced to drag all ten feet of his namesake behind him, its metal surface heavily corroded from the regular application of bodily fluids. By the time he took up his position against a small cluster of rocks, Coals was already lighting her fire.

"You should just leave it up here," she told him. "I couldn't be doing with dragging this lot around all the time." She gestured to her equipment, a ten-foot tall metal frame, pile of chains, hooks and the provisions for making her fire. "A small bag of coal," she said, "that's all I have to worry about, and coal weighs nothing."

"It's part of the punishment," Pole explained, wedging the end of his pole between the rocks, pushing it in deep enough that it stood firm, running parallel a foot or so from the ground.

"Let him struggle," said Nest, the third of the group, as he kicked at the base of the termite mound to get its residents thoroughly riled up. "Some people just can't help making things difficult for themselves."

Coals shrugged and began to sling her chains through the straps at the apex of the metal frame.

"Just because you're happy to take the easy route," said Pole, offering Nest a look of utter disgust. "Some of us will have completed their period of penitence a little sooner than others, that's all."

"You think this is easy?" Nest asked, unscrewing the jar on his pot of honey.

"By comparison," said Pole, squatting down in front of the metal rod and backing himself onto it. "Of course it bloody is."

"Maybe you'd like to swap one day?" Nest replied, angry at having his work denigrated. He began to slather the honey on his genitals, making sure he didn't work himself up into a state of erection as he often did. Pole would only use the sight of a boner to fuel the fire of his contempt.

"Personally," said Coals, satisfied that her fire had caught, "I'm not convinced either of you are really putting the effort in." She fixed the rusty hooks to the end of the chains and set to forcing the blunt points through the flesh of her nipples.

"This isn't about creativity," said Pole, forcing himself backwards so that the first few inches of metal were now lodged in his anus. "It's about punishment."

He gave a sigh and began the slow business of gradual self-impalement.

"Of course it's creative," said Nest, squatting over the termite nest and poking his genitals into the hole at its crown. "Suffering should be inventive." He gave a grunt as he felt the first wave of insects exploring the sweetness he offered.

Coals had climbed up her frame now, cinched the chains and, with a roar of satisfaction, set herself to swing above the glowing coals of her fire. "It should be transcendental," she said, teeth gritted so the words were little more than spit and percussion.

It was Coals who saw the procession first, thanks to her vantage point on the frame. "Someone's coming."

Nest, who just had—more food for the insects— thought for a moment she was referring to him, then he saw the trail of people entering the plain.

"Been a while since we had spectators," he said, shifting his position to work away at the itching in his balls.

"They don't look like tourists," said Pole, forcing himself back another half an inch.

"Friends," said the man at the head of the procession, "we bring excellent news."

"Christ," said Coals, parting her legs as she swung so as to give her groin a roasting. "That would make a change."

"My name is Arno," the man said, pointing to his female companion, "and this is Veronica. We have travelled all the way from the Dominion of Clouds to tell you that you don't need to suffer any longer."

"There's only one person I'll believe on that score," said Nest, "and unless He's amongst your number you're wasting our time."

"I assure you," Arno insisted, "this is completely unnecessary. Your sins have been forgiven, in truth they always were. We're spreading the word so that people like yourselves can return with us to the

Dominion of Clouds and experience its beauty and comfort."

"Don't deserve comfort," said Pole, who was finding it almost impossible to speak now as the pipe had worked its way up towards the back of his throat.

"You deserve whatever you let yourselves have," said Arno. "See all the others we've rescued? They've put their pain and misery behind them. They've suffered enough. God doesn't want your blood and tears."

"Well, tough," said Coals, bouncing up and down on her chains so that the hooks tore even deeper into the flesh of her breasts, rivulets of blood trickling down into the fire where it hissed and smoked. "Because He's going to get them."

Pole barked an agreement but it was unintelligible, his mouth now full of steel, blood and shit.

"Just mind your own fucking business," said Nest, removing his bloated and inflamed genitals from the nest to add more honey. "We're busy."

Arno opened his mouth to say more but Veronica tugged at his arm and shook her head. "There's no point," she told him, "they don't want to know."

After a moment he nodded and the procession about-turned and began its slow descent.

"Some people," moaned Coals, the sweat of exertion and heat stinging her eyes. "As if we'd be doing this if we didn't have to. I mean, it's not for pleasure, is it?"

"Of course not," said Nest, reinserting his genitals into the termite mound and grinding his hips against the dirt to force his swollen dick into it as deeply as he could.

2.

THAT NIGHT, ARNO'S people camped out in a clearing in the Forest of Lies. The whispered untruths from the leaves were quiet and easily ignored after you'd got used to them, certainly they were worth putting up with as a trade-off against the shelter the trees offered.

They had gathered a considerable number of souls in their travels through the Dominion. The first few had been the hardest, but now, with the weight of numbers behind them, people were coming over to the cause in droves. Alive or dead, humans would always be inclined to follow a crowd. Still, Arno dwelt on the souls they had not convinced, rather than the ones they had.

"It's just so ridiculous," he said, thinking of the trio on the Plain of Salt. "You'd think they wanted to be there."

"Some do," admitted a woman called Marrousia. "For all their pretence at penitence they just like the pain. Maybe that wasn't always the case but, over the years, they've developed a taste for it."

Arno shrugged. "I can live with that, I guess. I can't begin to understand it but if they're happy doing what they're doing..."

"Some also feel stupid," said Veronica. "It's not easy to admit that you're only here because you thought that's what you deserved."

"I blame the preachers," said Marrousia, "the people who spend their whole time telling you how deep you are in sin."

"And the parents," said Josiah, a boy who looked no more than thirteen years old but had endured the Dominion of Circles for decades. "They beat me every day for one thing or another."

They had found Josiah tied to a large rock several days ago. His stomach was missing, pecked out by birds. Veronica had tried to drape a poncho over him to obscure the sight of his innards but the boy had refused it. "I like the way the wind feels," he had explained, "it tickles."

Marrousia had been hanging from a tree to the side of the road, thin wire cutting into her ankles, her head a shining, swollen damson of gathered blood. When asked how long she had been hanging there she was honest with them: "After the first two years I began to lose count."

She couldn't walk but weighed so little the others didn't mind taking it in turns to carry her.

"There's a lot of people in the mortal world who deserve this more than we do," said Kane, an ex-soldier who carried his bitterness with him along with a stomach distended by years of being force-fed grubs and weevils at the tables of the Bastard's Banquet. However much he ate he could never sate his hunger. His guts, unnaturally resilient to the physical exertions of overeating, simply grew to accommodate and now hung around him like a wobbling skirt of fat. "I can't tell you what I'd give to go back there knowing what I know now."

"Once you've spent some time in the Dominion of Clouds," Arno assured him, "you'll learn to let go."

"I'm not sure I want to," Kane admitted. "I'm a soldier, all I know how to do is fight and there are plenty I'd like to take my bayonet to."

"He'll get over it," Veronica assured Arno that night, as they curled up in their makeshift tent. "Some people just take a long time to let go. A couple of days dreaming in the Junction and he'll have forgotten all his grudges."

"I hope so," said Arno.

3.

WHEN ARNO FINALLY slipped into uneasy sleep, other parts of the camp were not so quiet. The trees weren't the only ones doing the whispering and shadows flitted, carefully negotiating the sleeping bodies of their compatriots and making their way deeper into the forest.

The gathering was small, no more than thirty, but they made their way a short distance from the camp, coming to rest around the massive trunk of a large tree. Kane took his place at their centre, manoeuvring his unwieldy gut as he paced around the trunk. Every now and then he would see movement in its bark, insects and lizards that lived in the branches. He would pluck the creature from the wood and pop it in his mouth, more stuffing for the goose.

"You've all heard the stories," he said, "and I'm

not talking about Arno and his passage to paradise. They say that the way is open between here and the mortal world too. God is dead and all the barriers have fallen."

"You think it's true?" asked a voice from the crowd. Kane looked down to see Rachel Watson, who held her eyes in the palm of her hand. They had been plucked, she said, by a snake. Sucked out of their sockets and spat into the dust by her feet. They still worked, severed as they were, though sometimes she had to wash them in her spit as they grew dry and itched.

"I don't know," he admitted, "but I can't ignore the possibility, can any of us?"

There was a slight murmur from the crowd.

"How wonderful would it be to go home?" he asked them. "To find our families? To walk the streets where we used to live? Isn't that an idea worth taking a gamble on?"

Another murmur, this one growing in enthusiasm.

It wasn't nostalgia that would draw Kane back to the world he had left the day he had lain on his back in the smoke of cannon-fire, his body full of lead and his boots full of blood. It was something far stronger. He had died for a cause, and that cause had gone to the wall along with him; the war had been lost, the lives wasted. While he and men like him had rotted in the fields and rivers, those in power had talked their talk and made their compromises, uncaring of the blood that had been spilled under their orders. He didn't know how many of them were still living, the generals and the politicians, but he had years of Hell to show them if they still had breath to lose.

"How would we find the way?" asked another voice, this one belonging to George Oskirk, a man that Kane did not much like.

Oskirk had been part of a group they had found in the Draining Desert where bodies sank into the cold, clammy sand, choking on its grit until eventually they fell through only to re-emerge in the sky above and start all over again. Their skins were pale from years out of the sun, worn smooth by the movement of the sand. They had rescued them by throwing ropes over the sand's surface, fishing people out during the scant few minutes they were on the surface at the turning point of the cycle. Most of the group had been silent for many days after, the sand they had swallowed filling their bodies and clogging their throats. It had taken a lot of drinking and vomiting before they could work their lungs and their voice boxes. Not so Oskirk. He had been wearing a leather mask that had protected him from the worst of it. That mask, Kane had noticed before Oskirk had thrown it away, had possessed freckles. Kane had no doubt that Oskirk had taken advantage of another body that had come within his reach in the shifting sands. He had known his fair share of selfish soldiers during the war, men who only looked out for themselves, and he liked it no more now than he had then.

"How do we find it?" Kane repeated. "They talk about a town called Wormwood, a place that lies on the frontier between the Dominion of Circles and the world we left behind. If we can find that then we're free."

"You think Arno will let us?" asked someone else.

"He's not our keeper," Kane said. "We're grateful to him of course, but there's only one who could tell us what to do and if He is dead then I say we do whatever feels right."

Kane thought about that. Could God be dead? It seemed unlikely. Whether He still existed or not, He had not played a significant role in Kane's life. There had been no sign of His mercy or kindness on the fields of battle. He couldn't have been ignorant, didn't they say He heard everything? And His name had been called so many times by the dying. Hadn't Kane even uttered it himself as the bullet holes let his blood run out into the grass beneath him? Yes, he had. And if God hadn't cared to involve Himself then, Kane wasn't inclined to allow him a say now.

"And if He's not dead," Kane continued, "and the doorway to the mortal world does lie open, it can only be His doing. In which case He wants us to walk through it."

"Maybe it's all been part of His plan?" asked another voice. Kane didn't recognise the speaker; it was one of the many whose heads had been worn down to the bone, interchangeable off-white faces with unnaturally voracious smiles.

"Isn't everything?" he replied, not believing a word of it but only too happy to peddle such thoughts if it got the crowd on his side.

The murmurs turned into full conversation now as they all began to talk amongst themselves. He had set a fire burning here, he realised, and all it had taken was a few words.

"Be still," he said, waving his hands for quiet. "We don't want to wake the others."

"But surely we should all discuss this?" That was Rachel Watson again.

"Of course," Kane replied, "but there is something else to consider. You notice how they all talk as if the..." he left a pause here, for maximum effect, though in truth he had his audience well and truly under his control, "*things* that live here, the *demons*... don't wish us harm? That we were trapped here by our own guilt, or confusion?"

There was a mumble at this. Even though they had all taken the opportunity to leave once offered, the issue of culpability was still uncomfortable.

"Well," Kane continued, tugging at his belly, "I sure as Hell know I didn't do this to myself."

There was a mixture of agreement and humour at this.

"How about you, Rachel?" he asked, addressing her directly, "you pluck your own eyes out? Or you, George Oskirk, you try and suffocate yourself in that sand pit? All of you, look to your wounds, your pain, you do all that to yourselves?"

Again, a murmur of consideration. For most of them, they had fallen victim to cursed landscapes, wild animals or the traps they had subconsciously wished into existence. Certainly though, some had fallen foul of the demon castes. While they had not been charged with the heavenly role of chastisers, there was no question that some played merry with the mortal souls that cluttered up the Dominion with their wailing and begging. Some had done it to line their pockets, some simply because they could. Looking around, staring at each other's wounds, at the haunted look in their neighbours' eyes, Kane's words had weight amongst the crowd.

"Has it occurred to anyone that all of this... the offer of freedom, of paradise, might just be a trick? A way of torturing us some more? Building us up to knock us back down?"

"I don't believe that," came a voice. "Arno's a good man, he wouldn't play us false."

"Who says he knows?" Kane replied. "He might be being played for a sucker the same as the rest of us." He shrugged, his dangling fat quivering as it was hoisted up to reveal his feet. "All I know is that I don't trust anybody anymore, not completely. The first opportunity I get I'm going to make a break for the world I left, the world I know... I hope that many of you would want to join me. But I'm not about to make such thoughts public in front of all of them," he gestured towards the camp, "not until I know who's who and what's what. Who's my enemy and who's my friend. When we know who we have on our side we can either make a stand or a break for freedom. Until then, we play it clever, we talk amongst ourselves, we deal with only those we know we can trust. There could be demons hiding amongst us even now! Waiting for the chance to drag us all back to the pain and misery we've only just put behind us."

That caused a little panic, people looking around, judging, paranoid.

"We'll be careful," he said, "we'll be safe, and we'll talk again soon."

And with that, Kane left them to their private conversations, satisfied that he had begun the shift in power he wanted. Soon, these people would no longer be looking to Arno for leadership, they'd be looking to him.

WHAT AM I DOING IN THE MIDDLE OF THE REVOLUTION?

(An excerpt from the book
by Patrick Irish)

THE BRIEFEST GLANCE at Arno's progress reassured me that trouble was brewing for that noble man and his partner. Kane was almost a mirror of Atherton, the soldier who was not content to follow, who could never truly rest until he had stirred up a mob. What the result would be I would find out in due course, first I wanted to know what had become of Henry Jones. The man who had set all of this in motion, but not—as was unquestionably the case with Atherton or Kane—out of a lust for power but rather through bitterness and, as much as the word seemed unsuited to him, love.

Was there ever such a conflicted emotion? It brought euphoria and blood, creation and destruction. I would not wish to live in a world without it—though it had been some time before I had met someone towards which I was inclined to feel it, at least romantically—but I could only dream of the lives that had ended in its name. Perhaps that's the writer in me thinking, is it love that takes the blame or the person who cannot endure it? We are inclined towards the tragic, we inventors of fictions, an unhealthy desire, perhaps. Unhealthy or not, I asked the room to find the man.

CHAPTER SEVEN
A GUN FOR A HUNDRED GRAVES

1.

"NOW HEAR ME," said the voice of Henry Jones, echoing out over the plains outside Golgotha, "I am the God Killer, I am the wasting, I am the bullet in a thousand backs. I have taken the Exchange and toppled it. It didn't please me. Will you risk the same? There's a new power in the Dominion, and it is the ultimate power, the only power. It is me. And you would do well to remember before I come looking for you too."

Preacher listened to those words. He stirred them around in his head as if he were looking for a dead fly in a bean stew, then swallowed them. It would be what it would be, he decided, climbing onto his horse, despite its usual complaints, and continuing his slow progress towards civilisation.

He had been lost in Saul's Hex for the best part of three days. Allegedly, the area was named after a demon who had fallen foul of a local landowner. The demon cursed the soil and now it was a plot of land that stretched and contracted while you crossed it. In theory, the field was no more than an acre, in practice, some had been known to lose themselves in it for years. Preacher, having only skirted its edge, had been lucky he had camped out there, blithely ignoring the siren calls for help that came from deeper in. He was not a man naturally inclined towards helping others, so it was no hardship. He was lucky that he had enough provisions to keep both himself and his horse alive; had he chosen to eat the fruit that grew in Saul's Hex he would never have found his way off it. The apples that hung there brought confusion rather than nourishment. He had bought a couple of packs of dried meat from a vendor on the road outside Chatter's Munch. It was magically enriched, the vendor claimed, so that a small cube of it could keep your energy up for a whole day. That was certainly true, though Preacher found the hallucinations a distraction and he'd found riding with the runs almost as uncomfortable as the horse beneath him.

His first promise to himself on leaving the field had been to find somewhere that offered proper food and drink. His belly needed rewarding.

The outpost was the first opportunity to present itself and, despite the mess out back (when the trash in your bins appeared to be talking to itself, you just knew you had a major hygiene problem) he decided there was nothing they could serve that would make his guts riot any worse than the dried meat had.

The owner sat in a rocking chair outside the front of the hut, surrounded by ramshackle tables and chairs. The creature contained aquatic blood, vestigial fins jutting out from its wrists and ankles, its eyes large and resting on either side of its head. It sprayed itself with green liquid from a can, alternating between dousing its scales and smoking a pipe so large the bowl rested in a cradle on the ground next to it. The pipe's smoke bore a faint orange tint and when Preacher caught a breath of it, it made everything glow for a few moments.

"What is that you're smoking?" he asked.

"You've got to take your pleasure somewhere," it replied, "and who wants to look on a view like this without a little pharmacological enhancement?"

Preacher could see the creature's point. The landscape was a dirty yellow, the road lined with trees whose leaves looked like broken glass, glistening with the blood from careless birds.

"What's that you're riding?" the creature asked him.

"My horse."

"Horse? Never heard of one. Like a rakh, is it?"

The species was known to Preacher, though he had never owned one. "A different beast, but it serves the same purpose."

Not that his horse gave exemplary service. Preacher wasn't much of a burden, he'd been mortal once but his time in the Dominion had worn him down, altered him as sometimes this place did the most susceptible souls. He didn't know where the magic lived, whether it was in the air he had breathed or the soil beneath his feet, but over time he'd begun to change. Now his outside appearance better reflected the man inside. He had lost a couple of feet and a few stone, his skin dry as sand, his fingers and toes little more than claws. He was a nasty little runt, a wizened, ugly bastard. Still the beast struggled to carry him; tired and undernourished, it limped its way across the Dominion, always appearing to be minutes from death. He took some pride in the dedicated regime he put it through, consistently rescuing it from the point of physical collapse with a burst of food and rest only to run it into the ground once more. He figured he could keep the thing alive for some time as long as he kept alternating between the carrot and the stick.

"Hungry?" asked the outpost owner.

"Ravenous."

"I've got some ribs good to go. You like Gwanish?"

"No idea," Preacher admitted. "Is it a local dish?"

"I guess, maybe, I invented it. Some folks love it, others say it makes their stomachs bleed. I'll let you try a spoonful. Best not to risk a whole portion until we know how good your digestion is."

"Maybe I'll stick to the ribs."

The creature shrugged. "It's all better than dirt and fresh air, which is about all you've got to look forward to on this road for a few miles."

"Then I'll take my fill. You got drink?"

"I wouldn't get through the day without it. I'll get the gas on first then bring you beer. Tie your animal up and grab a seat."

Preacher did so, doing his best to be upwind of the pipe smoke so he might clear his head a little before the meal arrived.

"You hear that man earlier?" he asked the owner on its return. "Henry Jones?"

"The God Killer?" the creature nodded. "Always someone wanting to rise to the top of the shit heap. Why people can't be satisfied with carving themselves a little slice of life and eating it to the full I'll never know. Never satisfied, some people."

"Sounds dangerous to me," said Preacher, "like he wants to set the whole world burning."

"Good luck to him." The creature had brought a tankard of warm ale. "Shit don't burn so well."

Preacher took a sip of the ale. It was good and he set to work at it with enthusiasm, hoping the food would be of similar quality.

It was, though the ribs were small and, he suspected, more likely to have come from a domestic animal than anything found on a farm. The meat was tender and the sauce hot enough to clean his teeth. The Gwanish also turned out to be pleasantly edible, like a jambalaya made out of something that wasn't quite dead yet. It wriggled in his mouth but the spices kept it from making a break from his plate and he shovelled down extra portions.

Leaning back in his chair to enjoy another tankard of ale, he watched his horse work its way through a bucket of slops.

"Don't suppose you've got anything I can smoke that won't make me see visions for a week?" he asked the owner.

The creature went back into the hut and, after a good deal of rattling and cursing at the furniture, returned with a pouch of tobacco and some rolling papers.

"I think that's the stuff mortals like," it told him. "Toe Backs I think they call it, though it ain't got any toes or backs in it. Just leaves so they tell me, which seems like a stupid thing to burn up and breathe but what do I know of their ways?"

"Tobacco," Preacher said.

"Sounds about right," the creature replied, settling back into its rocking chair and taking a hearty lungful of smoke from its pipe. "Now, personally, I don't smoke anything I haven't caught myself. I'm a health freak about that sort of thing. You don't want to put just any old rubbish in your body."

"Very wise," Preacher said.

"You mortal?" it asked him, once the effects of the smoke had lessened enough for it to form coherent thoughts.

"Used to be," said Preacher.

"That's the thing with mortals, always changing their state. Easier to kill than a crotch fly."

"Some of us," Preacher admitted, "but what's death but a change of address?"

"A philosopher."

"I guess," Preacher replied. "I do like to think about things. The human condition." He looked at the creature. "Figure of speech," he shrugged, "human or demon, we're all just scratching out our time, aren't we?"

"That we are," the creature admitted, "the trick is to enjoy the fact."

Preacher nodded. "Oh, I do, I do." So saying he shot the creature in its amphibious belly, pulled on his gloves and forced its head into the glowing bowl of its pipe until it stopped screaming. The smoke gave him the most delicious visions as he watched the creature's face bubble and reform, features of rubber and oil in the heat. It made his philosophical heart soar to see the world grown fat in colour and sound through a mixture of the drug and the creature's expiring flesh.

Once the deed was done, he gave his horse some water, helped himself to a few more spoons of Gwanish from the pot on the stove and rode on.

2.

"I'D SAY IT was a pleasure," said Sister Franquesa, "but I never could abide a liar."

Jones took the glass canister she was offering, still not quite used to the way it buzzed in the palm of his hand, full of life.

"Business as usual," he told her. "You used to pay the Exchange, but now you pay me."

Sister Franquesa made a business of adjusting her robes, voluminous folds of crimson silk that had a habit of moving independently. "She needs to ensure she's completely covered," the Exchange had told him before they had entered. "One glimpse of her skin would kill a mortal."

"You realise," said Jones, as the sister continued to play for time, straightening her veil, "that you don't need to protect me from the sight of you?" He tapped at the patch of skin where his eyes should be. "Mortal I may be but you could be stark naked and it wouldn't mean a thing to me."

"Perhaps," she replied. "You think I should risk it? What's the worst that could happen? I end up with the God Killer's blood on my hem and the whole Dominion owes me a favour?"

"You make it sound like I'm a problem to be solved."

"Maybe you are. I don't know. At least we knew what the Exchange wanted: a cut of our profits."

"Am I asking for anything else?"

"No. Not yet, but we all saw your macho posturing in Golgotha. It's only a matter of time before you destroy something else."

"It's not my plan to destroy anything. I just want to bring order."

"When men say that it's always a warning of damage to come."

Jones couldn't see the point in arguing. She'd paid, his business was done. He didn't like being in the sisterhood's abbey, its geography was always on the move and the smell was driving his senses up the wall. "There is one thing I want," he admitted.

"And so it begins."

"I think you'll be surprised." He tapped at his head. "Take a look at this."

He had gone through this process a number of times now. He had shared the memory with the Triumph Ark, the forces of Sunday Crew, Mr Gristle and his army of bones, all of them had come up short. Perhaps this time it would be different.

Sister Franquesa took the memory of the face of Harmonium Jones and smiled. "Oh, how sweet."

"You wouldn't think so if you met her."

"Not the woman, the emotion that comes with the memory. I wouldn't have put you down as the loving kind. I'm tempted to keep this to warm me when the winter comes."

"I want it back."

"Of course you do. What else do you want?"

"To find her."

"She's here, in the Dominion of Circles?"

"I reckon."

"I'm afraid I don't know her."

"But you'll make enquiries amongst your people. Ask around."

It wasn't a request and she didn't treat it as such. "No problem."

"There's a healthy reward in it for you."

She shrugged. "If I find her I'm happy to give you the information for free."

"And why would you do that?"

"Because, Mr Jones, that's the first hope you've given me that you might not tear the Dominion apart. She's all-important to you. I assumed you craved power and blood, actually you just crave her. I find that reassuring. Besides, you're going to need friends. Have you paid a visit to Chatter's Munch yet?"

"On my way there next."

"Then prepare for the worst. They don't favour mortals. They'll die rather than pay you."

"Then I'll be happy to respect their wishes."

"And so," she sighed, "we're back to destruction."

3.

THE EXCHANGE WAS waiting for him outside, sat on the drawbridge that connected the abbey to dry land. Beneath her stolen feet the waves of the Crystal Wash did their best to reach up to her, the solid blades of spume eager to chop those dangled legs right off.

"They pay?" she asked.

"Of course," he replied, handing her the canister.

She weighed it up for a moment. "Either their profits are up or she was trying to flatter you," she said. She opened her mouth much wider than should be physically possible—beyond the teeth, the absence of the abyss—and dropped the canister inside.

"She hasn't seen Harmonium."

"And you believe her?"

"I do."

"Then on we go."

Jones climbed back on his rakh, pulling the Exchange up and sitting her on the front of the saddle.

"Tell me," she said, "what if we never find her?"

"Ain't going to happen," he told her and spurred the beast on towards Chatter's Munch.

4.

IN PHATTER-GEE'S tattoo parlour, the air was thick with Buzz vapour and the whirring sound of his tattoo iron. The man himself was flexing one of his dorsal arms, trying to get some strength back into it. He could always use one of the others for a while but the aching limb was his steadiest and he didn't want his client having any cause for complaint. One smudge and he'd likely have his beak snapped off. Last time that had happened he'd been off solids for weeks before it had grown back.

"You nearly finished?" asked Yuma. He kept getting cramps in his thigh and he wanted to get off the table and walk around a little.

"You think it's easy getting this done on your skin?" asked Phatter-Gee. "These scales of yours are so thick I keep having to replace the needles."

He took the opportunity to do so, Yuma stretching his legs and taking a blast from the Buzz pipe offered to him by Brinkle, his lieutenant.

"Shit, that's good," said Yuma, as the drug coursed through his system; the memory of a troubled birth, plucked from the mind of a mortal and condensed down into a blast of experience that set Yuma's muscles quaking.

"It's the best," agreed Brinkle, "some of the last from Greaser's private stash. Who knows when we're going to get more of that quality, that shit's getting scarce."

"No word from the farm?"

Brinkle flicked his forked tongue in the air, a gesture of disgust. "I don't think Shinder has the first fucking clue what he's doing. It's going to be an age before we've got a reliable supply."

Yuma sighed and took another hit. This time it was a fist fight in a bar, blow after blow, broken glass and flying teeth, boiled down into one pharmaceutical punch. He reeled from it, reaching out to grab hold of the bench he'd been lying on to get his ink.

"Who says mortals don't have their uses, huh?" laughed Brinkle, taking the pipe back and grabbing a hit of his own, this a one-night stand sweated out in a boarding house in Seattle.

"Damn straight," Yuma agreed. "I wouldn't be without them."

Phatter-Gee looked at the half-finished slogan on Yuma's back. 'MORTALS EAT MY SH' it said, only a couple of letters away from a culinary suggestion. He thought about mentioning the mixed message but decided he'd likely only get one of his limbs bitten off. Yuma was not known for either consistency or restraint.

"As long as they know their place," said Brinkle, happy to qualify his boss's opinion without fear of losing body parts.

"In the stable," agreed Yuma.

"What about Henry Jones?" Phatter-Gee asked, barely aware that he was saying it until the words had left his beak. Noticing that Yuma had bared his fangs, he decided to try and get his opinion in first in case it saved him a beating. "That fucker's sure got a cheek ain't he?" he said, "trying to lord it over the demonic castes."

Yuma's fangs didn't vanish but the man nodded and Phatter-Gee decided he'd got away with it.

"He'll soon learn," said Yuma, "when he comes around here looking for his cut."

"We'll give him a cut, won't we, boss?" laughed Brinkle.

"We certainly will," Yuma agreed, climbing back onto the bench and gesturing towards his nearly-finished tattoo. Phatter-Gee returned to work, the needle hammering its way through the inch or so of hard scale. The ink hissed, cut with extra Snark venom in order to give it clarity on this rough canvas. Phatter-Gee had spilled a couple of drops of it earlier and last time he had looked it was still eating its way through the earth beneath his parlour.

"Hey," said Brinkle, "you think we should try and turn some of his memories into Buzz? Imagine what it would be like to smoke the moment God got His."

Yuma snorted. "You believe that spongy little half-life managed to kill God and you'll believe anything," he said. "Fucker's full of nothing but shit and air."

"Guess so," Brinkle agreed. "He must have managed to take the Exchange out though. I know a guy in Golgotha who swears he was there when it fell. Saw that tower smack the earth like a felled tree. Way I hear it, he killed so many that day the Fundament's still choking."

"Yeah?" Yuma tried to stretch his leg, as it was cramping again. "Well, I reckon it'll fit one more if he shows his face around here."

5.

ON THE EDGE of Chatter's Munch, Henry Jones brought his rakh to a standstill and took a moment to centre himself.

"What are you doing?" the Exchange asked, impatient to get business done. "We won't get our due sat here."

"According to Sister Franquesa I'm unlikely to get our due anyway," Jones said. "These boys don't like mortals. It's a matter of principle to them. The only way we're leaving this town with anything other than bullets in our back will be if we kill for it."

"You think you're up to the challenge?" the Exchange asked.

"With you watching my back." Jones removed his guns from his holster, checked they were fully loaded and returned them. He hadn't needed to be sure but it was part of the ritual, running his thumb around the cylinder, feeling each bullet in its chamber. A blessing, a little prayer to the God of Gunfighters. "After this," he said, "it's time we set down some roots. A base to work from. People need to see me setting up a crew, making a statement."

"Perception?"

"Damn right. The most powerful force in the Dominion does not spend his days sleeping by the side of the road and getting sores on his ass."

"I thought you wanted to visit each of the other gangs personally."

"I do, and will, but we're raising empires here and that means staking your claim on a patch of land."

"You could have had a tower but you had us destroy it. I miss it."

"I bet you do, but you'll have a new tower soon. Something better."

"That would take some building."

"For an ambitious thing like you? You'll love every moment."

The Exchange smiled. "I grow to like you, Henry Jones. I hope you are not shortly to die."

"You and me both."

6.

THE TOWN OF Chatter's Munch had once been little more than a dirt pit infested with vermin. Its oldest residents claim with pride that it's never really changed.

While it may still have had a bacterial foot in the past it had certainly grown, like all good cultures do. It had become a thriving town, its streets radiating out from that central pit.

The pit itself was a place where nostalgists still liked to visit, tired of the sight of new buildings and businesses appearing on the outskirts, a seemingly bottomless hole where they dumped their unwanted shit. Over the next thirteen minutes its capacity was to be thoroughly tested.

The first four minutes were taken by Jones walking into town. That was how long it took for someone to recognise him and raise the alarm.

The next minute and a half saw Jones continue on his way towards the centre of town while Yuma rallied his gang together to intercept him.

The residents of Chatter's Munch were only too used to the control Yuma's gang extended over the town. It was, in effect, the gang's town. They were the dominant residents and the rest had two choices: oppose them (end up in the pit) or work for them (earn some money before probably still ending up in the pit). Unsurprisingly, most opted for the latter.

Of them all, Phatter-Gee was the resident who had succeeded in avoiding the pit the longest. That's not to say he hadn't come close to expiration on a couple of occasions. Indeed, he had once been thrown in there and was only still alive to tell the tale because, possessing such an extended collection of limbs, he had managed to hold on to the brim. He had hung there for four days, long enough that Yuma forgot why he was so cross with him and fished him out, his reptilian heart set on the notion of a flaming skull being etched onto his perineum. "I want something for the man-pigs to look at while I'm squatting over their soft, pink faces," Yuma had explained. Phatter-Gee had been back to work, scaly balls in one hand and iron in the other with nobody choosing to comment on his near death.

There were some, especially the younger folk, who looked to Phatter-Gee as a talisman of good fortune. To have spent so long in Yuma's company and still draw breath, they said, that was charm beyond pure good fortune, he simply must be blessed in some way. His answer was simple enough. "Yuma loves his ink and nobody else in this place can draw for shit."

Perhaps, however, for all his insistence to the contrary, there was something in people's claims. An inflated sense of self-preservation. If so, it served him once more on the day that Henry Jones came to town.

He was taking a piss break when the news came in and he was out of the toilet window, abandoning all but the clothes he stood in, before Yuma gave his first order. He was on the far side of town before he even bothered to tuck his dick away, patting it on its back and wandering off to pastures new.

Seven minutes in and Jones caught his first sight of the opposition. The Exchange had hung back but he felt her power with him, the hair on the back of his neck raised as if at the promise of a storm. She was the silent partner.

Two of Yuma's gang had decided they could earn a little respect by taking him out on their own. One carried a stubby rifle, the other a crossbow of some kind, its string groaning in complaint as it was drawn back.

"Be sure that you want to do this," Jones shouted, still walking, his hands hovering near the grips of his guns. "I ain't here to kill unless that's the way it has to be."

The first gang member, a hatchling of twelve months, had decided it would be cool if he screamed "Eat lead, man-pig!" at Jones while pulling the trigger on his rifle. In actuality, he didn't get further than the first syllable, his rifle at forty-five degrees, before Jones shot him, blowing his forked tongue out of the back of his throat. It flapped in a puddle of blood, trying to finish a whole word, and then fell still.

The second gang member had the sense to take cover before opening fire. The mortal man appeared blind and yet there were many unfortunate corpses who could attest to how little this had set him back. Squatting behind a half open door, he shot a bolt at Jones and had the opportunity of seeing for himself how well Jones could 'see' for a man who had no eyes. The gunslinger rolled to the left even as the bolt left the crossbow, dropping into a crouch from which he fired one shot, the bullet piercing the wood of the door and finding its target in a spray of blood and splinters.

Jones was back on his feet and walking.

Seven minutes and ten seconds.

Eight minutes and Jones reached the centre of town, strolling around the pit, knowing that he was being watched by both the residents and—inevitably—Yuma himself.

"I came for my dues," he said, barely raising his voice. "I came in peace. I am still willing to leave in the same way, despite the fact that your men struck first. That is the first of only two kindnesses I am willing to offer."

Yuma, only too aware that the longer he let this mortal talk, the more power he was conceding, shouted from the front door of Phatter-Gee's parlour, a hundred yards away. "You are very kind, man-pig." He took a blast of Buzz, mainlining the experience of an old man in India being shot with a rifle by British forces. Yuma hoped this wasn't a bad omen. "And what is the second kindness?"

"That kindness is only offered if you're stupid enough to want to fight."

"You're damn right we're going to fight, mother fucker!"

"Then I don't want you to come one at a time. That wouldn't be fair. I want every single one of you, every man you have, to come for me like you mean it. It won't do you any good but at least I can rest easy knowing I gave you some kind of fighting chance."

"I'll give you fighting chance, you piece of shit!" Yuma screamed, unable to tolerate another insult to his masculinity.

He ran at Jones, firing wild, anger and his running feet robbing his bullets of accuracy.

Jones sighed, raised his gun and fired once. The hand in which Yuma was holding his gun folded back on itself, until he was holding nothing more than a collection of half-severed digits. Still Yuma came running, partly because he was so high he hadn't fully appreciated his situation and partly because there was no way he could stop now and retain an ounce of authority.

Jones fired again, this bullet hitting Yuma's other hand.

By this time, Yuma was almost upon him. Jones waited until the last moment, turned and let a kick of a boot combined with Yuma's momentum send him flying into the pit. He rebounded off the far side in a shower of dirt and curses and then fell out of sight.

Nine minutes.

Jones turned his back to the pit and addressed the rest of the town.

"Come on then," he said, "let's have this done."

They didn't all rush him, of course. While there was a good deal of stupidity in Chatter's Munch, its reserves weren't endless. The locals finally saw a chance at freedom and the rest of Yuma's gang were roughly divided between feelings of ambition and terror. As a result, it was only twenty-nine reptilian, drug-addled, muscle-bound, bigoted creatures that bore down on him. They ran at him from the cover of shop doorways, back alleys, windows and parked vehicles. They roared, as much to fill themselves with confidence as him with fear. They knew he couldn't possibly shoot them all, and he couldn't, not if he'd been playing fair with the laws of physics, but Henry Jones didn't really give a donkey's dick about rules and he had the Exchange on his side. He reached into his coat and into the small pocket of the abyss that was stored there. His fingers touched ice and metal and withdrew a Gatling gun. He dropped to one knee, wedged the weapon against his foot and began to crank. Bullets embedded in flesh, plaster and brick as he described an arc. They took out windows in showers of glass, the locals diving for cover behind their shop counters or tables.

The gang's only real chance would have been to keep running at him; they might have reached him before he could bring the gun to bear. But it's hard to think clearly when the air is full of bullets, the natural response is to skid to a halt and panic, by which time you're already dead.

Nine and a half minutes and Jones began the laborious task of dragging the dead and dying into the pit. After a couple of minutes, some of the locals emerged from their hiding places and began to help.

And that's how Henry Jones became the new power in Chatter's Munch.

7.

SOME MILES AWAY, Preacher, the one man in the Dominion who could tell Jones for sure where his dead wife was, sat in a bar and listened to the news coming out of Chatter's Munch. He sighed, paid for his drink and then headed on.

WHAT AM I DOING IN THE MIDDLE OF THE REVOLUTION?

(An excerpt from the book
by Patrick Irish)

AGAIN, I EXPERIENCED that despicable pleasure in seeing these events unfold. A vicarious entertainment that brought me up short as I realised once again I was cheering on nothing less than slaughter. Of course, it would be a noble man indeed who would consider Yuma and his gang worthy of pity. They were terrible creatures, all and yet should I really take such enjoyment from seeing Jones despatch them?

Perhaps there was another truth here to appreciate. Rather than spend my time dwelling on the politics of Wormwood's presence, the dull conversations in offices of power all over the world as man's leaders tried to decide what they should do, I was following the simpler story. I was watching the tale of a man who wanted nothing more than to find his wife. Everything else in Henry Jones' story was peripheral. The empire he was building—and yes, it grows still, thanks to the Exchange and the power it brought him; the Dominion of Circles, much like everywhere else in existence, would not be the place it once was—was nothing to him. He wanted Harmonium Jones, and once he had her, he would let the power and violence continue to build around him, relieved to finally have someone of worth he could share it with.

But was it important?

Should I not be concerning myself with Wormwood? With the talks between Lucifer and the powers of America? Or the simple lives being carved out by those I had once travelled with? Of Brother William, now a happy shop boy, or the unfortunate Father Martin, wrought by indecision and a moral complication that now dominated his every waking thought?

Perhaps I should. But those concerns were constants. They would be what they would be. The smaller picture, the—in the loosest sense of the word—human picture was the one whose threads I couldn't help but follow. I wanted to know what would happen to the blind outlaw and his lady, the God Killer and the woman he would die for.

I would return to Wormwood soon enough, once I could bear to see the slow cogs of government grind out a miserable future for us all, the war that seemed inevitable, the pointless lives that would go on to be nothing more than footnotes in our history books. But first, I would see this one story through. I would see Henry Jones find his wife.

CHAPTER EIGHT
TWO CROSSES AT DANGER PASS

1.

IF ONLY ARNO had turned left. Not that it would have been easy; the trail would have led him to the Palace of Shines where the light had teeth and an unwary traveller could find themselves eaten by their own reflections. But even if the roaming Shimmer Queens had trimmed down the group's number, it would have been better than what lay in the opposite direction. Adversity brings people together and if Arno had fought hard for his people—as he most certainly would have done—then maybe the day would have ended differently.

Arno turned right.

"The road looks easier this way," he explained to Veronica. "I think the left hand fork was heading into higher ground and we've been breaking our backs enough today without a hill climb."

This was certainly true, it had been a long day of walking with little to show for it. Arno's hopes had been raised by stories they'd heard of the Crackling Field, a dark, moss-filled acre that, it was claimed, had been a popular haunt for penitents. They would stake themselves to the ground and begin the long, nervous wait for the will-o-the-wisps to come calling, tiny, incendiary beasts who loved nothing more than to toast those they found loitering in their domain. While there had been a few charred bones, nothing moved there, those who had made use of its horrors having moved on to the Fundament for a further go at life.

The group was getting restless, he knew. It was time they made the trip back to the Dominion of Clouds—and the chasm that lay between them, a problem Arno and Veronica had kept from them, reasoning that it was, perhaps literally, a bridge they would cross when they had to.

He had suggested to a couple of the other, stronger members of the party that they might split into smaller groups, spreading the word in different directions, but nobody was comfortable with the idea of trying to get into Heaven without him. He was the key, as far as they were concerned, the man who had promised them access. He hadn't pushed the point.

Perhaps it was best to stay together. The more they walked, the more he became unsure of how reliable his grip on the geography was. He had secured a map a few towns back and had begun the process of transcribing their progress, trying to form a clear route back to the Dominion of Clouds. After a few hours he had all but given up on the exercise because their route appeared to bear no actual relation to the map. Either they had repeatedly doubled back on themselves (and at one point somehow skipped a whole set of lakes and a forest) or the landscape shifted around. This seemed ludicrous but Arno wouldn't put anything past the Dominion of Circles.

Luckily they still had the orb that had led them here and he was sure that if asked, it would lead them back. That night, he decided, once they had made camp, he would announce his intention that they were going to return to the Dominion of Clouds. If that didn't improve the mood nothing would.

It was not an announcement he would ever make.

2.

PREACHER REINED HIS horse to a standstill and stared into the forest ahead. To avoid it was likely a detour of days rather than hours, the tree-line extending as far as he could see on either side of the trail. It was getting late in the day and the horse was tired, the only bed he was likely to find tonight would be at the foot of a tree. In the Dominion that worried him, the trees here could be unruly. Still, that could be said about most things and after a terrifying night being woken up by aggressive rain, the drops slapping him six ways from Sunday, he had vowed to never bed down in the open again.

He rode on. The forest was dense and filled with evergreens. Their needles were silent, which was some consolation given the talkative nature of much of the foliage around these parts. It was hard to get some shut eye when the leaves kept telling you what a miserable creature you were. He decided he'd give it another hour or so of riding and then stop at the first reasonable clearing he could find. He'd picked up a few provisions, nothing grand but enough to keep him off the dried meat. He was keeping that for the horse now, it was playing havoc with its digestion but the extra energy kept them both on the move. In truth, he half-suspected it was the only thing keeping his ride alive.

While the greenery kept its mouth shut, the forest wasn't silent. Every few minutes there was a loud crashing sound, as if someone were felling the trees. If they were, they were quick on their feet and indiscriminate about their work; one minute the noise would come from some distance away to his left, then closer but to the right. The sound bounced around the forest, both in front and behind. To begin with the noise put him on edge, but after it had happened many times without him dying of it, he grew to accept it. Perhaps the trees were rotten, he wondered, or it was the work of some indigenous animal. Whatever it was, he didn't appear to be in any immediate danger. As terrifying as the Dominion could be, if you ran for cover at the first sign of weirdness you'd never get anywhere. Besides, he had two choices, forward or back, and his preference was to keep moving. He knew that his enemy was on his trail now, had heard enough conversation on the road to suggest Henry Jones was close behind him. If there was a choice between moving forward into the unknown or turning around and bumping into Jones, he'd face the unknown every time.

3.

JONES WAS, INDEED, on Preacher's trail. Had been ever since a weapons dealer from Breaker's Pit had taken a look at the memory of Harmonium's face and immediately recognised her.

"She was with a guy they call Preacher," he had told him, "creepy little fuck, mortal once but you wouldn't know it to look at him. Like an underfed monkey with a drug problem."

"Who is he?" Jones had asked. "What does he do?"

"Not much. Kills sometimes. For a living I mean, though I hear he enjoys it. Mainly he just travels."

"Why's he called Preacher?"

"No idea, you know what it is with these people, they love to give themselves names. I worked with a guy once, called himself Thrasher. Real name was Bramblestalk. 'Who ever ran in terror from a man called Bramblestalk?' he'd say, guess he had a point."

Jones had paid the man a little extra on the weapons he'd supplied, everything from heavy artillery to knives, all the better to arm up the men and women who had descended on Chatter's Munch to be a part of his growing army.

The Exchange had been forced to admit that Jones had known what he was doing. The destruction of

Yuma's gang had been the final piece of theatre that he had needed to consolidate himself at the top of the food chain in the Dominion. He had been in Chatter's Munch no more than twenty-four hours before the first few enforcers and chancers had ridden into town, eager for the opportunity of allying themselves with the most powerful man this side of reality.

Jones had let them come. He knew how this worked, flies would always gather around corpses, eager to feed. He showed no favouritism—not yet at least—he just allowed his empire to begin its first steps.

Thanks to Yuma's ill-temper, if there was one thing Chatter's Munch possessed it was space and, soon enough, there would be more. The Exchange, eager for a new tower to rival the old, oversaw construction that would, eventually, see the small town reborn as a centre of power in the Dominion.

People soon got used to the idea that the Exchange, for all it might appear nothing more than a dead-eyed child, was powerful beyond its appearance. Looks meant nothing in the Dominion and, as far as all were concerned, 'Abyss' as it had taken to being called, was Jones' deputy and it need ask for nothing twice.

The only person in the entire town that would even think of standing up to it was, of course, Jones.

"I'm going after a man called Preacher," he told it, after concluding his business with the weapons dealer.

"I thought we agreed that you would let her come to you. Wasn't that the plan? To become so terrifying and important that she was handed to you as tribute?"

"It's not a discussion, I'm going."

The Exchange had cocked its head and stared at Jones in a manner that would have disturbed a man who had the eyes to appreciate it. As it was, Jones simply ignored it. "You can manage here," he said. "They do everything you say. Let them build, I'll be back soon enough."

"And if you're not? How am I supposed to control them then? What if this 'Preacher' puts a bullet in your back?"

Jones smiled at that. "Then he's a better man than most."

He had ridden out of Chatter's Munch half an hour later, leaving orders that, until his return, 'Abyss' was the voice of power.

On the road he soon experienced the fruits of his rise in notoriety. When they recognised him, people turned away or ran indoors. Others, perhaps braver or, more likely, eager for his favour, were quick to help him. A network of people keeping their eyes peeled for this man Preacher, all hoping they would be the one who offered the information that led to the man's capture.

Jones felt himself draw closer, arriving in towns and camps hours after Preacher had been spotted rather than days. Soon, he thought, soon I'll have that man in front of me.

4.

KANE WAS AT the rear of the procession. His
weight made speed difficult and while his legs
had grown thick, the muscles bulging, it was
still a considerable effort forcing his voluminous
body one step after the other. The soles of his feet
were flattened and hardened, his toenails yellow
claws, uncut for many years, now kept short only
by his rubbing them on the ground as he walked.
Sometimes, he dreamed of being carried in a
large chair, like the Roman emperors he'd seen in
pictures, a team of people on either side to bear
the weight. Maybe that would be the prize offered
to those of his enemies he could bear not to kill.
Maybe it would be the work he offered their wives
and children.

He knew that most of the people were now on
his side; their secret meetings had continued, with
the numbers growing steadily. Soon, he decided, it
would be time for Arno to follow rather than lead.
All he needed was one more mistake, one final
damning error that would turn those who still
wavered over to Kane's side. It had nearly come at
the Crackling Field, the weight of irritation that
the procession had felt at having marched so far
to be rewarded by so little. Kane had nearly struck
then, but had held back, certain that worse was to
come. So he continued to walk, swiping his nails
in the dirt, thinking his thoughts of dominance
and ruination.

They entered the forest and, looking from one side to the other, always on the lookout for danger, the day grew dark around them.

5.

THIS TIME THE sound had been mere feet away and Preacher had finally learned its cause. A full-size tree, with needles so sharp his fingers couldn't bear to touch them, had burst from the ground fully-grown. Nature had no patience in this forest it seemed, growth was not the business of years but seconds. A gentle spatter of blood and fur rained down around him and he realised that some wild animal had stepped on the patch of ground, triggering the growth of the tree. They were like the hidden explosives Preacher had heard of during the Civil War, buried just beneath the surface, their triggers covered with dead leaves and a sprinkling of soil. One false step here and he was likely to share the same fate as whatever creature now dripped from the brim of his hat. Was the trail safe? Did it offer a secure route through the forest? He had not known the Dominion to be so considerate.

"I think maybe we'll walk from here," he said, extending the reins on his horse so that it walked several feet ahead of him, testing the ground. "And I'll allow you the honour of going first, just in case."

The horse took slow steps along the trail, Preacher following on behind, mirroring its steps.

6.

THE FIRST OF Arno's people to discover the danger of the trees was a young man by the name of Warren. They had found him within the confusing corridors of the Wind Maze, a patch of land that appeared quite open until you entered it and discovered the thermal currents that blocked your path. Warren had been trapped within its airy confines for several months before Arno had led him to freedom using the orb to discover the route.

Warren had an annoying habit, picked up from his long time in the maze: he was perpetually tossing a coin. He'd picked up the British shilling from a confused soldier on the banks of the Bristle. The man had been using it to try and pay for a ferry ticket, unaware of the rules of the Dominion. Warren, taking pity on him, had taken the coin in return for his help and considered it a lucky charm. When trapped in the maze, crippled by indecision after the first couple of weeks of painful missteps, it had become his method of choosing direction. At least, he decided, if he gained a black eye from the pummelling winds thanks to random chance, he couldn't hold himself responsible.

Even though those days were now behind him, he had maintained the habit, flipping the coin high in the air, catching it, sometimes noting whether it showed heads (left) or tails (right), though more often not, just tossing it once more. He had become so adept at the action that he could flip it without even seeming to pay attention. He could be deep in conversation, the coin shooting up in the air and slapping back down on his palm, without him pausing in what he was saying or even glancing in the coin's direction. It had become automatic.

While the habit was harmless enough, there were those who found it annoying. Daniel Gonzalez Marquez for example, a young Spaniard they had rescued from the Lake of Lips, where the waves nibbled and licked you raw. Daniel thought that coin was just about the most annoying thing he had ever known.

As they were walking along the forest trail, Warren talking about his life before influenza had sent him to the Dominion, Daniel watching that coin fly up and then back down again, up and then back down again, up... Daniel had snatched the coin with a roar of frustration and flung it into the trees.

"Hey!" Warren had been distraught, "I need that..."

He had run off the trail in the direction of the coin, scanning the ground for a sign of it amongst the sharp, discarded needles from the trees.

There was so little light that he despaired of being able to find it, becoming more and more panicked by the second as he considered the possibility of leaving it behind.

Daniel, already regretting his behaviour, sighed and left the trail in order to help. "I'm sorry," he said. "I shouldn't have done that."

Warren wasn't even listening, he'd spotted a glint of light in the undergrowth and was reaching forward to investigate when his foot triggered one of the tree bombs beneath him.

The tree burst upwards with a crashing of limbs both wooden and flesh, Warren's screams filling the air as its trunk swallowed him. Daniel fell back, startled, a shower of blood hitting him.

"Madre de dios!" he cried, spinning on his feet and running back towards the trail where the procession had stopped, alerted by the sound of his and Warren's screams.

"The trees!" he shouted, "be careful of..." there was another crashing sound and Daniel vanished to be replaced by a solid trunk and the wet patter of blood.

Kane stared at the newly appeared tree as the procession fled in panic. In the bark of its trunk he could see Daniel's face, the skin dripping, loose and peppered with needles. "The trees," the face said, a trail of sap dribbling from the corner of its uneven mouth.

Behind Kane, the forest was filled with the sound of more tree bombs being set off, the panicked procession having left the trail, running blindly into the forest and into mortal danger.

"The trail," he shouted, "stick to the trail."

But nobody heard him above the sound of screaming and the creak of branches.

7.

JONES HEARD THE screaming as he entered the forest. It didn't delay him, the Dominion of Circles wouldn't be the place it was if not for the sound of death and agony.

His heightened sense of his place within the forest soon showed him its secret as he became aware of the trees multiplying around him. What was barely discernible to someone with normal sight, distracted by all the other sights, was clear to him. He stuck to the trail, riding fast, the sound of screaming getting louder and louder.

8.

PREACHER TURNED AT the sound of chaos on the trail behind him and he lost his footing as the horse yanked at the reins, the leather slipping from his grips.

"Get back here, damn you!" he shouted as it jumped over him and ran at a pace he hadn't thought it still capable of after being so mistreated. It was running back the way they had come, either wanting to leave the forest or drawn by the sound of others, he couldn't tell which.

"Fucking thing," he cursed, reaching for his gun. He'd have it dead at his feet before he let it run wild again.

Then a tree sprouted only a foot or two away from him, disrupting his aim, the bullet firing wild into the forest as his ride cleared a bend in the trail and vanished from his sight.

He sat there for a moment, wondering whether to go on alone or give pursuit. The idea of continuing along the trail without protection didn't please him, nor did the notion of travelling on foot for the foreseeable future. His legs were short and Jones was on his trail. "Damn it," he cursed, keeping his gun in his hand and moving as quickly as he could back along the trail.

9.

ARNO'S PEOPLE WERE in complete chaos, the neat procession lost as its members had run in all directions, uncertain of where the danger was coming from. Many of them found themselves prey to the tree bombs, their bodies extinguished by the brute force of the wood and the sharp piercing needles, their souls torn from their bodies to make the slow journey back to the Fundament.

Arno and Veronica, being at the front, had stuck to the trail, Arno shouting at his fleeing followers, trying to get them to stand their ground until they could discover what was attacking them.

Kane, some distance further behind, was trying to do the same.

As plentiful as the tree bombs were, many managed to avoid them, mainly because they had been triggered by others running ahead. The chaos lasted a minute or so, each new eruption furthering it as the crowds kept shifting direction, pushed back by the sight and sound of another of their friends dying in front of them.

Eventually what was left of the group, no more than a hundred souls or so, gathered once more on the trail, the danger now understood.

Arno looked ahead on the trail and saw something running towards them, a man... no, as she drew closer he could tell it was a woman, despite her beard and the leather straps that bound her painfully thin body. There was a bridle in her mouth and she gagged on it as she ran towards them, her eyes wild, her gait unsteady.

"It's alright!" he said, holding his hands out to her. "If you stay on the trail I think you're safe."

She fought him as he grabbed at her. "Help me!" he said to Veronica, grimacing at the sight of the woman, her body little more than bones, her skin covered in mud and faeces. "She's running wild, if she strays off the path she may get caught by one of the trees."

Veronica took the woman's arm, both of them trying to calm her down as she sobbed and roared against the bridle between her teeth.

"Get it out of her mouth," said Veronica, "she's choking."

Arno tore at the straps that held the bridle in place, finally freeing it from the woman's mouth. She gave a roar of animal anger and then a shout that was even more disturbing for its clarity. "Don't touch me!" she screamed. "Don't you dare touch me!"

Kane became aware of the sound of hooves behind him and just managed to avoid Henry Jones as he galloped past. "Careful!" he called after him, "the trees can kill."

But Jones didn't hear him. Nor the sound of the other members of the procession as they moved to avoid him. There was only one thing that existed in his world and it lay just a few short yards ahead. He might so easily have missed her, she was thinner and her scent was mixed with the dirt that covered her, but that scream, the sound of her voice. Harmonium Jones, his wife, even now under attack no doubt by the man they called Preacher.

"We were just trying to help," Arno insisted, letting go of Harmonium.

A figure appeared by the side of the road, unnoticed by either of them. One minute the edge of the forest was empty and then a man was standing there, moving towards them. A tree reared up next to him and he fell to one side.

Then a gunshot rang out and Arno saw a small red hole appear in Veronica's forehead. She stumbled back, her eyes rolling upwards.

"No!" Arno cried, reaching out towards her even as the sound of a second shot bounced between the branches of the forest. He felt nothing, just a sudden blindness as he toppled on top of her.

"Not them!" cried the man who had appeared at the edge of the forest. "You stupid bloody idiot. It wasn't them." With a sob, the man vanished once more, returning to the room where he had been watching these events unfold.

"Harmonium," said Jones, jumping from his rakh. "I'm here honey, it's me, I've got you."

He gathered her in his arms, pressing his face against her matted, dirty beard and whispering his love into her ears. "You're safe now," he said, "I killed those sons of bitches. You're coming with me."

She was like a deadweight in his arms, the shock and misery of her last few months suddenly overwhelming her. He carried her to his rakh, placed her across its back and mounted the saddle.

The rest of the procession were gathering around him now, staring past him at the dead bodies of Arno and Veronica.

"Get out of my way," he said, his gun extended towards them, "or I'll kill every last one of you."

They didn't need to be told twice, parting as he rode back the way he had come.

"Who was that?" one of them asked as Kane finally caught up, shoving his way through the crowd and coming to a halt by the bodies of Arno and Veronica.

Dead, he thought, looking down at them. As simple as that. Now the group, what was left of it, was his.

He looked up to see a tiny man walking towards them, his eyes nervously looking past Kane to the trail beyond.

"Has he gone?" the small man asked, scarcely able to believe he had come this close to Henry Jones, the husband of the woman he had so badly misused, and lived.

"And who are you, demon?" asked Kane.

"Demon?" the small man asked. "Me? I may not look much but I'm as mortal as you are."

Kane stared at him. He supposed it was possible, he hardly looked normal anymore, after all.

"Has he gone?" the small man asked again, peering around Kane's stomach like a child hiding behind its mother's skirts. "The man's a monster."

Kane didn't need telling on that score. As much as it might suit his plans, the rider had gunned down Arno and Veronica without a moment's hesitation.

"His name's Henry Jones," the small man said. "He's taking over the Dominion and I for one don't intend to hang around long enough to feel the results."

"Where are you heading?" Kane asked.

"Place called Wormwood," the small man said. "It's a gateway to the mortal world. Figured it was the safest place to go considering."

"You know where it is?"

"Sure, it ain't far, couple of days at most. Why, you want to come?"

"You'll show us the way." It wasn't a question, Kane wasn't about to hand over control of the group, not now that he finally had it.

"Sure," the small man said, "no problem. Happy to help."

"What's your name?" Kane asked.

The small man nearly said 'Preacher' but stopped himself. He had left a few graves behind him on the trail that could be linked to that name. Perhaps it was better to let it fall by the wayside and go back to the name he had always used, back before a bullet in the head had sent him to the Dominion and a new life. "It's been so long since I've used it," he said, extending his hand and shaking Kane's, "but I'm glad to make your acquaintance. You can call me Obeisance Hicks."

10.

ABOVE THE DEPLETED crowd, turning and twisting in the air like smoke on the breeze, the shades of Arno and Veronica intertwined.

"She was right," Arno said, his words almost as intangible as his body. "She always said my charitable nature would be the death of me."

"You can only die once," Veronica replied, "isn't that what we thought?"

"This doesn't feel like dying," Arno admitted, though he became aware of something, some force, pulling at him as he rose ever higher on the wind. "It feels like changing."

"I can't hold you," Veronica cried, "my fingers... my body... I'm nothing."

"No," Arno replied, "you'll never be that."

And they dispersed, on towards the Fundament.

WHAT AM I DOING IN THE MIDDLE OF THE REVOLUTION?

(An excerpt from the book
by Patrick Irish)

AND SO, TWO lessons were learned. Firstly, that casual, heartless pleasure I had taken in watching the stories unfold beneath me, as if they were nothing but fictions, was gone. It should never have been there in the first place. Arno and Veronica were dead, their souls moved on to the Fundament to be reborn in some other body, some other life. Even though they would exist again they wouldn't do so together, they wouldn't remember the people they had once been. There was no more Arno and no more Veronica, they would be fresh starts, ignorant of the love they'd known before. And for what? What purpose had their death served?

As a writer—and yes, I'm bringing this back to fiction even after having cursed myself for doing that in the first place, because it is the only frame of reference I truly understand—I had always condemned others for filling their stories with needless deaths. Characters expunged purely to make the reader feel miserable or sad seemed to me to be the laziest of actions. When you held the lives of your world in your hands then didn't it give you the freedom to make them mean something? I am not saying that any worthwhile drama can be wrought without a little misery, but why kill just for the sake of it? What are you trying to achieve? Can you not manipulate your reader more cleverly than simply slaughtering those you've created? Justify all you do in the name of telling your story.

But of course the real world doesn't subscribe to such dictates. Just as nobody is ever really able to call the story of life finished until death itself draws the line, people come and go pointlessly. They are not important. We are all the main characters in our own lives, but sometimes we have to accept that we do not have a starring role. Our narratives are blunt, boring and brief.

I had become distracted from the real questions I should have been asking, drawn into the tale of Henry Jones and the noble mission of Arno and Veronica. But they were not where the main action lay. That was in the town of Wormwood, the focal point of everything, the trigger that was soon to be pulled. No more viewing purely for the pleasure of it, from now on I would simply follow the threads of that town until their inevitable, catastrophic end.

But what of the second lesson? I had finally found my way into the world I was viewing. I had fallen through the floor of the Observation Lounge and onto the side of the road, narrowly avoiding death from one of the tree bombs. I had been there, for all the good it had done. I had cast no influence, I had been no more than a sobbing witness, but I had proven that it was possible. And if that were the case, could I really be nothing more than a spectator as the visions continued?

I wondered on that as I returned my attention to Wormwood.

CHAPTER NINE
THE BRUTE AND THE BEAST

1.

POPO HADN'T KILLED a sexual partner in decades. While not a claim many would feel the need to take pride in, for an Incubus it was a surprising achievement. It was all very well being of the higher caste, a rank of demon respected and feared throughout the Dominion, but if it meant you couldn't sleep with someone without reducing them to a lifeless husk it was murder on a long term relationship. So he had adapted. It had been a surprisingly easy process but not one he chose to explain to the world at large. While an Incubus, like a Succubus, was a sexual demon, the force it fed on was not purely carnal. It was, for the sake of a term, 'life force' and while it was the act of sex that channelled that force, opened the mouth so to speak, he had soon found that he didn't need the donor to be aware of the fact they were donating. This realisation provided a simple change to his dining habits, one that he had adopted ever since.

In the early hours of the morning, just before dawn, when most people were fast asleep, he would find himself somewhere quiet to sit, close his eyes and tap into the dreams of those around him. That was where the sex normally came into play on the part of the donor, it caught them at their most honest. However much people liked to pretend in the bedroom, dressing up in costumes, slipping on characters, it always boiled down to flesh and hunger. It was animal, it was real. For all the theatre leading up to it, there could be no lies at the point of orgasm. Sleep was similar, a time of dreams and lowered defences.

Popo would slip into a dream state, working himself to orgasm, becoming part of the subconscious world around him. Then, at the moment of climax, he would breathe in. In this way he could take all he needed, a little from each, nothing they would notice, but a feast that kept him healthy all the day long.

He kept the method to himself, not because he was ashamed of it but because he didn't want people to view him as a danger. He took nothing from them they couldn't afford to lose but they might not see it that way and the last thing he wanted was to be hounded out of town as an onanistic leech.

Since taking over the hotel he had taken to performing this ritual on its roof. From up there he could look out over the whole town, imagine each and every one of the sleepers around him as he teased himself with spit and thumb. Sometimes, when the connection was particularly strong, he could even visualise the dreams of the sleepers. He would sift through them, lifting out the erotic as extra fuel (another thing he would not have admitted to, as few like a voyeur). These little pornographic shows were fascinating to him. From the romantic to the bizarre, the simple to the bacchanalian. He knew all the town's secret loves. He had witnessed Billy the engineer admit his lust for Elisabeth Forset, and she for him, but only within their separate beds. How he had longed to simply force the two into a double room and demand their honesty. Now, at least, it seemed he no longer needed to intervene, the barriers between them had fallen and they were finally together. He witnessed Biter, lost to a dream of countess jiggling rear ends, nose to buttock in a delirium of scent. He witnessed the ever fecund Fenella, her brood the eager helpers on the Land Carriage repairs. She was like him, a solitary lover, she needed only to dream to impregnate herself, each of her many children the product of nocturnal imaginings. What would the fathers think, he wondered, if they knew how their dream seed had helped to grow flesh? What would the noble Lord Forset say if he realised that the cheeky creature he had played peek-a-boo with the day before was his own dream child? Popo didn't think the old man would approve.

He also witnessed the nocturnal thoughts of the governor's aide Elwyn Wallace and his partner

Meridiana. There was another solution to the long term problem of being a sex demon, he thought, find yourself a partner who can't die then you can get up to whatever you like in the bedroom without fearing fatalities. Lucky for her.

He had finished his morning feed with a shiver and a sigh when he noticed movement on the street below. Crouching on the edge of the roof he recognised one of Fenella's young, escaped from the house no doubt, and eager to play while others slept. He tried to see which child it was, they were all so similar with only the slightest variation in their features to differentiate them. He wondered if one of them was his. It would be a considerable blow to his pride if not.

The child was running towards the edge of the town and Popo decided he had better be the good citizen and capture it before it became lost.

He descended through the hotel, the nighttime chorus of snores and creaking bedsprings following him down the stairs.

Outside, he couldn't see the kid. Adopting a gentle jog—he couldn't move too fast, not so fresh from feeding, a process which left him bloated and dizzy for half an hour or so—he moved up the street in the direction he had seen the child running.

He passed the general store, the square, and jogged on towards the far side of town.

He finally caught sight of the child, dragging a length of wood behind it. It was an off-cut from the repairs to the Land Carriage, Popo guessed, now turned into a toy to draw lines in the dirt of the road.

"Hey kid," he called, keeping his voice low for fear of disturbing the sleeping town. Perhaps it was too low for the kid to hear, or maybe it was just feeling willful as it continued to run towards the barrier, bursting through it and out into the world beyond. Popo growled. The kids were under strict orders from their mother to stay within Wormwood's limits.

He gave chase and crossed the barrier, momentarily disorientated by the sudden light that hit him on the other side. He had forgotten how time shifted differently on both sides of the barrier. Who knew what day he had walked out into? Who knew what day would greet his return, for that matter? He could be out here for minutes only to find he'd been missing for a day on his return. Damn kid.

He rubbed at his eyes, cursing the dizziness that still coursed through him. After a feeding he liked to do nothing more than lie back and doze. All this running around was throwing his equilibrium. Certainly, if he had been at his best, he'd not have let the mortal that had crept up behind him get so close. There was a loud crack as the length of wood the kid had been playing with hit the back of his head and he fell to the ground, suddenly aware of the presences around him.

"Foul beast," someone said, "look at the state of him! Shameless!"

"I think we all know what he was going to do to this thing when he caught it," said another.

He was clubbed once again and he felt consciousness slipping from him. The last thing he saw was the sight of Fenella's squealing child, held aloft by one spindly foot, being scrutinised like a fish netted from the river.

2.

"WAKE UP," A voice said to him. The pain in his head had spread it seemed, both his hands and ankles throbbed so hard he dreaded to think what he was going to see when he finally opened his eyes. He decided it was probably for the best to keep them closed.

"I won't ask again," came the voice. "I'll just set to work on you with something sharp until you find feigning sleep impossible. Perhaps I should just remove your eyelids, that might force you to be more polite and look at the man who is talking to you."

"Is this violence really necessary?" asked another voice.

There's hope yet, Popo thought, if at least one of these people has the spirit to ask that question.

"Perhaps it would be better if you left, Father," the first voice replied, "I have no wish to upset you. But before you do, I'd advise you to take one more look at this beast and reassure yourself that we're dealing with something beyond God's mercy, and therefore beyond ours too."

"I thought God was supposed to be all-merciful?" Popo asked, scared at the way his voice sounded so weak. He opened his eyes. "Isn't that what mortals always say?"

He was in a small tent, five men surrounding him. He looked at his hands, sickened to see they had been nailed, rather than tied, to the chair he was sat on. No doubt the same could be said of his ankles, though he was in no position to strain and check.

"See how he mocks the Lord?" said one of them, the one who had been doing most of the speaking, "like a true child of Satan."

"Actually," Popo replied, trying not to let his fear show while taking the opportunity to assess the man, "Satan was one of God's most loyal helpers." The man was tall, his moustaches full and preened, a man who took pleasure in his image. There was nothing to be ashamed of there. Popo, while not one for clothes (there wasn't a pair of trousers that could accommodate him) had been known to succumb to vanity on many occasions. The look in the man's eyes, however, was worrying indeed. Despite his words there was no sense of fervour there, he was not a man who thrilled at the good book, his gaze was calm and cold. His religious affectation was a means to an end. "Last I heard," he continued, "he'd retired from a life of testing the faithful. I believe he's now running a trout farm somewhere in England."

The cold-eyed man feigned anger. His mouth contorted but his eyes told the truth, chilly and practical, as he stepped in and dealt Popo a slap with back of his hand. "No more blasphemy," he said.

He turned to the man Popo assumed was the 'Father' due to his monk's robes. "Leave us," he told the man, "this is not going to be quick or pleasant and I have no wish to upset you further either with his words or my responses."

The monk hesitated for a moment and Popo realised he had misplaced his flippancy. He had played into the cold man's hands with his talk of Satan—though he had spoken truthfully as far as he was aware. The monk nodded and stepped outside the tent, leaving Popo to the attention of the cold man and his three colleagues.

"There," said the cold man, "that's probably for the best. We don't want to distress the Father any further, do we?" He looked to the other three men. "Are the rest of you happy to stay and do what must be done?"

"It's clearly a devil," said one, a pudgy man with yellow skin.

"You can count on me, Mr Atherton," said another, "I won't blanch when the going gets tough."

"I know you won't, Phil," said Atherton, "you've a strong heart."

"Me too," said the final man, ageing disgracefully beneath an unruly mop of grey hair. "I'm only too happy to take a swing at the cursed thing."

No doubt the old codger felt he had to compensate for Phil's enthusiasm, Popo thought. He even placed a wonderfully heavy emphasis on the last syllable of 'cursed'.

"I don't know what you think needs to be done, gentlemen," said Popo, realising it was likely fruitless to try and talk his way out of the situation but willing to try, "but I've done nothing to you. I was merely trying to fetch back the child of a friend."

"You call that thing a child?" asked Yellowskin.

"Yes," said Popo, "I do. Where is he?"

"You don't seem too distressed at your situation," said Atherton, not answering the question. "You like a bit of rough treatment, do you?"

It took Popo a moment to realise Atherton was referring to his erection. As a permanent fixture he sometimes forgot how distressing some mortal men found it.

"If so," Atherton continued, "I can promise you're going to very much enjoy what lies ahead."

"It's just the way I am," Popo explained, then, unable to help himself, "though I'm gratified it's taken your fancy so. In other circumstances I'd let you indulge yourself with it but I'm not feeling particularly loving at the moment."

For the first time, that coldness in Atherton's eyes thawed and he beat at Popo with a ferocity the Incubus was barely able to endure.

When he finally stopped, Popo found it hard to breathe and his mouth was filled with blood.

"You think you're funny," said Atherton, flexing swollen fingers and regaining his own breath as he took a step back, "but you will learn. I want to know all about that town. How many of you are in it. What abilities and weapons you have. Every last detail. I'm not going to ask you now. I'm going to let you rest a while, let you really enjoy the pain, then I'm going to come back and we'll talk a little more."

With that, he stepped out of the tent. Popo realised he'd probably struck a nerve, for all the good it had done him as Atherton had certainly struck a few in return.

"Well," said the old man, "that sure told you, huh? Maybe you'll watch your damned mouth next time."

Again, that emphasis, damNED, it would have been sweet were Popo not in such pain. He spat blood onto the floor, only to feel his mouth begin to fill up again. And was that a tooth working itself loose? Popo thought it probably was.

"I asked a question earlier," Popo said, no humour in his tone now. They had gone beyond trading insults. "I asked where the child was."

"That thing weren't no child," said Yellowskin.

"Some kind of demon," said Phil, "the way it chattered and screamed."

Popo clenched the arms of the chair, though it was agony to do so.

"Phil smacked the shit out of that thing until it quit its noise," said the old man, "took some doing too. Used that length of wood to turn the ugly thing to paste and still it cried."

"And if you don't tell us what we want to know," said Phil, "I'll be doing the same to you."

Popo spat again. It took him a moment to realise he was crying, his face was so wet from his own hot blood. He always had been one for tears. Opera turned him into a sobbing wreck.

"You may find I'm not such easy sport," said Popo.

"Oh I don't know," said Phil the Child Killer, "you don't look all that much to me right now."

"I can take a beating," Popo admitted, tensing his arms, "that's not the measure of a man. It doesn't matter how long it takes to knock him down, what matters is how long it takes for him to get back up."

He yanked his arms upwards, wrenching the nails from the wood of the chair. The old man and Yellowskin were closest and they made the fatal error of grabbing him, meaning to force him back down. He slammed the bloody points of each nail down into their heads, pounding on their skulls with his forearms and using the leverage to pull his ankles free. They burned with pain as he stood up and grabbed Phil, clamping a hand to his mouth before he had time to scream. The nail on that wrist, half of which had snapped off and was now jutting from the scalp of Yellowskin like the stalk on a rosy red apple, pierced Phil's cheek. Popo held him hard, stifling his screams.

"I'm a higher caste, bitch," he whispered into Phil's ear. "That gives me the sort of strength and tolerance a mortal like you can only dream of. And I fed not long before you caught me, putting me at the top of my game." His mouth was filling with blood again, the loose tooth finally snapped free and rolling on his tongue. "You want to know how I feed, Phil? Well, I've adopted a more gentle attitude to that of late but in the old days it was different." He reached forward and yanked at Phil's belt, loosening the man's trousers. "Tell you what, why don't I just show you?"

He stepped back slightly. "I can't promise to be soft," he said. He spat the mouthful of blood and loose tooth onto the weapon he hadn't put to fatal use for some time. The tooth glistened on its tip, the ruins of a great smile.

If Popo's hand hadn't stifled them, Phil's cries would have been the equal of the child he had killed.

3.

ATHERTON PACED THE edge of the camp, wanting to cool his anger. It did him no good, this rage. The beast, every bit as infernal as those creatures in Wormwood, that he kept caged in his belly. Sometimes, deprived of light and food, that beast grew weak, so weak in fact he might almost believe it had died. But then, something would awaken it again and it would return, as big and powerful as ever.

To his employers, that rage was a weapon, but that was only because they didn't know how hot it could burn, how much Atherton had to keep a grip on it. If they saw the real power of it, the screaming, pent-up lunacy of it, they would have shot him years ago. Which showed how little they understood the job he did; did they really think it was possible for a completely sane man to travel the world getting gallons of blood on his hands?

He climbed up to the edge of the crater rim, looking down over the plain in front of Wormwood. Over the short time he had been here he had watched that plain fill up, the traffic to and from Wormwood getting busier almost by the hour. They had had to move carefully, he and his men, to get close to

Wormwood and capture someone without being seen. He didn't trust those that gathered down there to have seen the importance of what they had been doing, seen how vital it was to gather information about the enemy.

The talking was soon to begin. There had been official envoys and messengers moving to and fro all day. That poisonous stew, politics, was on the boil. And now, to add a little urgency, he understood the President was on his way to visit.

He filled his pipe and let the act of smoking calm him down.

Ten minutes, that was how long he allowed himself to find clarity and focus, to bury the monster. Then he climbed back down into the camp and down the short path to the tent they had erected a distance away. Atherton had known that it would be a mistake to have pitched this tent with the others, it took a special kind of soul to retain their conviction even when the screaming started. Father Martin, for example, a man that would throw words at his enemies but nothing more.

Atherton peeled back the flap and looked at a horror of blood on canvas. He saw the desiccated remains of Phil, his trousers loose at his ankles, his skin wrinkled and contorted. He saw the absence of their prisoner. And with that, the monster in his belly returned.

His course of action was barely even deliberated, he simply reacted. He ran, not further along the trail, where the creature had undoubtedly fled, but back to the camp. He grabbed his rifle from his tent and then scaled the crater once more, ignoring the questions of those around him. He skidded down the outside edge, running over the rocks with such dexterity it was if they weren't there. Descending at a steep angle, his only chance was to cut off the creature further down the mountain before it could make a break for the plain and aid. As much as Atherton might hope that any right-thinking human would refuse such a thing assistance, he could not rely on the fact.

He jumped down onto the trail the creature would have used when exiting the tent. Momentarily, he dropped to his haunches and studied the ground. It was peppered with blood, a mixture no doubt, of the creature's victims' and its own. There was no part of Atherton's mind that saw the creature as a victim itself, of course, it was simply the enemy and he ran down the trail, shifting his attention between the blood and the way ahead.

4.

POPO KNEW HE was being followed. While his pursuer was athletic he wasn't silent, small rocks tumbled at his passing and, to someone with ears as sensitive as Popo's, the man's breathing echoed off the corridors of stone around them. Popo's ankles burned, blood pumping from his wounds. If it weren't for the energy he'd gained from a dual feeding he wouldn't have been able to walk, let alone run. That said, the energy wouldn't last forever, his pains would get the better of him soon and, as much as he wished for nothing more than to turn and fight the bastard that had dealt them, he knew his only hope was to escape. Once healed, once strong again, he promised himself he would return. He had a score to settle with the man behind him, and he wouldn't rest until it was done.

5.

ATHERTON CAUGHT A glimpse of the creature ahead. He stopped, raising his rifle, resting the barrel on the rock to steady its aim. You'll not run, he thought to himself. Nobody escapes from me.

With Popo in his sights, he placed his finger on the trigger and gently squeezed.

WHAT AM I DOING IN THE MIDDLE OF THE REVOLUTION?

(An excerpt from the book by Patrick Irish)

NO MORE. As the Observation Lounge continued to pummel me with sights I could hardly bear, I made that promise.

Hadn't Alonzo said it was impossible to simply observe? He had been right. I couldn't be a spectator, not to this. Not to atrocity after atrocity, themselves nothing but drops in the ocean of blood that was sure to flow soon enough.

But what could I do?

Everything was a chaos. Atherton and his army; the impending President and the soldiers he would bring with him; the gathered masses in the plain, observing and judging; Lucifer and the forces of the Dominion of Circles who, soon enough, would no longer be his to control.

How could I resolve any of this? It all seemed too confused, too disparate. Were this a story on a page how could I ever hope to bring it to a conclusion?

The honest truth was that I would not have allowed it to become such a mess in the first place. There were too many characters following too many journeys of their own. What sort of story would this have been? Was it Elisabeth and Billy's love story? A broad comedy, with Abernathy in his store? A political drama with Lucifer and his conferences? Atherton's brutal tale of horror?

It made my head swim. It was no story of mine. I had crafted simple adventures of a noble hero facing monsters. Where were the monsters here? The demonic caste? The humans that hated them? It was all the most terrible, unpleasant mess and I didn't have the first idea how it could ever be brought together.

I left the Observation Lounge for a while and walked the corridors outside, because, in the old days, when this sort of thinking had been my bread and butter, I had often found that most plots gave in if you just paced around enough. Of course, back then, if the pacing hadn't done the trick I would just have taken the cap off a bottle and drowned the problem, but that was a solution I was determined to avoid for now. If I started drinking I'd simply never stop.

There had to be a way. There had to be something that could be done to bring all of this together. What strings could I pull, what extra chapters could I write? What story could I force upon that mess of life below me?

I returned to the Observation Lounge, looking back over the lives I had encountered. Not just re-watching moments I had already seen but also looking earlier. I followed Lucifer's passage through the Dominion of Circles, hunting for the power to lift his curse of being 'non grata'. I watched Elwyn, the nervous young man now made immortal through a mistake in a hand of cards. I watched...

And then I decided.

CHAPTER TEN
BETWEEN GOD, THE DEVIL
AND A WINCHESTER

THE BEAST WAS dead and that was the only good thing that could be said of it.

Leonard Oliver hadn't always been a man of the city. He had spent his formative years on his father's ranch before swapping the corralling of horses for a life of politics. He saw the skills learned in one life as perfect training for the other. When dealing with his father's horses he had often felt his control was illusory, now as a White House aide it was doubly so. He did his best to herd those in power from one appointment to another, the clean white fences of his father's ranch swapped for the enclosed walls of governmental office. The men in beards and suits were just as unruly, and liable to bite, as those willful colts had been. Now, he had to herd that most unruly horse of them all, President Benjamin Harrison, not through the streets of Washington but rather the open grasslands of Nebraska.

"What in hell's teeth is it?" asked Corker, the Army Captain currently charged with keeping the convoy safe. His platoon maintained their positions, rifles at the ready, big guns cold but their keepers ready to load at a moment's notice. They looked like they were en route to a war rather than a conversation.

Corker poked at the creature in front of them with the gleaming toe of his boot. It made a noise like sponge engorged with broth.

Oliver, who had been wondering much the same thing, squatted down and risked lifting one of the beast's leathery wings. Beneath it was a mess of meat and fur that offered no further clue as the animal's identity.

"Is that its eyes?" Oliver asked, pointing to a glutinous mass at the centre.

"If so, what the hell are these?" Corker replied, pointing at a pair of cream spheres at the other end of the creature's body.

Oliver shook his head.

"With all due respect, gentlemen," came a voice from inside the presidential coach, "we're here to do considerably more important things than marvel over grotesques. Would you please get us moving again? I wish to achieve more today than a numb posterior."

"I appreciate that, sir," said Corker, "but it's my duty to assess whether there are any threats to your personal safety."

"It's deader than my grandma, son, the only way it's going to hurt me is if I have to smell it a moment longer. Let's get under way."

Corker sighed and nodded at Oliver, both returning to the convoy as it rolled on towards its destination.

2.

AGRAT HAD ENDURED a tiring morning reading *Venus in Furs* and consuming a small sack of peaches. She claimed it was 'research into the mortal domain' and vital in fostering 'a continuing understanding of their mores with a view to potential co-existence'. When Elwyn had asked her opinion thus far she had simply replied:

"Delicious."

"The book or the fruit."

"Both."

Having announced to the household that a morning's work was more than should be expected of a woman of her importance and nobility, she had retired to the verandah to drink brandy and bully passersby. She was not, therefore, best pleased by Lucifer's request that she be pressed into service once more.

"Can't you get one of the others to do it?" she asked. "One of the more unimportant ones?"

"Such as?"

"Ask Elwyn, he's a mortal, he knows what mortals talk about."

"That's rather missing the point, I want the president to be met by someone from the Dominion. Someone who can show a charming side."

She stretched out on her sofa and basked in the glow of the compliment. "I am terribly charming."

"You're capable of pretending as much," Lucifer agreed, looking out across the square at the bustling streets beyond, "and that's almost the same thing."

"Still," she insisted, "I don't see why I should put myself out. Ask Meridiana, she can show him some of her attractions."

"I want to impress him, not kill him."

"I think she's strictly monogamous these days. Certainly she shouldn't be hungry, I hear them at night. She moans awfully, egging his withered genitals on to further acts of heroic savagery. It's quite disgusting."

"They're happy."

"Oh, to be so easily pleased."

Lucifer sighed and tried his best to keep his anger in check. He had swapped a life of wandering for one of complication and responsibility, two things he had happily given up long ago. "The American president is a very important man."

"That's a contradiction in terms," she smiled, "present company excepted. He's King Ape of a trifling land mass, I fail to be impressed. Now, Queen Victoria..."

"She's not paying a visit, President Harrison is. Besides, America is hardly a trifling landmass, it's young but growing in power all the time."

"So you talk to him."

"I'm intending to, clearly, I'm just asking you and Forset to be the welcoming party."

"Sat out there in the dirt waiting on a monkey. In the company of another monkey. It is not an attractive proposition."

"Nonetheless, you'll do it." Lucifer's patience was running thin. "Because I'm telling you to."

Agrat sighed and threw her arms in the air. "Very well, as a favour to you."

"A favour given freely," he insisted, knowing full well how Agrat might choose to turn the situation to her advantage otherwise.

"Naturally," she replied, begrudgingly. "When is he due to arrive?"

"Forset's calculations are far from precise, there may be a couple of hours in it either way, but he thinks it'll be around noon our time."

"You're not making this seem any more attractive, you know."

"Take a book." He stepped back inside the house, before briefly reappearing. "But not the brandy."

"Spoilsport," she said, draining her drink and setting her thoughts as to what she should wear.

After some consideration, she settled on a frock hand-woven by the Needle Babies of Albeer. She decided it was intimidating enough to create an impression and yet not as violent as some of her wardrobe; Lucifer would hardly be pleased if she wore something potentially fatal. She took a few passes in front of the dressing room mirror, delighted by the noises the frock made, like a host of chattering teeth.

Satisfied, she went looking for Forset. He was hiding in his room at the hotel, hyperventilating.

"I can't abide this sort of thing," he wheezed, "ceremonies and handshakes. I was tempted to crawl under the bed and stay there."

"I'm not exactly brimming with enthusiasm either," she admitted, "but if I have to suffer so do you."

She led him out of his room, he still fussing over his tie as they descended the stairs.

They met Elisabeth and Billy in the foyer.

"You look very respectable," Elisabeth told her father, pulling his hands away from the knot of his bow tie. "But stop trying to choke yourself."

She readjusted it for him.

"I don't suppose either of you have seen Popo?" Billy asked.

"Certainly not," said Agrat. "I make a point of avoiding doing so wherever possible."

"You wouldn't have had to try hard for the last day or so, nobody's seen hide nor hair of him."

"No doubt he is soiling some poor creature's bed linen," she replied before snapping at Forset, "Are you coming or not?"

"Of course, of course..." he gave Elisabeth a grateful kiss on the cheek and followed Agrat out of the building.

Agrat had drawn to a halt, looking up and down the street. "Where in damnation's name is he?" she wondered aloud.

"Who?" Forset asked,. "Popo?"

"Of course not!" she muttered to herself and began striding towards the edge of town. "He'd better already be there, that's all I'm saying."

Forset decided against cross-examining her, she was clearly singularly disinterested in his having the first idea what she was talking about and he had enough to worry him already. With a fatalistic sigh, he followed the sound of her chattering frock and began mentally rehearsing what one said to Presidents when one met them.

3.

HICKS MISSED HIS horse. He just wasn't built for getting anywhere fast on foot. He looked around the ramshackle group and wondered if he might convince any of them to carry him. Perhaps he could feign some sort of ankle injury and throw himself on their mercy. Then he saw the kid who was striding on with nothing but fresh air and flies where his stomach should be and decided a sprained ankle probably wouldn't cut it. These people made corpses on a battlefield appear in good shape.

It wasn't far, that was some consolation. The confidence with which he had claimed to know the route to Wormwood had been somewhat exaggerated—when you found yourself outnumbered and disadvantaged you made yourself indispensable, that was his thinking, and it had saved his neck several times. Not that the last time he'd played that particular hand it had fared him so well, he decided. He'd been heading towards that elusive damn town, with Henry Jones and his band of outlaws in tow, and earned a bullet in the head for his trouble. While it hadn't been Jones or his damned hoity-toity wife that had pulled the trigger they'd not exactly leaped to his defence. In fact, the last words to pass through Hicks' head before the bullet swept them away had been Harmonium Jones wishing death on him. Well, as much as he might miss the feel of her scrawny neck between his thighs as she carried him around, he could at least reassure himself that she'd had a considerable time to regret making him her enemy. Nothing quite enriched the soul like emptying your bowels over the back of someone you hated.

For all his concerns over the precise location of the town—and quite how he'd avoid a beating, at best, when his fellow travellers realised he didn't have its precise location to hand—things had worked out just fine. They'd bumped into a man on the outskirts of Sepulchre Heights who had given them precise directions. Quite why the man, a strangely refined gent for that part of the Dominion, had been so eager to tell them the way, Hicks didn't know. They'd stopped for some provisions when the man had suddenly walked up to them and begun listing the route, step by step, answering a question that nobody had asked. Hicks wasn't complaining, and would have offered thanks towards the divine if there was such a thing anymore. He'd made a good show of agreeing with the man's advice, pretending he was only being told something he had already known, and they'd carried on their way, following the man's directions to the letter.

"We'll be there in an hour or two," he said to Kane, who was also struggling with the pace, dragging that fatty carcass mile after mile. "Then we can both get some rest."

"We'll rest when we're on mortal soil," Kane replied, "and not a minute before."

"Fine," said Hicks, "you do that. Me, I'll just be glad to see another town, book myself a bed and someone compliant to lie in it with me."

They continued to walk and, after a short while, the landscape grew emptier around them, the landmarks falling away so that their surroundings became more insubstantial.

"We're on the cusp of it!" Hicks shouted, "can you feel it? We're crossing over from the Dominion."

Kane, who certainly could feel something, beyond the usual gnawing in his ever hungry gut nodded. "Come on!" he shouted, determined to be the one who was seen to lead, rather than their wizened little guide. "We're almost there! Follow me!"

4.

ATHERTON'S BULLET WENT wide as a polished boot nudged the stock of his rifle.

"God damn you," Atherton said, turning his rifle towards the newcomer.

"No," the man replied. "He's beyond such things. You're still pointing your gun in the wrong direction."

The man was English, Atherton noted. Was he one of the people who had travelled over here with the monks?

"I was sent by Admiral Clemence," the man said, adjusting his cuffs, as if nothing were more important out here in the middle of nowhere than maintaining a civil appearance. For some reason, this ludicrous affectation helped convince Atherton as much as the accent. There would always be a certain breed of Englishman abroad that considered the state of their tie of the utmost importance.

"Where are the others?" he asked. "I was led to believe there was to be a sizeable party arriving."

He had lowered his rifle but not yet discounted the notion of using it. He wasn't about to let his moment in authority pass painlessly. If this man was from the ministry then he'd adjust his plans, but quickly. Once the diplomats took over his window of opportunity would be closed.

"They're still en route I'm afraid," the man replied. "I came ahead. Shipped up from Mexico where I've been keeping an eye on Diaz. A little interim assistance, if you will."

"Don't need any," Atherton replied. "I know what I'm doing."

"Not a criticism old chap, it's just that I have new orders."

"Let me guess, you want me to set up talks with these things?"

The man frowned. "I hardly think that's a good idea, we want them wiped out not befriended."

Atherton's hand loosened on his rifle. Was it possible that his lack of faith in his employers had been unjustified?

"Even more importantly," the man continued, "we need to ensure that the Americans don't try and form an alliance. The last thing this troublesome country needs is friends of that calibre."

"So what are the orders?"

The man nodded at Atherton's gun. "First we want your people to stage an attack on the town."

"Already planned," said Atherton, relishing the fact. "Though they don't stand a chance, as I'm sure you'll appreciate."

"Naturally not, but their noble sacrifice will make excellent reportage for the gathered press, there's quite a representation down there by now."

"Second?"

"Ah... well the second part of the plan involves you and that rifle," the man nodded at the weapon, "and the very important targets we wish you to point it at."

5.

AGRAT AND FORSET had taken up position on a large wooden bench just outside the barrier to the town.

It seemed to Forset that they were sat on a stage, their audience the gathered crowds of journalists and spectators that now filled the plain outside the town in anticipation of the President's arrival. He had never felt quite so uncomfortable in all his life. Including, he decided, during the several recent instances when he was being shot at or threatened with immolation.

A large party of workmen had constructed a tent housing a meeting table and refreshments, the venue where the President and his colleagues would sit down with the Governor of Wormwood and his chosen representatives and discuss exactly what the future held. It was no great surprise that the President refused to enter the town itself. That, it had been accepted, would be a security risk too far. Better, his people had suggested, that the initial meeting took place out here in neutral territory, where initial discussions could be carried out in an open and friendly manner.

Forset was quite sure that the gathered crowd would be as unwelcome to the President as it was to him—he knew of no politician that relished such delicate conversations being carried out in the public eye—but this situation had gone past the point of secrecy. The world was hearing all about Wormwood, better then that the American government seemed to be conducting itself in as open and frank manner as possible, both for the confidence of its people and the fears of foreign governments.

The notion of the plain being a place of neutral safety was, of course, an utter nonsense. Several divisions of infantry were surrounding the area, their guns not quite pointing directly at the town. "Security," one of the officials had said, "you know how it is."

Indeed, Forset did. He had no doubt that those guns would be aimed more directly at the very moment the men commanding them felt it necessary.

Perhaps they thought that such a show of strength

would intimidate the people of Wormwood. Forset, knowing the sort of strength that lay within, and indeed beyond, that small town, knew better. Not that it reassured him particularly. Knowing that the mortal army could not win the day didn't mean they couldn't clock up a few casualties in the attempt. Forset was not a man who enjoyed the experience of having a gun pointed at him. Though even that was preferable to the lens of a camera, several of which were aimed in his direction, ready to pounce. He made a point of crossing and uncrossing his legs as frequently as possible, worried that if he sat completely still one of the photographers would take advantage of the fact.

"Do stop fidgeting," Agrat told him, "you're aggravating my dress."

Unsure of quite where such aggravation might lead, Forset did as he was told.

There was a distant shout and he saw one of the lookouts signalling to those gathered below.

"I imagine that means he's nearly here," Forset said.

"Hooray," Agrat replied, with very little enthusiasm.

6.

"ALMOST THERE, SIR," said Oliver, peering out of the carriage window. "There's quite a crowd."

"Naturally," said Harrison. "This is a piece of theatre as much as it is politics."

"Is there ever really a difference?" asked Levi Morton, Harrison's vice-president.

Harrison sighed into his beard. "Perhaps not." He tugged at his jacket, trying to make himself look as presentable as possible. Morton always looked so damned dapper, he thought, whereas he could never quite shake the feeling that someone had altered the fit of his suit overnight, making it pinch and bulge in all the most uncomfortable places.

"Historic times," said Morton.

"Historic indeed," Harrison agreed, "and the problem with history is that it will always be judged by those who follow. Let us hope what we do today is judged fairly."

"There will be those who consider us heroes and those who consider us villains," Morton replied. "That, at least, will never really change."

7.

FATHER MARTIN WATCHED as the people from the camp began to descend the mountain, nigh-on a hundred and fifty souls, all ready to fight for something they believed in. Ready, perhaps, to die for it. On one hand he was distraught at the idea of the impending violence, on the other he found he envied them their conviction. He watched them recede down the mountainside, likely never to return. Behind him were the remains of the Order of Ruth, excluded from the fighting due to their age and the few fragile convictions they had left. Some were praying, the others just stood silently, as lost as their superior.

"What is my purpose?" Father Martin asked, no longer expecting an answer.

"Well," came a voice from behind him, "I would say it's the same as the rest of us: to be a better man."

Father Martin turned to see Patrick Irish. In the writer's arms was Popo, barely conscious, his wounds leaking onto Irish's shirt and pooling in the ground at their feet.

"Patrick? You came back?"

"Temporarily. I am, for once in my life, committed to tidying up after the mistakes of others." Irish lay Popo down on the ground. "You need to bring whatever medical supplies you have. Clean water, dressings, whatever you can find."

Father Martin stared at Popo. "That's... the creature we..."

"Nearly killed, yes. But you're going to learn to be a better man than that and you're going to look after him. You're going to help him heal and then you're going to take him home."

"I am?" Father Martin stared down at Popo, at his bright red, bloodied face, the skin torn to reveal the muscle beneath, and he remembered the visions that had plagued him on his journey to Wormwood. The red-faced man that had appeared to him nightly, taunting him—or so he had thought—an omen of the very worst to come. He looked down at Popo and realised that the omen had always been about him, about the horror he would not only witness but endorse. Oh Martin, he thought to himself, you lost your way so long ago, I only hope there's time for you to find your way back. "I am," he repeated, "of course I am. Fetch everything you can find!" he shouted at the monks, "this man needs our help."

8.

THE PRESIDENT'S CONVOY arrived on the plain and the barely restrained chaos that had held sway for the last hour or so finally burst. The reporters and spectators were shouting and crowding around the carriages as the army did their best to hold them back. Orders were barked, shots were fired into the air, defensive formations were struck and somewhere, at the heart of it all, two middle-aged politicians stepped out into the sunlight and wondered what the Hell lay ahead.

"Spare any change?" asked the demon who had taken up residence on the edge of town, restraining a sneeze that would set his facial fronds into a financially disastrous mess of mucus. Nobody even heard him—though a few had given him a wide berth when he'd ambled over earlier, bowl held out hopefully towards the gathered members of the mortal public.

Jolted by a small gang of reporters, he tumbled to the floor, his bowl spilling its pathetic contents. Cursing under his breath he tried to retrieve his funds; at least he hoped they were funds, being new to the world of dollars and cents he was a little baffled by some of what he'd been given.

Retreating to a safe distance he shoved the mixture of coinage, buttons and small stones into his pockets and sat back to watch the pageantry unfold.

Agrat and Forset were on their feet and making their way towards Harrison and Morton, the crowds finally forced back by the enthusiastic efforts of the military.

Harrison looked at Agrat and her chattering frock as if he were about to be buttonholed by a glamorous, six foot shrimp.

"My name is Agrat," she said, "the other creature is Lord Forset, we have been sent to welcome you on behalf of the Governor of Wormwood."

"Charmed," said Harrison taking her hand.

Agrat looked to Morton. "Is this your wife?" she asked.

"Vice-President Levi P. Morton, ma'am," Morton said, giving a polite bow.

"You didn't answer the question..."

"Not wife, no," said Forset, nerves having robbed him of all but the most vital words. "Pleased to meet you, gentlemen," he said to Harrison and Morton. "I have agreed to assist the governor in diplomatic matters, as I hope has been explained. I do not represent my home country in any way, I speak on behalf of Wormwood only."

"Understood," Harrison smiled. "I'm sure we're grateful for your assistance."

"These are complicated times, sir, I'm just hopeful they can be turned to everyone's benefit."

"You and me both."

They moved towards the tent that had been constructed for their talks, a sea of shouted questions washing over them as they approached it.

"That's an interesting gown, ma'am," said Morton, looking at the roving hem with a mixture of concern and curiosity.

"Just mind it doesn't go for your fingers," she warned him, "the threads get a trifle unruly in crowds."

He took a slight step back, unsure whether she was joking.

"Unruly or not," he said, "it's most..."

He didn't get to finish his sentence. A rifle shot rang out and he was startled to note a blossoming of red on the front of his shirt. "Oh Lord," he said, "I think I've just been..."

A second shot, and this time Harrison was the target. Later, when the gathered representatives of the press tried to evoke that moment they would write of that startled face, his thinning hair flicked skywards, the blood covering half of his face, the eyes that spoke only of confusion. None of the descriptions were printed, many were not even accurate, dramatising after the fact. At the moment that the shot was fired— the second shot that would change the world—the panic was so widespread, the confusion so total, that nobody really had the first idea what was happening.

It was Agrat that reacted first, that much would be accurately reported. Indeed, even in the calamity that was to follow, she was impossible to miss.

"Get behind me," she roared, seeming to grow in size, her dress writhing around her, her eyes burning.

If there was one thing the mortals would never forget, she decided, it was that Agrat was not a woman you pointed a weapon towards, not if you wanted to retain your soul.

The rifle shots were only the beginning. Even as their noise continued to echo between the mountains, they were joined by the roar of a crowd of people, Atherton's devout army, breaking from cover and advancing towards the town.

9.

ATHERTON REACHED INTO his pocket to reload. As accomplished as he was in the art of killing, he was by no means sure that he had administered a lethal wound to either of his targets. Even if he had, there could be no harm in adding a few more corpses to his ever-increasing tally.

He felt a hand grip his wrist and, as he turned, a fist connected under his jaw and his rifle was snatched away from him.

The sun shone in his eyes as he tried to focus on the figure hovering over him. A demon? Here to punish him?

"That's your lot, British," said the Geek, squatting down over him. "I promised God I'd help, see? And I'm not a man to say no to the Almighty, my folks brought me up better than that."

Atherton lifted his knee, meaning to dislodge the Geek, get that foul face and rancid breath away from him so that he could regain the upper hand. He was a fighter, it would take more than this brutish freak to get one over on him.

But the Geek was fast. Atherton may have been a fighter but the Geek was a hunter and he'd spent his whole life subduing his dinner.

"Uh uh," he said, avoiding Atherton's leg and dealing another blow to the man's head. He stepped back, Atherton's rifle now pointing at its owner.

"Now," said the Geek, "you're going to tell the folks down there who you are and who you just shot."

"Like Hell I am," Atherton replied, spitting at the Geek. "Who do you think you're dealing with? I've engineered entire revolutions, I've squeezed out a final beat from the heart of kings, I'll die before I say a word."

The Geek smiled, his metal teeth glinting in the sun. "I kind of hoped you might say something like that," he replied. "I was looking forward to convincing you."

10.

OSCAR BURIED HIS head in hands and wished to be anyone but the man he was. Life had become far too hard over the last week. Surrounded by people demanding answers and owning nothing but questions, he had come close to barricading himself in his office and refusing to come out. Realising that, however much he might wish it, this was not possible, he had at least taken to locking himself away for half an hour every day. Shut in with silence and a decent brandy he would try and clear his thoughts of their own unproductive chatter so that he might be able to do something useful once forced back out into the world. He never could, but he did at least have a small portion of the day he could now look forward to.

"This really is a very good brandy," said a voice from one of his two armchairs. He looked up to see a man sat there, perfectly at home, sipping at some of his liquor. This was impertinent but not his uppermost concern, his uppermost concern was how the devil the man had got in here in the first place. The office had been empty when he'd locked the door and drawn the curtains, refusing the outside world entrance. There was no doubt about that; his office, though spacious, was not so cavernous as to be able to hide people in it.

"I'm glad you approve," said Oscar. "If it's not too much to ask, who the devil are you and how did you get in?"

"I'm the person who's going to help solve the Wormwood problem for you, and I got in by methods that you will scarcely be able to comprehend."

"I can comprehend a great deal."

"Very well." The man placed his brandy on the small table next to his chair and promptly vanished, only to reappear again sat on the corner of Oscar's desk. "Can we take that part of things as read now? It really would save a great deal of time if you simply accepted I'm working with powers and abilities you can't begin to imagine."

"You've left your brandy behind," Oscar nodded towards it, terrified but suitably trained after a life in government not to show it.

"I shouldn't be drinking anyway," said the man. "Patrick Irish," he announced, extending a hand for shaking. "A pleasure to meet you, Oscar."

"Likewise, I'm sure," Oscar replied, ignoring the handshake.

"Time will tell on that," said Irish. "I'm afraid I have some bad news. Atherton, the man Admiral Clemence set to keep an eye on the Wormwood situation, has just put you in a very awkward position."

"Has he now?"

"He has. He's just shot both the President and the Vice-President of the United States of America. Not only that but he's managed to get caught and identified himself as an officer of the British Empire."

As well-trained in appearing casual as Oscar was, this was a step too far and he couldn't quite conceal his discomfort. "That is an awkward position," he agreed, reaching for his own brandy.

"Indeed. He has quite possibly placed you at war. A war, I hasten to point out, that you couldn't possibly win."

"We can win most wars," Oscar replied. "Eventually."

"Not ones like this. You know that America has a new ally. One that no other force in the world could hope to defeat."

"One hears rumours."

"One also sees a man appear and disappear in your room, Oscar, I think we can afford to take those rumours as read too, don't you? We have power and strength that even the British Empire can't defeat."

"You sound English yourself."

"I've emigrated. The point is this, I can assure you that war will not happen unless you take steps to instigate it. The forces that lie behind Wormwood have no urge to fight. They are content to co-exist peacefully. If you don't threaten them, they will not threaten you. They will leave the Empire to its business."

"And you have the authority to promise that, do you?"

"I do."

"Bully for you I do not."

"But you have enough authority to convince those who do, not to sharpen their sabres, Oscar. And you need to do so. Quickly. Because this is an offer you need to accept now, I can't promise how long it will be extended to you."

"The British government does not respond well to threats."

"I'm not offering one. Right now myself and several other important spokesmen for the powers behind Wormwood are working hard to ensure this situation doesn't escalate. We want this awkward situation to end before it becomes an even bigger problem. It's in your own best interests to do the same. Work with this new power, Oscar, don't fight it. Because, right now, the only act of aggression that matters is one undertaken by your man. If you issue an immediate and unequivocal statement clarifying that he acted under his own aegis and was not carrying out his government's orders we can nip this in the bud right now before anyone else is hurt."

Oscar thought about it for a moment. "I'll see what I can do."

"Good enough, I shall take you at your word. It's the right decision, old chap, I promise you that. I'm acting just as much in your interests as I am anyone else's."

Irish stood up. "Now, if you'll forgive me, I have a dead President to deal with."

With that he vanished.

11.

KANE THOUGHT HE saw movement in the mist ahead. Finally, a sign of life in this insubstantial barrier that lay between them and the real world.

"I see it!" he cried, eager to be the voice that brought his people home. "We're here!"

He stepped through the mist and found himself facing a large chasm that stretched to either side of them. Stood on the chasm's edge was the man he had seen Hicks talking to back in Sepulchre Heights.

"Wormwood?" he asked, an awful feeling spreading through him, the earliest sense that all was not as he had hoped and imagined.

"No," admitted Patrick Irish as the procession gathered around Kane, staring out over the chasm into the whiteness beyond. "Not Wormwood. Somewhere better."

The man closed his eyes and suddenly the air was filled with glowing lights, orb after orb descending as it chose a member of the procession to call its own.

"You goddamned cheat!" shouted Hicks. "You gave me the wrong directions!"

"You could look at it like that," Irish admitted, "or you could accept that I brought you where you needed to be. There's nothing in Wormwood for you, nothing in the mortal world. That's done, it's behind you. Ahead is somewhere better, ahead is what you all deserve."

He looked at Kane and his eyes narrowed slightly. "Even you." Several orbs clustered around the fat man. "Though you may need a bit more support than most."

He raised his voice so that they could all hear him. "Two wonderful people left this paradise to come and rescue you. You repaid their kindness by turning your back on them. By deciding you knew better, by choosing to follow anger rather than love." He shrugged. "But that's fine. They would have forgiven you and so do I. Take hold of the orbs, get a firm grip."

The orbs moved behind Kane and pressed against him, forcing him to topple back onto them, bouncing on their support.

One by one the members of the procession rode into the air. Marrousia, the woman who had hung by her feet for years; Josiah, the hollow boy; Rachel

Watson, her eyes held out in front of her as she floated over the chasm; even George Oskirk, who had once taken the skin from another to protect himself in the Draining Desert. They all drifted on, towards the Dominion of Clouds and a better future.

Even Hicks, draped across an orb, sailed upwards, a wary look in his eye as Irish watched him go. "One way ticket to paradise, eh?" he shouted. "I guess I can go along with that. Especially if there's an eager woman at the end of it!"

Irish watched him go. "You're half right, I suppose," he said as the orb suddenly shifted direction and Hicks began to sail back the way he had come, his orb rising higher and higher as it raced away from the chasm, back through the mist and on and on towards a destination of its very own.

Irish looked up into the air, the light of the orbs receding now that their charges were almost at the other side. "If God were here," he said, "maybe He'd be better. But He's not, and I'm only human."

12.

As ATHERTON'S ARMY charged, a roar to match their own emerged from Wormwood as the Forset Land Carriage burst through the barrier and charged forth towards them.

On its roof, a solitary figure, Lucifer, the wind whipping his jacket around him.

Mere moments after the crowds had acknowledged his arrival, the large wooden bench that Agrat and

Forset had been sitting on while they waited for the President creaked and expanded, rearing up to cries of panic. But those gathered had nothing to fear from Branches of Regret, his mission was not one of destruction. This had been explained to him by the curious Englishman who had visited him— and several others—a few hours earlier. His job was incarceration. He expanded wider and wider, branches forming branches forming branches as he towered over Atherton's army, who cowered together, their advance halted by the sight of this mobile forest that seemed intent on attacking them. He did not attack. He simply dropped forward, encasing every single one of them in a cage made of his own body.

The Land Carriage turned and slowed, drawing to a halt a few yards away. Its doors opened and one by one, its passengers alighted. Billy and Elisabeth; Elwyn and Meridiana; Biter, the excitement of his situation making him howl, his face lifted up to the sky; William, Abernathy, even Knee-High, the latter couple slightly the worse for drink though they covered it well as they dropped to the ground and stood next to their fellows; several residents from Wormwood, the human and the grotesque, stepping down in front of the eyes of the world. Even Fenella and her children were there, the excitable young things clambering around the outside of the carriage, jumping to either side of Lucifer who stood firm at the centre.

Above them a figure soared in the air, the bird-like creature Atherton had first noticed on his arrival at

Wormwood. It flew past them all, on towards the mountains.

"No more!" Lucifer shouted, his voice carrying over the plain as slowly, but surely everyone grew quiet. "There will be no more blood spilled here today. Your enemy is not in front of you. If you want the assassin look to your own people, not mine."

Agrat, her face still terrifying enough to live forever in the nightmares of the first few rows of spectators, lowered her hands.

Forset, down on his haunches, holding the President in his arms, called for help. "He's still alive!" he shouted. "I need medical help!"

Captain Corker was shouting at his men, ordering them to hold fire. As terrified as they all were, the man was right, the shooter was in the mountains behind them, not the town. He shaded his eyes with his hand and stared up into the rocks, looking for a sign of their attacker.

A field medic rushed forward, giving the Vice-President a cursory glance—more than enough to show him that Mr Morton had passed beyond his help—and dropped down next to the President.

"Head wound," he said, examining Harrison's scalp, which peeled away in his hand. "Not a chance."

Forset stood up, looking down at the dying man and the crowds that pushed forward to see his final breath. Leonard Oliver was at his side. "Presidential aide," he said. "We should..." His words failed him. The man he was responsible for was expiring and with him, Oliver's sense of purpose.

"We need to get him inside the tent," Forset said. "If all we can give him is privacy then that is what he deserves."

No sooner had he finished speaking than Fenella's children were surrounding him, swarming around both Harrison and Morton before carefully lifting them and carrying them into the tent that had been constructed for their talks. It was an image that would be remembered, the children of Wormwood and the care and respect they showed the elders of the mortal world. The field medic simply stared, Forset grabbing him by the arm and pushing him towards the tent. "Come on man, now's not the time, just do what you can."

"These men came to me in peace," said Lucifer, addressing the crowd, "and were struck down by one of their own. You're afraid, I understand, and perhaps we are worthy of your fear. But we come to you under the same promise of peace offered by your government. Would you reject that? We don't come as enemies, we come as friends. That town behind me is the doorway to other worlds and places, and it can never be closed. So why not take comfort from it? Instead of fearing what you do not know, why not embrace it? We are with you now, and we're staying. I have offered the people of the Dominions my protection, and I offer that same protection to you. To all of you. Please take it, it is freely given."

There was the call of the flying creature again as it descended into the open ground between the crowds and Lucifer's party. In its hands it held Atherton, who stumbled free and walked towards the reporters.

"My name is Richard Atherton," he said, "and I came here under orders of the British government. I'm the man who killed your President."

He dropped to his knees, his energy spent, and those gathered couldn't fail to notice his right arm was torn apart up to the elbow. The reports that followed would choose to ignore the fact, because nobody quite knew how to explain the wounds. The skin was ragged and appeared to have been bitten by some wild animal. Besides, the man's own government claimed him soon after. While they disowned his actions, they accepted his provenance. Nobody was inclined to question.

The silence that had fallen in the wake of Lucifer's appearance broke again as the crowd began to talk. The plain was awash with shouting, tears and questions. Lucifer lowered himself from the train and stood with his companions.

"This is the turning point," he told them, "as I'm reliably informed by an influential observer."

Irish appeared amongst them, his face solemn. "Thank you," he said, "for all playing your parts. We have offered a show of strength today but the only blood to be spilled is not our responsibility."

Lucifer raised an eyebrow. "That rather depends on who told Atherton to shoot, doesn't it? Was it really his government's orders?"

Irish shrugged. "According to them he was acting on his own and that's how it will be left. But the world has seen you all, standing together. They have seen you come in peace. The entire future now hangs in the balance, and there is one more card that must be dealt in order to ensure things pan out for the best." He looked at Lucifer who, after a reluctant sigh, nodded.

13.

HICKS' ORB BEGAN to descend, his wiry little fingers digging into its skin as he screamed curse after curse at it.

Below him, he saw the signs of building, foundations being laid, concrete being poured, great crowds of people milling around as they set to the art of building the biggest, most awe-inspiring tower the Dominion had ever seen. Lower and lower he dropped, the people growing larger, their faces distinct. He saw what he would have taken to be nothing but a small child were it not for the fact that her eyes were empty holes, opening onto a limitless darkness. She smiled as he floated past, giving him a wave.

Finally, the orb came to rest, hovering over the pit at the heart of Chatter's Munch, Hicks forced to grip as tightly as ever in case he should fall into it. On the brim of the pit he saw two people he knew only too well.

"Hello again, my kind and considerate rider," said Harmonium Jones. She was looking much improved from the time he had seen her last. Her hair and beard were clean and brushed, her skin scrubbed. Several meals had put some weight back on her and given her skin a more healthy glow. Her husband stood next to her, his head cocked, his face half in shadow beneath the brim of his hat. He was pointing his gun at Hicks.

"I believe you owe my wife an apology," he said. "A considerable apology." He cocked the gun.

"Fuck you!" shouted Hicks. "You're going to shoot me whatever I say. I loved every minute of it! Every single damned mile grinding my old balls against the back of her lousy neck. Every tug of the reins, every single crack of my whip. So get it over with! Kill me!"

Jones put his gun back in his holster. "Kill you?" he asked, leading his wife away from the pit. "Where would be the fun in that? You can hang there a little longer first. Maybe a day or two."

"Or a week," said Harmonium.

"Or a month," said her husband.

"Or a year..."

They joined Patrick Irish, who was stood watching at a distance. "You're satisfied with our deal?" he asked.

Jones nodded. "The Exchange is happy to concentrate on business here in the Dominion for now. As for me, I couldn't care less. We won't interfere with the mortal world. Not yet, anyway."

"That's good enough," said Irish, "things are delicate for now. It'll take time for us all to adapt. I just needed room to breathe. Let the Dominion of Circles keep itself to itself for a little while, just until people get used to what they're now sharing reality with."

"What about the Dominion of Clouds?" Harmonium asks. "Now God's dead, who speaks for them?"

Irish smiled. "Me, I suppose. Not bad for an alcoholic old hack, eh?"

14.

THE PRESIDENT DIED as the sun began to fall low on the horizon.

If the crowds had been large before, the hours of the afternoon had only seen them swell yet further as people continued to gather, a never-ending procession from Alliance to the strange, ill-matching mountain range that stood in that Nebraska plain, and the town it surrounded.

The mourning was cut by a sense of wonder, an awe that passed through them all as they moved in and out of Wormwood. Demonic caste and human intermingled both in the streets of the town and the land outside it.

Elspeth Gorman and her son, Hodge, sat out on the street, smiling at the passersby. Their next door neighbours, Remy and Boo, recently from the Bough, had decided to organise a barbecue and the air was thick with cooking food. Abernathy's till was fit to burst with the sudden upswing in trade and he was caught in a state of euphoria and irritation, trying to fulfil orders.

"We need to set up a run to Alliance," said Knee-High, "get more supplies coming in."

"We?" Abernathy asked.

"Don't tell me you don't need a business partner," the dwarf replied. "You wouldn't have the first idea what you were buying."

"I already have a business partner!" Abernathy replied. "He's around here somewhere with a mop. William? William? Where in the name of duck teats is the tower of a bastard? William?"

But William couldn't be found, so Knee-High got his deal.

Popo was returned to his hotel, dressed in a spare monk's habit loaned by Father Martin, who accompanied the Incubus along with the rest of his brotherhood.

His return was well-received by those who had all but given up on him. "You'll never get rid of me," he'd said, twirling somewhat weakly in his borrowed clothes. "I'm far too fabulous to die."

Father Martin, overcome by the sights around him but determined to try and retain an open mind hung back. He and his brothers had done their best to help Popo but it had become clear that the Incubus healed only too well on his own. All he'd really needed was a bit of rest. Father Martin suspected Irish had known that, but had wanted to force Father Martin into choosing the route his future would take. In that, he'd succeeded.

"You know," said Brother Clarence, looking around, "it's not quite as awful as I thought it would be."

Father Martin nodded. "It never is."

"What about..." the old monk hesitated, "well, what they were saying about God. Do you think He really can be dead?"

Father Martin thought about Irish. "Not in any sense that matters," he said, and led his monks along the street in search of food.

Not everyone welcomed the intrusion of course, certainly not Fingers and Nyctos who stared out of their window at the influx of mortals and felt their thoughts turn to murder.

"Look at them all," said Nyctos, the dark pulsing with anger. "We're infested with apes."

"Not for long," Fingers replied, clicking his fingers in irritation, "just you wait. There'll be more like us, willing to band together and drive these monkeys out."

Which was undoubtedly true, but while there would be dissent on both sides, the union held, not least because of Lucifer's announcement a few hours later.

15.

THE YOUNG MAN who up until recently had been a novice in the Order of Ruth and then a shop boy to Abernathy was on the edge of the Dominion of Circles, having decided to leave Wormwood behind and see where his feet took him. William looked out onto its rough and blasted landscape and wondered where he'd be tomorrow.

"Wherever I want," he said aloud, smiling at the freedom of it.

"Who are you talking to?" asked a voice from beside him. He looked down to see a young girl.

"Where did you come from?" he asked, looking around. "Your parents around somewhere?"

"I don't have any," she replied. "I'm on my own. Unless I can walk with you for a little while?"

William thought about it, but didn't see he had much choice. He could hardly leave her here by the side of the road. "I guess," he said.

"Thanks."

So they walked off towards Hell together, he with his sack of provisions and her with her wooden toy train, trailing behind her in the dust.

16.

LUCIFER WAITED UNTIL the dawn to address the people. He knew he had to allow a little time to pass after the death of both Harrison and Morton, but he also wanted to make his statement while the memory of those gentlemen's passing still lingered. The crowds were in mixed spirits but that was when they would be at their most amenable, Irish had assured him, so he climbed on top of the Land Carriage, still stood out there in the plain, and held up his hands for silence.

"Ladies and gentlemen," he said, "thank you for allowing us to join you in remembering those who were so recently taken from us. I want to assure you that what I'm here to say is intended to honour their memory rather than taint it. Your leaders came to me wanting to form a union between my people and yours. I respected that and hoped to achieve the same. So, with that in mind, I want to announce my intentions here and now. You have lost a great leader, I only wish I could have arrived here in time to save him. But I could not. I can, however, honour his wishes by saying that I intend to honour his last wishes for the future. In order to do that I intend to run for President."

The response to this was beyond measure, the reporters ecstatic as they scribbled in their notebooks, the people unable to quite believe what they were hearing.

"Your country wisely believes in democracy," Lucifer continued, "so the choice will be yours. Let this be my final proof to you that I do not come here to do anything but build a union between us. I am not your enemy, I am not your invader, I am a man who wishes to serve you and protect you. I am yours if you'll have me. What comes tomorrow is up to you."

WHAT AM I DOING IN THE MIDDLE OF THE REVOLUTION?

(An excerpt from the book
by Patrick Irish)

I NEED HARDLY tell you whether Lucifer achieved the position. It is, after all, a matter of history. The Vote Lightbringer campaign—that name, Lucifer, always so contentious and better avoided—the attempts by Democrat and Republican alike to derail his rise to power. They claimed it unconstitutional, that he was unfit as a candidates until, of course, it was shown that Lucifer had been a citizen of the country since the Constitution itself was drawn up (indeed, he had walked its roads long before it) and thereby perfectly eligible under law.

They claimed it would herald an era of terror and violence, and, certainly, there were times when that seemed to be so. Yet the fighting, the riots, the attacks on his party in general and his person in particular, they were all nothing compared to the destruction that might have been. The vast majority accepted him, as the landslide vote proved. People are very simple creatures, they want to feel safe, they want to be reassured. With Lucifer in power most citizens felt that their fears were needless; if there were one candidate that could guide them through the turbulent times ahead it was the candidate that knew the dangers Hell had to offer. Not only did he know them, but he could fight them. All a voting public ever really wants is a steady, safe hand on the rudder and that was what Lucifer offered.

So it was that six months later, the results of the emergency ballot were unveiled and a new man sat beneath the roof of the White House.

I visited him that night. Possibly I was feeling smug. As you will have gathered by now I can be susceptible to the more base human emotions.

"Happy?" he asked, sat in the solitary light of the lamp on his desk, a scattering of papers in front of him.

"Yes," I admitted. "It worked didn't it?"

He didn't answer that, just stared out of the window at the remnants of the celebratory banners and ribbons that hung from the trees and the windows.

"I spent so long avoiding authority," he said, "preferring to live my own life, out of His shadow."

"His shadow has long since dispersed," I said.

He looked at me. "It never will," he replied. "But I shall continue to do my best while it falls over me."

I left him to his brooding, knowing better than to argue.

I thought I might return to the mortal world, give up this temporary pretence of godhood for an honest life amongst my peers. Somehow it's never happened. I still sit here, watching life unfold beneath me. Sometimes I visit, but I'm determined not to get too involved. I think it's time we all made our own way, don't you?

I warned you that stories never really end. Of course they don't, they just change. The day that Lucifer took his place in the White House was a beginning, not an ending. The years that followed, the crises and the victories, the bad years and the good, were all, in their own way, just as—if not more—important than the events of those few months that saw our world become something fresh and new.

I could tell you more. About Elwyn and Meridiana's child and the chaos it brought? About Black Tuesday, when the Exchange finally made its mark on the mortal world? How Biter took on the Chicago gangs? About the Texas assassination, and the attempts on behalf of the grassy knoll—or Branches of Regret as we know him—to uncover the murderer? Or what about the Great War? Demonic castes and mortal soldiers fighting side by side while the world burned?

No. Stories never end. They just become history.

And, for better or for worse, this was mine.

ACKNOWLEDGEMENTS

THE HEAVEN'S GATE books have lived in my head for far too long. Unwanted lodgers who cluttered up the place and never did the washing-up or contributed towards the rent. Naturally, once I finally brought them outside and looked at them in daylight they bore no resemblance to the shadowy, indistinct creatures I always imagined them to be, but it's a relief to finally evict them from my brain and put them into yours. The fact that I was able to do so rests entirely with the frankly gorgeous people at Solaris.

In the Rebellion Oval Office, President Jason and Vice President Ben could easily have pressed the large red button but resisted.

Jonathan Oliver (Calamity Jon as we've never thought of him but might now) pointed out the targets; David Thomas Moore (whose hairy face brings the banks of the Gristle to the minds of fearful onlookers) polished the ammunition; Michael 'The

Moustache' Molcher (who sounds like a really shit Cab Calloway song now I come to think on it) ensured there was a crowd to see the first shots fired; Lydia 'I Fed it to the Fucking Dog' Gittins ensured the crowd continued to grow (despite my best efforts); Kit 'What Is it with this man and commas?' Scorah steadied my aim; Jake 'Pretty Boy' Murray and Dominick 'Tentacles' Saponaro designed my jackets and Pye 'O' Parr and Sam 'Sam' Gretton stitched it beautifully together. Finally, Gareth 'sign here' Busby and Marytyn 'The Dollar' Wiggins ensured the papers were legal and the funds were there for gunpowder.

I cannot thank all of them enough. These books mean a great deal to me and the fact that the above folks allowed it all to happen puts every single one of them in my debt.

As always, my posse had my back. Mother wasn't quite as disgusted with this one as the last (though she was VERY cross about the horse) and Debs just laughed at the nasty bits, proving that there's nothing more satisfying in life for a despicable man as the love of a despicable woman. I love them both.

And if you've read this far I love you too, you mad, word-starved fool.

GUY ADAMS

'Guy Adams is just magnificent.'
Fantasy Book Review

THE GOOD THE BAD AND THE INFERNAL

One day every hundred years, a town appears, its location and character different every time. It is home to the greatest miracle a man could imagine: a doorway to Heaven itself. The town's name is Wormwood, and it is due to appear on the 21st September 1889, somewhere in the American Midwest. There are many who hope to be there: travelling preacher Obeisance Hicks and his simple messiah, Soldier Joe; Henry and Harmonium Jones and their freak show pack of outlaws; the Brothers of the Order of Ruth and their sponsor Lord Forset (inventor of the Forset Thunderpack and other incendiary modes of personal transport); and finally, an aging gunslinger with a dark history.

They will face dangers both strange and terrible: monstrous animals, predatory towns, armies of mechanical natives, and other things besides. Wormwood defends its secrets, and only the brave and resourceful will survive...

 WWW.SOLARISBOOKS.COM

Follow us on Twitter! www.twitter.com/solarisbooks

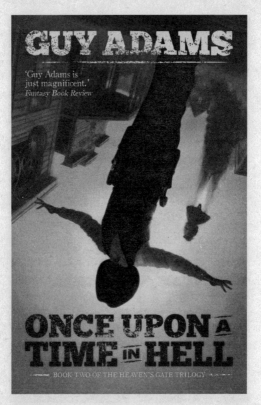

GUY ADAMS

'Guy Adams is
just magnificent.'
Fantasy Book Review

ONCE UPON A
TIME IN HELL

BOOK TWO OF THE HEAVEN'S GATE TRILOGY

Wormwood has appeared, and with it a doorway to the afterlife. But what use is a door if you can't step through it?

Hundreds have battled unimaginable odds to reach this place, including the blind shooter Henry Jones; the drunk and liar Roderick Quartershaft; that most holy, yet enigmatic of orders, the Brotherhood of Ruth; the inventor Lord Forset and his daughter Elisabeth; the fragile messiah Soldier Joe and his nurse Hope Lane.

Of them all, Elwyn Wallace, a young man who only wanted to travel west for a job, would have happily forgone the experience. But he finds himself abroad in Hell, a nameless, aged gunslinger by his side. He had thought nothing could match the terror of his journey thus far, but time will prove him wrong.

On the road to Hell, good intentions don't mean a damn.

CHILDREN OF THE DROUGHT BOOK ONE

ONE NIGHT IN SIXES

ARIANNE 'TEX' THOMPSON

Appaloosa Elim is a man who knows his place. On a good day, he's content with it. Today is not a good day. Today, his so-called "partner" – that lily-white lordling Sil Halfwick – has ridden off west for the border, hell-bent on making a name for himself in native territory. And Elim, whose place is written in the bastard browns and whites of his cow-spotted face, doesn't dare show up home again without him.

The border town called Sixes is quiet in the heat of the day, but Elim's heard the stories about what wakes at sunset: gunslingers and shapeshifters and ancient animal gods whose human faces never outlast the daylight. If he ever wants to go home again, he'd better find his missing partner fast. But if he's caught out after dark, Elim risks succumbing to the old and sinister truth in his own flesh – and discovering just how far he'll go to survive the night.

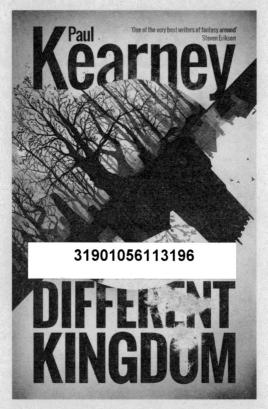

'One of the very best writers of fantasy around'
Steven Erikson

Paul KEARNEY

31901056113196

DIFFERENT KINGDOM

Michael Fay is a normal boy, living with his grandparents on their family farm in rural Ireland. In the woods—once thought safe and well-explored—there are wolves; and other, stranger things. He keeps them from his family, even his Aunt Rose, his closest friend, until the day he finds himself in the Other Place. There are wild people, and terrible monsters, and a girl called Cat.

When the wolves follow him from the Other Place to his family's doorstep, Michael must choose between locking the doors and looking away—or following Cat on an adventure that may take an entire lifetime in the Other Place. He will become a man, and a warrior, and confront the Devil himself: the terrible Dark Horseman...

WWW.SOLARISBOOKS.COM

Follow us on Twitter! www.twitter.com/solarisbooks